THE ELF AND THE ARROW

Alora's Tear, Volume II

NATHAN BARHAM

BARHAM INK
MOSCOW IDAHO USA

Table of Contents

For Pops, because the stories go on.

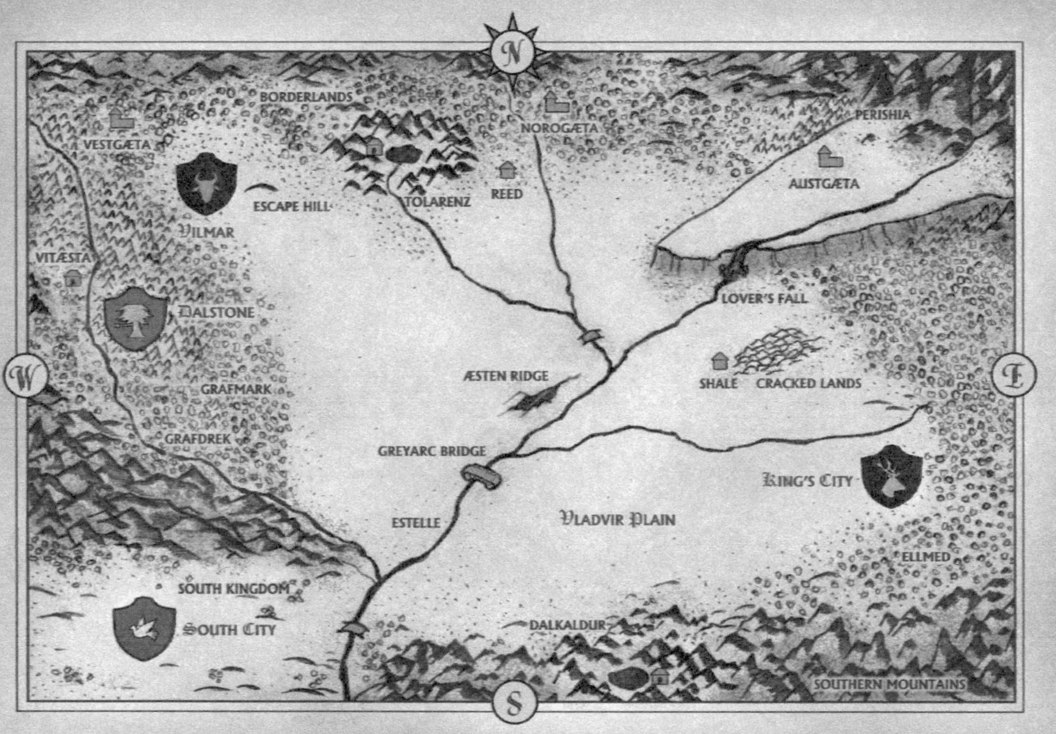

N
BORDERLANDS
VESTGÆTA
PERISHIA
NOROGÆTA
AUSTGÆTA
TOLARENZ
REED
ESCAPE HILL
VILMAR
VITÆSTA
LOVER'S FALL
DALSTONE
ÆSTEN RIDGE
SHALE
CRACKED LANDS
W
E
GRAFMARK
GRAFDREK
GREYARC BRIDGE
KING'S CITY
ESTELLE
VLADVIR PLAIN
SOUTH KINGDOM
SOUTH CITY
ELLMED
DALKALDUR
SOUTHERN MOUNTAINS
S

THE ELF AND THE ARROW

CHAPTER ONE

A Prince and a King

Edward's boots clicked and scraped across the cold stone floor. Above, heavy buttresses and support beams framed the vaulted expanse, as if to lift the sky in order to accommodate the huge rooms of the castle. His mind wandered back to days long past: days spent playing in these halls, hiding behind red velvet curtains only to be discovered as his feet peeked out from the bottom; days spent studying stealth and self-defense, policy and propriety, each test ever more difficult, until they blurred together into a shapeless cloud his mind called 'education'. Memories of stolen pastries crept back as the smell from the kitchens wafted into the entryway. They were simpler days, easier days.

The daydream ended as the immense doors slammed shut. The guards slid the bolts into position and fitted the metal-banded crossbeam into its slots, a command which carried great consequence if overlooked.

"Master Edward, the king will see you now," said the guard, who then dutifully led him to his father's quarters. The need for such formality had always irritated Edward. Every step, every turn, another reminder that Codard—and *only* Codard—was king. The guard pulled back the expensive drapery that separated cold stone entryway from cold wood-paneled throne room.

The cloth slid back into place silently behind him. Finally alone, the two men surveyed each other. Edward, tall and strong, dark of hair, gray of eye. Codard, glowering and graying, though the tangled locks atop his head had once been as black as his son's.

Edward bowed his head. "How may I serve you, Father?"

The king did not bow in return.

"I summoned you for one reason and one reason only. You are the only heir to my throne, and thus the only soldier trustworthy enough for this task." Codard motioned for his son to have a seat. His eyes narrowed. "It seems only logical that the future king should retrieve what he lost in the first place!"

Edward nearly fell from the chair as a wave of new memories washed away the old.

"Take the hill!" The sergeant screamed. "They'll never hold us now!" Edward's strength was failing him. The hours of battle drifted in and out, both as real as the open wounds on his arms, yet somehow as illusory as a dream.

He ducked behind a tree to shield himself as another in the endless series of arrow volleys smashed against his squad. The corpses that had once been his friends and followers lay scattered across the grassy hill. Their open eyes—glazed yet watchful—pleaded for an end to the fighting. Only a dozen remained to defend the position, a third of whom were injured.

"They're charging us! What should we do Master Edward?" called one. The young man had evaded danger for most of the battle. At this dark hour, Edward could see the boy trembling in fear.

In truth, the king's son was out of ideas. Their attempt to breach the gates had failed miserably. The enemy was aware of their plan. After the first charge, the gates had opened, and they were overcome. A precious few managed to retreat to the hill that now, it seemed, would be their graveyard.

Far too much effort had been wasted, and for what? For Alora's Tear. Edward laughed, a grim sound, hollow and dry. As if such a thing even existed. A real leader, a truer king, would have sent his company to fight the Norill. At this very moment Edward's friend, Askon, would be leading a company to Austgæta, where the General was already entrenched against the threat from the north. But Edward had instead been sent on a fool's errand, a mission to find a shortcut for his father, a quick solution to all their problems.

It made the death surrounding him all the more tragic. Edward knew that he and his men could defend the hill for some time, but they weren't prepared for a siege. Originally, Edward had tasked a small contingent with infiltrating the castle gates while the remainder of his men would stay behind as a precautionary defense unit. However, when they arrived at the stronghold, the enemy had been ready for them. Now, with only a few soldiers remaining, Edward braced himself. "Prepare to defend yourselves," he ordered. "Prepare for the end."

The enemy crested the hill, their faces twisted in grimaces and open-mouthed roars, a demon-army of men. They held their weapons high and the blades gleamed, casting light into the shadowed faces. Edward and his men rushed at the opposing ranks, but just before their weapons clashed, a blinding flash of light sent both sides reeling. The light surrounded them; blade, army, grass, rock, and tree disappeared. Edward closed his eyes to protect them from the whiteness. He awoke just a few miles from home, as did the remnants of his command. But it was empty-handed and empty-hearted that they returned.

"I apologize, Father. Everything just disappeared. We gave our all, and lost most of our men doing so." Edward swallowed hard against the anger. "How many will you send? How many will ever be enough?" A rim of water filled his eyelids. He blinked it away.

"I should send you to your death for surrendering. You expect me to believe your fairytale return?" Codard shook his head. "No. You will go, and you will bring me Alora's Tear, or I shall find someone else to take my throne! Now get out of my sight." Instantly, the guards reappeared and roughly led Edward back through the curtain.

Under his breath, so quietly that the swish of silk masked his words, Edward swore an oath. "One day our people will be free from your greed and cowardice."

His childhood memories seemed to scatter as he stormed through the entryway. His bleary eyes betrayed him, and he ran abruptly into three men who were approaching the king's quarters. They moved with urgency, nearly knocking over the prince who stood in their way.

"Move yer precious self aside there, ya li'l princeling. We've got business needs tending to here," said the first. The others stood unmoved and stunned. Edward bristled.

"Take care to show some respect—" Edward cocked his head slightly, blinking. "John?"

"O' course, you pampered couch-lounger. Who else'd have the guts to talk to you that way? Don't you have a festival or a ball to get to? Ya know, somethin' important like that." He smiled wide, showing his already decaying teeth. Still in disbelief, the two men flanking John remained silent.

Edward laughed, a heavy choking laugh that overrode his anger. His gray eyes brightened, the heavy brows lifted, and his shoulders relaxed. "Kneel now at my feet, or suffer the consequence for your transgression, peasant!"

A cool silence hung between the prince in his fine clean clothes, standing straight-backed, and the three men in their weather-stained uniforms. He lifted an arm, gesturing to reinforce the command. The two men at John's sides bowed their heads and drew back one foot each, attempting, awkwardly, to kneel. John slapped the backs of their heads.

"Get up, ya gullible couple of—" John pulled at the shoulders of each uniform. When their eyes lifted, they found a broad smile on Edward's face.

He laughed again. "I'm sorry; it's a tired old joke. John and I enjoy it a bit too much, I think. There is no need for that kind of formality with me. In there, however," and he pointed to his father's quarters, "you'd do yourself a favor to do that and then some. King Codard loves his rules and codes and social graces." He looked to John.

"Ah, I should introduce you proper. This," John said, pointing to his left, "is Christopher: scout and intelligence gatherer. And this here's Thomas." He indicated the young, nervous looking man to his right. "All around fool and general halfwit." Both men bowed, slightly this time.

"I am Edward, commander in the king's army, and as you know, also his son. It is a pleasure to have met you, though your choice to follow John calls your judgment somewhat into question."

"Oh it ain't by choice," John interrupted. "They're soldiers in my company."

"Your company?" said Edward, eyebrows arched in surprise.

"Aye. Mine now, that is. Assigned by Victor after Askon went deserter on us."

"Hardly!" said Thomas, now looking a bit more lively. "We saw the smoke, Christopher and I. Who knows what he found there."

"Oh shut it, Thomas," John barked. "Askon left his command to go back to Tolarenz. That's disobeying a direct order. Far as I'm concerned, he's a deserter."

Edward reached out and let his hand rest on John's shoulder. "I'm sure Askon had a good reason to leave, John. You know him as well as I do."

"Yeah well give his good reason to the dead men at Austgæta. An' what if these two hadn't made Norogæta in time? He's craftier in the woods than 'bout anyone we got, an' he leaves one scout with a green first-timer, expectin' them to carry the whole mission. It ain't right."

Edward tried to let his friend's anger pass. "Well, we will know what Askon was thinking when he returns," he said. "What is this about Austgæta and Norogæta?"

John chewed at his lower lip, obviously still irritated. He looked at Thomas. "Yer an information specialist in training. You tell him."

The nervous young man turned to Edward. His shoulders hunched, and he ducked his head, letting it swerve left and right as though he were dodging invisible blows as he spoke. "Uh, we—we were all at Austgæta preparing for the battle to attack the Norill colony. The—the mission failed, and the General's men were wiped out. The enemy has some sort of weapon that allows them to dispirit and debilitate our forces." As he continued, Thomas grew more fluent and animated.

He told Edward of the battle and the overwhelming power of the Norill weapon in the underground passage. He explained the late arrival of Askon's company and the devastation that they found. Then he addressed the splitting of the scouting group from the main company, Askon's separation from the scouting party, Patrick's death, and finally Christopher and Thomas's arrival at Norogæta only hours before the Norill. When he had finished, John nodded approvingly.

"Not bad, for a first report. Might have to beat that stuttering outta ya, though." He stepped forward, leaning in so that only Edward could hear him. "Both forts are gone. The army is headed this way, on the retreat. We left a lot of good men holding their ground so that the majority could escape. We won't know if they got out until the enemy is right on top of us, I figure. These two and I, we rode out ahead, as fast as we could to get this information to the king. Somebody has to decide what to do. Victor's dead; the general's dead. Can't say what'll happen to the defenders on the retreat. They should arrive in a couple of days. Depending on the defenses, the enemy won't be far behind."

"Gods," said Edward, blinking. "Strange things are happening all across the kingdom, my friend. This weapon, this darkness, and I at the same time in battle at one moment, a clear defeat, then miles away at the next."

"Oh, really?" said Christopher. "Some say you turned and ran, like Askon."

Edward scoffed at the comment. "It sounds as though that is what we all have done, Christopher. My men gave battle to the last and were then transported away. I can't explain it, but my company suffered great loss before the event." He turned, lifting a hand to indicate that they should pass into the king's quarters. "I think you'd be well served to take your information to Codard before he no longer has time to organize the remaining forces."

The three men passed by Edward. John slapped him on the back as they went. "Good to see ya," he said. "Let's hope this gets better, eh?"

"Let's hope," said Edward.

Waving a goodbye to John and the others, Edward stomped past the remainder of the castle guard and into the front courtyard. With each step, his anger toward the king returned. Green hedges filled the area between the castle and its outer wall. His father made sure that they were cut frequently and kept neatly. Edward tripped over the cobblestone walkway toward the gate, his mind wandering. Could the outposts at Austgæta and Norogæta really be gone? They had held for years against the disorganized attacks from the Norill. Perhaps the enemy had grown somehow in intellect, or adopted tactics used against them by the king's own forces.

The black iron ring of the gate handle stung Edward's hand. He closed his fingers tightly around the cold metal and pulled the door back. The hinges creaked. Outside, the people of King's City bustled on obliviously, unaware of burning forts and crushing darkness and the coming threat.

The city itself formed a half-circle around the castle and its major defenses. Between the stone wall and the paneled buildings was a wide strip of garden. The shrubs and scrub plants had overgrown their appointed areas and now twisted into each other, a nest of bramble and vine. Instead of a broad lane leading directly from the gate to the city's main street, a winding trail had been unceremoniously hacked through the brush.

Edward walked the path and laughed to himself: inside the wall, perfect tidy hedges; outside, a wild forgotten snarl of weeds. It fit his father all too well. He rounded a corner, still surrounded by brush and half-grown trees. He turned, looking back in the direction from which he had come and saw nothing, only thorns and branches and snaking vines. He scratched at his shoulder. Beneath the soft sound of fingernails on fabric came the swish of leaves. He stopped, silent; but no sound came again.

So quickly that he barely deflected it, a gleaming blade flashed toward his neck. Edward parried with an armored wrist and instinctively turned to face his assailant.

The figure moved fluidly, like a snake or an eel. In his left hand, the knife gleamed. He slashed down again. Edward sidestepped the stroke.

"I know only one left-handed swordsman," Edward said, grinning. "It's a disadvantage." Another slash came down with lightning quickness, but it fell wide.

"What? Being left-handed or knowing a left-handed swordsman?"

"Either way. However, I should hope that I never meet him in battle. Unless he now fights like this." Edward laughed, dodging a final, halfhearted stroke from the knife, then bowed low, a mockery of the stilted formality his father so adamantly enforced. The knife slid back into its sheath.

Straightening, Edward found himself standing before a figure hooded and cloaked in deep green. A pair of deft hands moved from sheath to hood, pulling it back, revealing a sharp, angular face. Dark hair fell to just below the ears, long enough to cover their points. The stubble on his jaw gave him a rugged look, but his face was free of battle scars or wounds. Two distinct eyes looked up at Edward: one green as the hedges in the courtyard, the other brilliant blue. The eyes and the ears gave away his half-elf heritage and his identity.

"Askon," Edward said. "It's wonderful to see you again—especially now—though your choice of greeting is, as usual, unorthodox."

"Someone has to keep you on your toes," the figure replied, smiling. His eyes gleamed. "But why is now such a good time for my arrival?"

Edward shook his head. "Not here. That story can wait. What about you? What brings you to the castle? I've just run into John and two of your men from the company at Austgæta."

Askon gripped Edward's shoulders, shaking him excitedly. "You've seen John! He's alive? That is excellent news, my friend. And what of the other two? Who were they?"

"Excellent news it was not," said Edward, pushing Askon's hands from his shoulders. "Austgæta has fallen, and the enemy is headed toward the city."

Askon was unmoved by the revelation. "They had already set fire to Austgæta when I sent John with the company to defend what was left. It's not surprising that it could not be saved. Hopefully most of the defenders were able to escape. But what about the others? Who was with John?"

Edward tried to remember. It had only been moments before, but the two names, and the faces that corresponded seemed vague and nondescript. Then he remembered the nervous, first time soldier. "One of them, the younger and less experienced, was called Thomas, I believe."

"Thomas!" Askon fell to his knees, laughing and holding back tears at the same time. "He made it, then. I knew there was a soldier in there. He just needed a reason to find it. I suppose the other was Christopher?"

"Indeed, it was. A good guess. I'm not sure I would have remembered his name had you not hit it aright."

"He's a scout and infiltration expert," said Askon, rising from the ground. "The training makes him forgettable, elusive. You're not the first to lose track of him, and you won't be the last, I'm sure."

"Well, let's hope he isn't tracking you." Edward pointed at his friend. "When I left them, he and John were calling you a deserter. The boy stood up for you, though."

"A deserter?!" Askon replied angrily. He paced back and forth across the narrow pathway. "They know why I left. And I wish you wouldn't call Thomas *boy*. He's no younger than we were when we joined the ranks." Askon stopped. "Are you sure it wasn't just John making jokes? You know he has an active sense of humor, sometimes too active."

Edward shook his head. "No. It was no joke. In fact, I'm not sure that I've ever seen John more serious. They lost Norogæta as well. The other two only arrived there just in time to prevent the defenders from being wiped out."

Askon resumed pacing. "First Austgæta, now Norogæta. That leaves only Vestgæta still intact, and I fear it won't be long until it too is gone. Then our northern border will be completely undefended. Iramov will have the last fortress north of King's City. If he stops the Norill, he will look like a hero."

"Lord Iramov?" Edward's eyes grew wide, recognition sweeping over his face. "Askon, I was just there, at Vilmar. His forces are amassing, and there are many—more than we thought—far more than my father's allotment for him."

Askon turned a skeptical eye on his friend, remembering Morrowmen's warning. The old man had said to trust Edward, but not the king. "Why were you in Iramov's stronghold? And how did you return so quickly? It's four, maybe five days straight riding from there to here."

Edward began to form a response, his face apologetic and slightly injured at Askon's mistrust, but he did not have the chance to speak. A guard, patrolling from the palace gate, had closed on them as they talked. He approached Edward, placing himself firmly ahead of the prince, in case Askon posed some sort of threat.

"Is this… *man* bothering you?" said the guard with some relish. He seemed hopeful that Edward would ask for his help. "As I came down the path, I saw him put his hands on your person, sir."

Edward laughed. "No, not at all. This is Commander Askon of Tolarenz. We were discussing official military business. It does not concern you."

"Yes, sir," replied the guard. "Commander," he said, turning to Askon. Then, without another word, he proceeded down the path to finish his patrol. When he was a few feet away, Askon heard him mumble to himself. It was soft, spoken under his breath. "A half-elf commander, in our forces? The king must be desperate."

A tide of emotion surged within Askon, and the memories from the powdered circles flooded back. Iramov had used the same sort of language in his tirades against the villagers and Caled. Without thinking, Askon's hand was on the long knife. He drew the blade and launched himself toward the muttering guard. But in a flash, Edward was at his side, gripping Askon's wrist.

"Don't," warned Edward. "It isn't worth it. What is the matter with you anyway? I've seen you ignore much worse than that."

Askon ripped his arm free of Edward's grasp. "You know nothing!" he snapped. "And how did you even get over here so quickly?"

"Maybe you were indecisive," said Edward. "Honestly, I was surprised that I got to you in time. It was like you were a step behind, held back by something."

Askon sheathed the knife again. He had now twice found himself outmatched in speed by an opponent: first in his empty home against the unskilled swordsman, and now against his friend, Askon's equal in skill but not athletic ability. He cast the thought aside. "It's about Tolarenz, Edward. I have to explain."

"You know as well as anyone that Tolarenz is a part of this kingdom just as any human town or village," Edward said, loudly enough that the guard could hear, even at a distance.

Askon hushed him and started to walk. He jerked his head slightly, expecting Edward to follow. Edward complied, and the two friends walked in stride down the path past the guard who now stood at attention near the outlet to the busy street. As they passed, Edward took an extra step forward, placing himself between the guard and Askon.

CHAPTER TWO
King's City

King's City murmured and droned as the two men walked the crowded street. Many of the buildings showed evidence of great care in their construction and maintenance. Some had fallen into disrepair or abandonment, but their sagging doorways and half-rotted eaves were the exceptions. Here and there, animals passed through the gaps between people: dogs brought in by merchants or customers, pigs to be sold, various chickens, and a stray cat who slinked from stall to stall. Merchants from outlying villages shouted deals, and blacksmiths hammered loudly at their work. Askon and Edward covered their faces as the acrid smell and heat burned their noses. And they passed guards, sometimes in pairs and often in threes, always armed and always ready to silence opposition.

Soon, the two came across a tavern. Its peaked roofline and heavy shingles bespoke its age amongst the newer construction on either side. The entryway crouched beneath an overhang that jutted like a nose into the street. A short set of stairs climbed to the wide patio where a painted sign dangled from two small chains. "The Goat's Beard," it read, and next to the words was a rough painting of a goat's head whose beard had been exaggerated for effect. Askon eyed a trio of guards who had just settled a dispute between a merchant and an angry customer. One cocked his head suspiciously, but Askon had already looked away and moved into the shadow of the tavern stairs. "Let's get out of this street," he said.

Askon stepped through the door and into the dim light of the tavern, Edward following closely behind. Pipe smoke and the smell of the open fire drifted freely through the half-light. To their left was a table-full of drunken merchants, all chanting some slurred and off-key song. To their right a decrepit old man sat hunkering over a wooden mug. The elder raised an eyebrow at the arrival of the two friends.

"Let's sit down before I'm noticed," Askon said, turning his back to the old man. "You know how they treat us in the city, especially the older generations." Spotting a table in the far corner, they moved to sit. Askon pulled a chair so that it was half facing the doorway and half turned away from the other patrons; he lowered his head to avoid drawing any extra attention.

Edward paid the bartender and brought two mugs brimming with the tavern's finest ale. Setting the wooden vessels down and pulling out a chair for himself, he asked again. "What brings you here, old friend? I assure you, in this place, we are safe." Askon's brow lifted, and several thin lines appeared on his forehead. He tilted his head slightly as the words struggled to arrange themselves.

"Years ago," he began, "after my parents fled from King's City, they took up with the other half-couples and families that had also been chased out. They wandered together with Caled and the others, looking for the right place to start their dream city; a city with no special rules for half-elves, a city that accepted those who were as accepting as they were. After their years of searching, they found the perfect place. A wide flat valley floor, green with tall grass for pasture and growing, steep mountains surrounding it, and a crystal clear river twisting through like a shimmering ribbon." Askon lifted the wooden mug to his lips and paused, remembering.

"You speak of Tolarenz as if it no longer exists, Askon, and as though I've never seen it before. What has happened? Have you spoken to Caled?" Edward waited, but Askon extended the silence, his eyes tracing a winding scratch on the table's surface.

He set the mug down and went on. "As you know, I was on assignment at Austgæta. The general wouldn't allow us entry, and the enemy attacked during the night. We prevailed in the battle and were granted access. After our victory we did not remain idle in our plans. The general had been prepared for the ambush with a counterstrategy of his own. It failed. As far as I know, he and all of his men are gone, killed in our assault on the Norill colony near Austgæta.

"It might seem, to the eyes of a passing observer, that it was the fault of my men that the plan did not succeed. That is not the case. We arrived late at the rendezvous point, but we merely escaped the slaughter." Askon tilted the mug to one side; his finger traced the etching of the same bearded goat that graced the tavern's sign. "We couldn't attack the Norill directly; we were too few. And in our attempt at reconnaissance the news got worse. Not only had the enemy routed our forces at the colony, they had planned an attack of their own. I sent John back to Austgæta with the majority of my men, while four of us made for Norogæta in hopes that we would be able to warn them of our defeat. But our adversaries had gained a new confidence; we were ambushed again. The Norill had matched us step for step in our plans. We lost Patrick in the attack. He and Christopher were great friends. It was a sad parting, as they always are.

"That is when we saw it, and Marten confirmed it. Smoke in the distance, rising from Tolarenz. It was there that I made my choice, apparently marking myself as a deserter. I had to go to them, Edward. I couldn't leave them to burn!"

A brief smile moved across Edward's face and vanished as he too stared at the scratch on the table. "No. You couldn't. I remember the inside of that Norill cell. You refused to leave me behind that day. I'd expect nothing less from you concerning any of your friends," he said.

"But I did leave them!" Askon protested. "I left Thomas and Christopher; I left John and Victor. Maybe they're right, and I am a deserter."

"It's over, Askon," said Edward. "The decision was made. There is no use in guessing at what might have been. You were confronted with an impossible situation, and you made the best of your options."

"Did I?" Askon seemed sullen now.

"Why don't you finish the tale, and I'll tell you what I think?" Edward suggested.

Askon ceased his tracing of the goat on the mug. "I broke ranks from the others and struck out for Tolarenz. I stole a horse." He laughed, shaking his head slowly. "It's here in the city. I didn't know what to do with it after it was all over. When I made it back, the town was empty."

"Empty?" asked Edward, puzzled.

"They were gone, and the houses, the farms, stables, forge, mill, everything was empty. In the square, they had piled all of the belongings and set them on fire. There was enough fuel that I could see the smoke at a day's ride distant."

"Who piled everything, the people?"

"I thought maybe that some illness had come while I was away, that they had decided to purge the valley."

Edward nodded. "I've heard of villages doing that. Burn the belongings and you burn the disease. Something to do with angry spirits and too many possessions. I didn't know there were people in Tolarenz who believed that."

"Neither did I," said Askon. "And there weren't. They were *forced* to burn everything."

"By whom?" Edward asked, indignant. "Caled would never allow someone to force his people to do anything."

"Caled is dead," Askon replied coldly, and the words fell like heavy stones plunging into deep water. "I saw it with my own eyes."

"Who would do such a thing? Who could, even?" Edward's bewildered eyes ranged across the darkened tavern. Caled's prowess and power was well known throughout the kingdom. Of course, he had only been one man; but news of his passing was absurd, as if someone had claimed the sun had been struck from the sky.

Askon's response was venomous. "Iramov."

"I don't understand. Iramov's forces are gathered at his stronghold south of Vestgæta. I saw that with my own eyes. There aren't enough men in Vladvir to marshal that many in addition to my father's army and still have enough to assault Tolarenz. Granted, the third would be the smallest force, but the townspeople would not go without a fight, and a good one, especially with Caled leading them."

Askon nodded. "So it would seem. But Iramov didn't need men to take Tolarenz, no more than a handful anyway."

The table of singers finished their latest selection and had taken again to the round of mugs brought by the bartender. Askon lowered his voice as the room quieted. "Iramov's desire for control is well known, but his treachery is greater than anyone has yet suspected. Or, that is my belief, at least."

Edward still wasn't convinced. "My father sent me and my men to Vilmar for a reason, Askon. Iramov is a problem, surely. I think he intends to challenge my father. But if the entire army gathers, he would be greatly outnumbered. And how many of his new recruits would follow him if they knew that as we speak, the Norill are marching on the city? A hostile takeover doesn't seem likely."

Askon ground his teeth. "It didn't seem likely that he'd wipe out Tolarenz either!" he shouted and moved to upend the table. He had come here believing that Edward, of all people, would listen. Even Morrowmen had said that trusting Edward was the right choice. In his anger, Askon lifted the table's edge, expecting mugs, decorations, and chairs to scatter. But they did not. Instead, as though Edward had been able to read Askon's thoughts, he pressed Askon's side of the table down, barring him from his display of frustration.

"Sit down," said Edward. "Aren't you supposed to be keeping a low profile? It's like you wanted someone to notice."

Askon sat heavily, and the chair creaked under his weight.

"Well, I'm sorry for upsetting you," Edward said, even quieter than before. "Tolarenz is important. And not just to those who live there. It's an example for all of us."

"Not anymore, it isn't," Askon replied. "Edward, that's what I haven't said, yet. There's still so much I haven't said. Tolarenz is gone, at least, the only part of it that really mattered. The buildings are there and the valley, but not the people; Iramov killed them all. And by destroying everything they had or that they ever made, he effectively erased Tolarenz and everyone in it."

Edward lifted a hand to his face, rubbing his brow. Askon could see that he did not understand. "How?" Edward asked after a moment. "I mean, I hope you don't see this as disrespect for the dead, but what did he do with all the bodies? Even if he could have somehow killed everyone with only a few men in his service, you said the town was empty."

Reaching across the table, Askon put a hand on his friend's shoulder. He spoke in a low voice, so low that even Edward had to strain to hear it. "Iramov wields a power so great that he needs no more than a few men to take a town like Tolarenz. And I think he's using it in concert with the Norill. The same power that subdued us in the battles against the enemy is the same that I saw Iramov use against my people." Askon laughed awkwardly, leaning back in his chair again. "You would never expect it. It looks like a walking stick. But at the end of the staff there is a jewel."

"The Tear!" Edward said abruptly. He dropped his mug on the table where it fell and rolled to one side. Its contents spilled out, spreading slowly across the surface, finding the channel of the winding scratch and there racing out ahead of the rest of the thin pool of ale. Edward was standing now. Askon made to set the mug upright, but Edward had his arm in a tight grip. "We need to go." He threw some coins down on the table where they clattered noisily.

"Aren't you going to clean that up?" the bartender said gruffly.

"The king sends his regards. I'll let him know that the ale at the Goat's Beard is exemplary," Edward said, nodding and allowing the bartender to get a look at his face.

"Prince," stammered the bartender. "I—uh—thank you, sir."

The two emerged into the street, Edward still dragging Askon by the wrist. Askon wrenched his arm free, but Edward moved swiftly to an alley between the buildings opposite the tavern. Confused and emotionally drained from recalling the events at Tolarenz, Askon followed him into the shadows.

Between two buildings whose construction only emphasized the age of the Goat's Beard, Edward stopped. The space spanned only slightly more width than the two men standing shoulder-to-shoulder. Clay shingled eaves protruded from the rooftops above them and provided shelter for a ragged looking man in grimy, tattered clothing who huddled, deeply asleep, on a wooden box. He woke with a start and scampered away upon seeing the two armed men approach.

"I apologize," said Edward haltingly. He scanned the now empty area between the buildings. "We had overstayed our welcome, I think. Too many of the people were watching us. If what you say is true, and you've seen Iramov with Alora's Tear, then my father is actually right."

"What do you mean?" said Askon, pulling his hood over his head. In the streets of King's City, half-elves often used such guises to avoid being noticed. Though not as strong as during the Scouring—when half-elves had been hunted and executed by the thousands—emotions still ran deep, and conflicts often erupted when those of elvish decent were recognized among the crowd.

Edward continued to eye the end of the alley facing the Goat's Beard. "My mission, given to me only moments before we met in the garden outside the castle, is to find and recover Alora's Tear," he said. "It's the reason we were sent to Iramov's stronghold and the reason I was chastised so strongly when we returned empty-handed. I thought it was a myth, yet here you are telling me that you've not only seen it, but seen it in use!"

"I have," said Askon lowering his eyes and shaking his head slowly. "And it isn't something I would want to see again." Askon paused, waiting for Edward to lead the conversation. He considered explaining what he knew to be the truth about the Tear: that it was, in fact, five separate stones and that Edward's father, Codard, had one of them already. However, it was obvious that Edward was unaware of the fragment hidden somewhere within the castle. Codard had kept the information from his son deliberately.

"This is at least useful intelligence, Askon," Edward said awkwardly. Askon could tell that his friend did not want to present the revelation as good news, but that he welcomed the tactical advantage. "My father will want to hear of this at once. Perhaps he will have a plan."

Askon had listened, many times, to Edward's complaints about the king. The prince needed a reason to continue trusting his father. Their relationship was known throughout the kingdom to be tenuous and often adversarial. And so, the secret would stay as such, Askon decided. Morrowmen had cautioned him concerning his dealings with the king, and it seemed better to err on the side of secrecy than to reveal too much too soon. For the moment, as far as Edward son of Codard would know, Alora's Tear was still whole.

"I think the king should hear your story, Askon," Edward said. "We should go back to the castle and inform him while there is still time to move against Iramov."

CHAPTER THREE

Desertion

The sun, westering in the late afternoon, warmed the twisted briars and vines of the overgrown garden. Branches crisscrossed one another only a few feet from the path where strangled trees struggled against the weedy undergrowth. But instead of providing relief for passersby, the foliage only increased the humidity, stifling Askon and Edward as they approached the gate. The outer wall's designers had constructed several gates at intervals dispersed unevenly throughout the outer garden. Some, after years of neglect, had been covered entirely by crawling ivy and other brush, while a few had clear pathways tended by the patrolling guards. Askon and Edward walked one such path.

They passed the same guard from earlier that morning without incident or interruption. Askon felt the man's eyes upon his every step. For a moment Askon considered confronting him a second time, but Edward increased his stride, hoping, Askon guessed, to avoid conflict.

Upon entering the gate, the contrast between the outer and inner gardens became readily apparent. The two men continued briskly along the manicured hedges and crisp fragrant flowers until they reached the entrance to the castle. There, Edward stopped.

"I apologize, Askon," he said quietly. "For you, the telling and retelling of this story is such a burden. I'm so sorry for the loss that you were forced to endure. If you don't want to tell it again—"

"Edward," Askon interrupted. "We're soldiers. Even when it is our own people who are under attack, it is our duty to report what we have seen and done. I accept that responsibility." He took a step toward the door, reaching for the thick handle. In his mind, he agreed with Edward. It was his duty to report his actions and the movements of the enemy, but Edward's apparent lack of information concerning the division of the Tear weakened Askon's trust toward the king. Not only that, but the possibility existed that Edward himself was hiding the information as part of some conspiracy with his father. If that were the case, Askon would be walking into a trap. He shrugged off his wavering faith in his friend and pushed the door open, organizing his thoughts and his story.

He would be forced to play the same game as the king, revealing only what was necessary, while still appearing to be forthcoming on all counts. The tragedy which had befallen his home would be an advantage. The emotions would cover the adjustments to accuracy, but he would have to remain calm and collected. As they paced down the long hall toward the king's chamber, Askon felt the sharp edge of the fragment against his skin. Under the heavy cloth, it pulsed with faint green light. Askon tried to recall both Caled's icy, emotionless expression as he stood his ground against Iramov, and Morrowmen's advice to beware Codard's motives. Edward pulled back the heavy curtain, and Askon entered the king's chamber.

Once inside the lavish room, Askon met a welcome that he had not expected. To one side of the king's throne stood Thomas with his head and shoulders stooped slightly. Only a few feet away, with his arms folded across his chest, was Christopher. He looked worn and beaten, his face drawn in physical and emotional exhaustion. Both faced the king, who gestured widely, explaining something. Askon heard only a few words. Opposite them on a long bench, John sprawled, arms spread across the thick wooden backboard, legs stretched comfortably to length and crossed at the ankles. He flicked the toe of one boot rhythmically and stared into the distance as the king spoke. A long yawn escaped his mouth. Codard stopped mid-sentence.

"Commander!" growled the king, but John appeared to be unaffected. He sat up, looking back in Codard's direction with only the minimum of attention.

Askon and Edward waited awkwardly for the moment to pass, for the king to begin again with whatever topic John's inattention had interrupted. Instead he turned to his son.

"Edward," Codard said with the same irritation he had used with John. "Your orders were clear. Am I to take this as direct disobedience, or simply incompetence?" Edward took in a quick breath and stepped toward the throne, but was intercepted by Askon before he had the chance to speak.

"I made him come back," Askon said. "He informed me of the prior orders, Your Majesty, though he refused to disclose the details of his assignment. What I have seen is far too important. We need every commander and captain that can be assembled." As he answered, Edward faded from view into a corner near the heavy curtain. "I have reason to believe that the threat against this kingdom, your kingdom, is greater than we had imagined."

Codard's brow pinched slightly above the nose, thick wrinkles appearing in the olive skin. Whether the information came as news to the king, Askon was unsure. He tried to study the thin face, but it turned away.

John perked up. "Yeah? And what do you know, ya chicken-heart?" He swung his legs around, planting his feet firmly on the floor. "I didn't see you around when we fought through rank after slimy rank of Norill at Austgæta. Takin' a message you were, to the northern outpost, lettin' 'em know what happened, how the general got wiped out. That's what ya told me. Well, I did my job. Where were you when these boys showed up at Norogæta?" He gestured to Thomas and Christopher who looked from John to Askon to Codard expectantly. "Not with 'em! That's where. Ya wanna tell us what was so important that ya leave a rookie and one scout to fend for themselves?"

"Sir, if I may," Thomas stuttered, "he left us in order to investigate another, possibly coordinated attack."

"That's enough," said the king. "Your commanding officers are addressing one another. Askon will answer Commander John's question without your interference."

Askon stepped forward again, fully eclipsing Edward who had now become almost invisible in the shadowy corner. "John—I mean the commander—is correct, Your Majesty," said Askon. "I did leave these men and deviate from my original plan to carry the message to Norogæta; however, what I found may be of greater importance to us than the defeat at either outpost."

Codard's eyes narrowed, and he lifted a hand to his face, running the knuckles slowly along his upper lip. "Proceed, Askon, but keep in mind that you have been accused of desertion. A person such as yourself would be at, let us say, a disadvantage, were the accusations to come before a military court."

Deep within himself, Askon felt the old anger swell. After the events at Tolarenz, every slight against his people, no matter how minor, pricked like thorn. He mastered the emotion, thinking at once of Caled's stoic control in the face of Iramov, and suddenly a sense of tranquil calm swept over him. He read on Codard's face a series of almost imperceptible movements: twitch of the eye here, tilt of the head there. The king had anticipated an explosive response, and now he was surprised by Askon's restraint. It was as if Codard's face had transformed into an open book which Askon now read with ease. He turned to John and found a similar story, though the opinions written there projected more from tense posture than facial expression. Quickly, Askon turned to Christopher. In that face—that entire body—deep-seated rage stood boldfaced against the seemingly tempered visage. Then the moment passed.

"Commander?" prompted the king impatiently.

"There was fire and smoke rising from Tolarenz," Askon began. He recounted each step of the journey, including the stolen horse, the burning pile of belongings, and even the powdered circle in front of the town hall. He omitted the connection between the Norill darkness and Iramov's Tear fragment; he left out the Tear fragments entirely. Throughout, the king stopped him to question this point or that, often making disdainful comments toward Tolarenz and its inhabitants in the process. Each time, Askon felt the same surge of emotion, yet each time, he resisted it. As he did so, the feeling of unnatural calm swept over him again and again. In this state he continued to read the unspoken reactions of John, Christopher, and Codard, finding only more evidence that he spoke no longer to his friends and leaders. He now stood amongst a ring of adversaries, with the blatant exception of Thomas. Askon's story, though personally tragic, did not yet justify his desertion, nor could it justify the loss of Patrick. But now he came to the point: Iramov had led the attack, had killed Caled, had killed Askon's family, had erased an entire city.

Edward stepped from the corner into which he had receded. He stood proudly now, a prince in bearing and lineage. "Iramov used the Tear, Father! This is why I returned with Askon. Not only that, he is using it in tandem with the Norill. Tell him, Askon."

Codard seemed to notice Edward for the first time, as if he hadn't admonished the prince for returning so quickly from his mission. The king's gaze lingered momentarily before passing slowly back to Askon. Askon had not anticipated Edward's abrupt contribution. It skewed his strategy and revealed much of the critical information concerning the events at Tolarenz. To Askon's relief, though, his friend still showed no knowledge of the fragments or their properties. Edward, and Thomas as well, could be trusted. But the more the conversation progressed, the more certain Askon became that the other men in the room could not.

Askon controlled the urge to address Edward directly, to scold him for saying too much too quickly. Instead he focused on carefully clarifying the information for the king. As he did so, the emotion faded and the unnatural calm returned. "Yes," he said slowly, waiting for the king's reaction, "Iramov has recovered Alora's Tear." At this, a subtle change coursed over Codard's whole frame. Was it relief? The movement was too slight for Askon to completely understand, even in his heightened state of awareness. He continued. "Iramov's intent, I think, is to use the Tear's power against us to take control of the kingdom."

"Lord Iramov is our ally, Commander, and of higher rank and authority than you. I would proceed carefully, were I in your place." Codard had taken on the overwrought formality for which he was known, but Askon saw through it. The king knew that Iramov posed a threat, yet would not stand against him.

"He is no ally of Tolarenz," said Askon forcefully. "In the white circles, those left behind by the dead, I saw what he did to them, to all of them. I watched him use the Tear to kill Caled. Iramov is our enemy. And it would be wise to plan a preemptive strike against him."

There would be no plan. To Askon that was absolutely certain. The king had risen from his seat, and Askon saw everything clearly. Codard knew that Iramov had the Death fragment. Morrowmen had told Askon as much directly. But in this moment, Askon became aware that Iramov and Codard had worked together, that at the very least,

Codard knew about the planned attack on Tolarenz and did nothing to stop it. A blink of the king's eyes and the slightest glance to the four corners of the curtained room betrayed his purpose. The conversation had progressed from merely adversarial to openly hostile. Guards moved in. Askon had been right. The meeting with the king *was* a trap, one that Codard was not yet ready to spring. Askon could be easily charged for desertion, but that would not be enough to convince Edward or Thomas. Codard's eyes jumped from one to the next. He wanted all the men in the room on his side before he struck.

Askon knelt before the throne, hoping the gesture would demonstrate his commitment to the kingdom. "We must fight against Iramov," he said, lowering his head. But as he did so, something happened which he did not anticipate. The fragment, hanging from the chain around his neck, tumbled out from beneath his shirt. It fell heavily, the chain arresting its motion only a few inches from the ground. There, it pulsed green in the silent room. Askon looked up.

Codard's eyes went wild as they alighted on the gleaming stone. "Guards," he ordered. "Arrest the commander on charges of desertion!" His voice strained as he shouted the instruction. But the men did not move. For a moment, all was still.

Askon cursed himself for the mistake. His concentration faltered, and the clarity of perception crumbled. Christopher was the first to engage. He seized Askon's right arm, relishing the chance to exact even the slightest revenge. One of the guards slammed into Askon's left side, twisting the arm behind his back. The speed with which they crossed the room was greater than Askon would have thought possible. In an instant they surrounded him. John, now standing, scowled behind the throne, and the green fragment swung from side to side as the guards forced Askon to his knees.

Askon writhed and twisted, but to no avail. Christopher and the guards brought several heavy blows down upon his head and shoulders. The strokes came quickly, in rapid succession. Still, Askon continued to fight against their grasp.

"You knew!" Askon screamed as another guard approached with a heavy iron collar. "Iramov has won you to his side. You allowed him to attack Tolarenz." A heavy hand pummeled the base of his neck in an attempt to silence him. "You even recognize the Time fragment, do you not?" Askon spat the words and more blows assaulted his senses. "Where is yours? Why have you not used it to stop Iramov!"

"Silence!" Codard bellowed.

Askon felt something heavy, something hard, strike the back of his head. Dazed, he fought to arrange the stream of accusations that flowed through his mind but managed only a short series of senseless noises. As he balanced on the edge of consciousness, the king approached. "Kill this traitor now," said Codard coldly. "He speaks heresy and questions my rule. These people, these *things*," and at this he spat in Askon's face, "sow only the seeds of discontent and rebellion."

The guard who held the iron collar dropped the heavy metal ring. All around the room, the thick curtains dampened the clatter and clang. The man produced a sword, first glancing toward the king. At a terse nod from Codard, the guard lifted the blade. At the apex, strong arms flexed, bringing the sword flashing down.

His life left him before the stroke fell, as did his comrade's to Askon's left. With the same inhuman speed which the guards seemed to possess, and a deadly silence, Edward and Thomas had come forward. As the guard had lifted the sword, Thomas thrust his own through the man's back, the point emerging from the opposite side. At the same time Edward kicked the guard on Askon's left, driving him into the path of the blade and Askon into the hard stone floor. Thomas retracted his sword from the fallen executioner and rounded on Christopher, but the latter spun away, deftly drawing his own weapon. The final guard, pierced by the point of Edward's sword, died reaching for the back of Askon's cloak.

Silence fell on the room. Edward and Thomas circled the ring of dead and dying guards, weapons at the ready. The king stood, mouth agape, as Askon regained his senses and began to climb to his feet. Christopher's eyes searched for an opening between Askon's defenders, and John, sword pointed downward, rocked back and forth with indecision.

Knees bent, eyes darting from side to side at the foot of the throne, Thomas waited, showing none of his old tentative fear. When Askon was on his feet and Edward had circled to his side, all three faced the king. Much to the surprise of everyone in the room, it was Thomas who spoke first.

"Your Majesty," he said calmly. "M-My orders are to follow the commander, to defend him in battle at my own peril." He faltered as Christopher shifted position, their swords tracking one another; but he continued, though his eyes followed his opponent. "And I will do so."

"O'course ya would, ya fool farm boy," said John, whose sword still pointed to the ground. "If he'd a let ya, you'd have been with me at Austgæta 'stead of running with Christopher. Probably be dead by now. The king says this coward's a traitor."

"Enough," said Edward, his voice clear and final. "More guards will be here at any moment. Father, Askon speaks the truth. I will not stand by and watch his execution. I declare him to be under royal protection, by order of the prince of Vladvir."

Codard gave no response, only a twisted grimace as he stood impotently before his throne, staring at Askon's chest where the Time fragment pulsed like a slow, laborious heartbeat.

"So, what is it?" continued Edward. "Are you in league with Iramov? Did you allow him to attack Tolarenz? And what are these *fragments*?"

"Ravings of a traitor," spluttered the king. "If you defy me, beware. Royal proclamation or no, I am king, and this criminal will be apprehended. As will all who aid him." At this Codard paused. Askon, head throbbing, tried to focus, but no calm passed over him. He glared at John and Christopher in the dim light. He blinked, trying to cast off the haze as Codard finished. "I am your father and the lord of this realm. Obey or be charged with treason."

Edward lowered his weapon. He stood stock still and erect, taller and more imperious than Askon had ever seen him.

"Then you choose to give no answer," the king said. "That is all the evidence I need."

Footsteps thundered an approach at the back of the room. Outside the curtain, the remainder of Codard's guard had assembled. Even through the thick fabric and muffled blur from his wounds, Askon could hear voices as they ordered themselves for the attack. Evidently, Edward heard it too as he turned from his father to glance at the back curtain. He spoke once more. "You can still stop them," he said.

Codard stared down: Edward standing tall, kingly, and unwavering; Thomas still tracking Christopher's every movement; and Askon only barely staying upright. But the king's eyes ever returned to the glowing gem. No word came to stop the guards who passed through the curtain in a tight line, two men deep. They marched forward, and Askon faced them. He drew his sword. As the guards advanced, the three men backed toward Codard's throne. With only a few feet remaining before they would reach the back wall, Edward pivoted on his heel, crouched, and with a shout, shot forward into the line of guards. The thrust pierced heavy mail, and the line quavered. In their moment of shock, Askon lunged, felling another.

"Follow me," Edward shouted.

He turned again while the guards reformed the line and stepped over their fallen allies. Christopher and John stood in front of the king, swords at the ready. Edward charged them, Thomas following closely behind. Codard shrank to one side and covered his head. But Edward did not stop, nor prepare to cross swords at all. He ducked quickly, narrowly avoiding both blades and drove his shoulder into John's chest. Christopher stood hesitant as Edward passed, followed by Thomas and finally Askon. John tumbled to one side, but Edward thundered on at a dead sprint to the far wall. To Askon, it appeared that he would slam against it.

He did not. Instead of solid stone, Edward met only the resistance of the curtain which billowed and twisted behind him, revealing a narrow passage directly behind the throne. Thomas passed through next, and Askon strained his eyes as he watched their blurred figures disappear down the corridor. Behind, he could hear the guards, clanking and clattering in their heavy armor.

The passage ran a long straight path before making several sharp turns, each with another straight span in between. Edward followed the turns with such confidence that Askon surmised he could have done so in the dark. They came then, still at a run, to a place where the hallway turned a circular bend to the left. It then forked, with one path remaining level and another descending gradually.

They stopped at the fork. Askon peered down the level path, which led no more than fifty feet before it terminated in a small room. There, on a marble pedestal, rested a velvet pillow fringed with gold. Atop the cushion, a deep blue gem pulsed with faint light. Askon gaped. Looking down at his own fragment, he watched as the light grew brighter than he had yet seen it glow. The luminance expanded until it cast all three men's faces in lurid green. Askon stepped into the hall.

Edward yanked him back. "It's one of my father's personal storage rooms, Askon. We can't get out that way." Armored footsteps drew closer. "The servants' quarters are down the other fork. They have many entrances and exits. We have to go, now."

Askon fell back as his friend pulled roughly on his arm. Codard's fragment vanished from view as they passed down the hallway. Thomas followed dutifully behind.

A few moments later they spilled out of the passage one after the other: Edward, Askon, Thomas. At first, Askon could see nothing. The large chamber into which they had entered was much brighter than the long dark of the passageway behind the throne room. Above them several wide skylights allowed the sun's rays to shine through into what Askon assumed to be the main hub for castle servants. Here, many men and women bustled about carrying laundry, firewood, trays, and dishes. It all progressed so smoothly that Askon felt as though he were watching a complicated mechanism rather than a roomful of people.

Edward's eyes darted from side to side, searching. He picked up speed as they passed the servants. Several of them raised a hand to greet the prince, while others turned their gaze. The waves were returned with a simple nod of the head as the three men moved quickly through the large room. Following a huge, bearded man, Edward led them to the door furthest from where they had entered. Askon tried to track the twists and turns of the passageway in his mind, but found his sense of direction baffled. He assumed that they were heading away from the center of the castle and toward the outer wall.

Edward placed a hand on the bearded man's shoulder. "May I?" he asked calmly, indicating the door. The man stared back, blinking slowly, eyes wide.

"O' course," he managed with an awkward bow.

"Thank you," said Edward. He flipped a silver piece toward the man, who smiled back broadly.

Askon slipped through the door first, followed closely by Thomas, and finally Edward. He stood just on the other side of the threshold while the others came through. The door swung shut, and Askon peered back into the room. There, the troop of guards emerged, single file, into the servants' quarters. Askon closed the door, hoping that the size and bustle of the room, as well as their friendly reception by the bearded man would provide enough cover.

Unlike the passage at the back of the throne room, the tunnel from the servants' quarters showed its age and use more readily. The floor was covered in flecks of bark and pieces of wood. On the walls a damp film covered the rough-hewn stones, and here and there moss and lichen clung to the mortar. Every thirty feet or so, a torch burned or lay cradled in a rusty iron bracket. Soon these gave way entirely, and Askon detected natural light somewhere far along the tunnel. The pavers lining the floor ended, and he felt the soles of his boots press into packed earth. But the light was not as far away as Askon had at first guessed. Only a few feet from the change in the floor, the tunnel broke hard to their right and descended gradually. At the bottom of the descent, an archway opened in what Askon perceived to be the castle's outer wall.

Outside of the archway, the king's servants had cut a wide lane clear of trees. Long before Askon or Edward or even Codard was born, the king's great-grandfather had begun construction on the castle. Its initial design incorporated mostly wooden beams and panels, as did the town hall in Tolarenz. To supply such an immense undertaking, a large source of trees was required. Codard's ancestors had found it in the forest of Ellmed, a huge expanse of broad-leafed trees that bordered the grasses of the Vladvir plain. Many had explored the forest, and some claimed to have emerged safely on the other side. What was there, only a few knew. Common belief held that the world came to its end with the ending of those trees. Askon held no such belief, but a shiver ran down his spine as they stepped into the lane.

CHAPTER FOUR

Ellmed

Beneath the canopy of leaves, a soft glow warmed the dampened earth. Three silhouettes perched atop a web of fallen trees that rested lightly on a bed of rustling bracken. The leftmost figure sat hunched, with one ankle crossing the opposite knee, plucking briars from his trousers. At every third or fourth briar, the figure would flinch and recoil at the sharp prick of thorn. As he did, the end of the tree would bounce and sway wildly. Leaves and dead branches crackled; the figure wobbled, almost toppling to the ground, and the remaining two silhouettes watched impassively for a moment before returning their attention to something that lay on the ground before them.

"Ow!" Thomas whispered with a sharp hiss. He flapped his hand, and the knuckles snapped together. The tree shook.

"You'll never get them all," said Edward flatly. In his hands he held a pointed stick, the sharp end of which he had pressed into the soft soil.

"And," added Askon, who held a pointed stick of his own, "when we begin again, the thorns will only recollect on the trousers." He returned his attention to the place where the two sticks converged, attempting to ignore Thomas who continued picking and wincing alternately through the thorns.

On the ground between Askon and Edward, a crude map had been scrawled into the dirt. It coarsely but accurately depicted the Vladvir plain, Codard's castle, and the approximate dimensions of Ellmed forest. For clarity's sake, Askon had crushed several dead leaves and sprinkled them in a line indicating their respective paths to the castle, then one line leading away into Ellmed. A few inches from where the depicted forest began, the line stopped.

"Alright," Askon said, pointing with the stick. "You came from Iramov's stronghold, west." He tapped a dot of dead leaves, then arced the stick across the makeshift map to the castle. "But you were somehow transported, rather than crossing it on foot, thus arriving before Thomas or myself."

"Correct." Edward nodded.

"And I," continued Askon, "came from Tolarenz, here." He tapped the stick at a rounded divot in the map's northern extreme. "From there, I went southeast to reach the castle." The line of dead leaf bits trailed from the top of the image to the point where the paths intersected. "Then Thomas," he said with emphasis on the younger man's name, hoping to get his attention, "came down from Norogæta with Christopher."

There was a pause. "Right Thomas?" said Edward.

"Oh-uh-yeah…" Thomas responded.

"Pay attention!" Edward grumbled.

Thomas relinquished the leg of his trousers and the numerous thorns still resident there, sidled along the tree trunk until he was within a few inches of Edward, and rested his elbows on his knees and his chin in his hands.

They had crawled, sprinted, trudged, and padded through the trails and trackless spaces of Ellmed for hours. From the castle their path first led them east. Soon, the low stumps and piled brush ceased, and a wall of trees and shrubs replaced it. On into that dark barrier they plunged, where the wild weeds of the harvested area pushed into the border of the forest. The thistle and brush, dense for only a short while, had provided much-needed cover. Somewhere behind them, the king's men still followed, and did so even into the thickest trees and brambles. But where the forest had aided Askon and his friends, it hindered the castle guards. Their heavy, ornamental armor became hopelessly tangled in the plants and vines. Some of the guards had remained behind, helping those who had become stuck.

Those not caught up, Askon found, were relatively easy to confuse at any distance from the main trail. By then, however, the forest had given Askon time to think. He sent Edward and Thomas in opposite directions and himself in another. Each of the three was to loop and crisscross not only his own path through the trees, but the others' as well. At one point, their scheme had worked so beautifully that from a bluff at the top of a rise, they were able to rest and watch as four guards crossed and recrossed each other's paths.

After having watched two of the guards stumble into the forest to the west, while the other pair went east, Askon and his friends seized the opportunity and rushed along the spine of the rise until they reached a well-worn game trail. They followed it north as quickly as possible, breaking from the path, struggling against the brush, careful to leave little mark or sign. In the late afternoon glow, the three men had emerged into the clear space with the overlapping windfalls.

It was Askon who suggested the halt. They had not seen or heard anything or anyone since the confused guards had stumbled into the trees below the bluff. Now, tired and thirsty, the three sat on the bouncing tree trunk in an attempt to decide where they would go next.

"We could stay in the forest," said Edward. "You said that no one is following us anymore."

"Marten has seen nothing," Askon replied. The falcon had pursued them along their journey north and now hopped from one unsteady tree to another, eyeing the low bushes for movement.

Edward shook his head, his dark features brightening into an incredulous smile. "I wish I knew how you did that," he said.

"What?"

"Talk to Marten. You know that's one of the things that makes people uneasy around you, around elves."

Askon rose, his face dark. "You know better than that," he snapped, a little too loudly. "I can't talk to animals any more than you can. But I do *see* them, understand them better than most—"

"Humans?" offered Thomas.

Askon gritted his teeth, and his upper lip curled. He stepped across the space, scowling at Thomas, and shot out a hand to grasp the young man's collar. But the hand never found its mark. With almost no effort at all, Thomas leaned to one side and watched Askon's hand pass harmlessly by. He batted it down and laughed as though Askon were playing a game. What had begun as irritation now bloomed into anger, and Askon struck again, only this time more earnestly. Thomas again leaned effortlessly out of reach and batted the hand away, laughing. Furious now, not only at the offense toward his race, but also at his inability to strike, Askon drew his sword.

"Whoa!" Thomas managed, standing with both hands in the air. "I thought you were just playing around."

"Askon!" barked Edward. "What is the matter with you?" His hand already gripped Askon's sword arm. In the blink of an eye, he had moved, almost impossibly so, from his seat to Askon's side.

Bewildered by the surprising agility of his comrades, Askon paused. The frustration receded, and he lowered his sword. "Don't tell me what it means to be human or half-elf," he said, breathing deeply.

Edward released Askon's arm.

Thomas's eyebrows lifted as a smile appeared on his face. "I'm sorry if I offended you, Askon. But I laughed because I thought it was a joke. You moved as though you were under water. If I knew you were serious, I would never slap your hand away."

Askon paused, reaching to his chest where the Time fragment hung from its silver chain. He pulled it from beneath his shirt and into the light of the forest. There it glowed, green on green with the leaves of the canopy above.

"I think it's time I explained something to you two," he said. "When I arrived at Tolarenz and witnessed all that Iramov had wrought, I lingered in the empty city after he and his men had gone. It was then that I saw the events in the powdered circle in the square. What I have not yet spoken, Edward, to you or anyone, is that a circle was left behind by Caled as well. In it he somehow managed to convey a message to me."

Thomas's eyes widened. "He spoke to you from the realm of the dead?"

Askon laughed, a short snuffling sound. "No," he said, smiling. "Before his death, he knew that I was there watching. The circles seem only to provide a vision of the victim's final thoughts.

"In his message he said that I should wait for a man called Morrowmen, that this man would find me. And so he did, in the Tolarenz town hall that night. He had been hiding in a secret chamber which Caled kept as a personal study."

Askon proceeded with the details, telling them everything, even of Morrowmen's dry, biting sensibilities and his own collision with the pillar in the darkness of the hall. Then Askon explained the Tear and its several fragments. Edward began curious, but was soon angry, then dejected as Askon told him of the piece held by his father.

"He sent me to Iramov's stronghold knowing the danger? I knew that he cared mostly for himself, but not so much as to send me and my men to certain death."

Askon placed a hand on Edward's shoulder. "Morrowmen also said that *this* Iramov—as he is but one in a long line of that family name—seems to have a command of the Death fragment which his predecessor did not. Perhaps your father was unaware of the power Iramov could wield."

"Perhaps," said Edward, grudgingly.

Askon continued. "Caled also carried a fragment: this one." He held up the glowing green gem so that the others could see it. "This is the Time fragment. For Caled, it extended his life, paused the progression of age, effectively freezing him in time from the moment that he decided to carry it. Morrowmen bears another, Life, and it serves a similar function. While it is in his possession, he will not die, though age has beaten down his body for many generations. Caled was, and Morrowmen *is*, very old. The fragments were separated long before the Scouring."

"That would make them at least a hundred and fifty years old," said Thomas, astonished.

"And a great deal more if I understand what Morrowmen did not outwardly state. Twice that, maybe even more. It is hard to say once you go beyond our grandfathers' grandfathers." Askon shifted his position on the fallen tree, forcing the others to adjust as well. The branches rattled and swayed. "That leaves two of the five unaccounted for. One of those two, we know, is in Codard's possession. I saw it myself as we made our escape. The owner of the last is none other than Lord Apopsé of the South Kingdom. The five men who carried the fragments were known as the Greats in the time of the Tear's separation. Apparently as the years went on, Apopsé, Iramov, and Codard passed the fragments on to their heirs. Morrowmen and Caled never accepted the title, though, and their names, as well as the title itself, faded from use."

Edward stood and the fallen tree shifted. Thomas wobbled precariously, swinging one arm widely in an attempt to regain his balance.

"I don't understand," Edward said after a moment. "My father possesses a fragment of Alora's Tear, but he sends me to Iramov's stronghold to retrieve another. Then, he sets the guards on you for accusing Iramov."

Askon looked up from the crude map they had drawn in the dirt. "Ah, but your mission was a secret, was it not?"

"And what of that?"

"Well," Askon continued, "I think we can safely say that Iramov intends to collect the fragments and keep them for himself."

Thomas, now holding steady on the tree trunk, tilted his head in Askon's direction. "We can?"

"Yes. On his way out of Tolarenz, Iramov took the scepter that Caled carried. In that scepter is set a large blue gem, but it is not one of the fragments. Iramov had no way of knowing what to look for and in his haste carried off a very valuable, but not very useful souvenir." Askon smiled, amused by Iramov's overconfident mistake. Edward however, remained serious.

"How does my father fit into all of this, Askon?"

Askon thought for a moment. If he painted a picture of the king that offended Edward, he might weaken his friend's support. But if he suggested that Codard's motives were noble, he could possibly avoid sounding accusatory. He settled simply on the truth. Back in the city, at the Goat's Beard, he had chosen to hide details from his friend, but no more. Edward and Thomas had proven their loyalty at the foot of the king's throne. That would be enough.

"I believe," Askon said, "that your father is trying to collect the fragments for himself before Iramov can. Each is playing against the other. Each believes that he has a friend, or at least an ally, in the other. And in the throne room, when I accidentally revealed the Time fragment, your father saw an opportunity to gain the upper hand. But Iramov has an advantage that the king didn't know about until you arrived, Thomas."

The young man rose awkwardly, backing away. In doing so, he nearly fell as his boot caught on one of the tree's branches. He stumbled then righted himself. "What? I didn't mean to—" he stammered.

"Don't worry," said Askon calmly. "You've done nothing wrong. I was referring to Iramov's secret allies, the Norill. With them under his command, or at least his influence, he can threaten the king, maybe even coerce him into giving up his fragment, or take it by force as he tried to do against Caled."

Edward nodded. "And force might be all the more likely if Iramov believes that he has two fragments in his possession."

Marten alighted on the leather guard at Askon's shoulder. Over the course of the conversation, the bird had taken to the sky and returned to the clearing several times. He stooped his head once, twice, then again, and the shimmering gray feathers on his back flashed in alternation with his speckled white chest. Askon leaned in close, studying the creature's movements.

"Someone is out there," he said, pointing to the opposite side of the clearing where they had entered. "We may have squandered our lead."

Quickly and almost silently, save for a few awkward missteps by Thomas, the three lowered themselves behind the fallen tree. Over the smooth gray bark, Askon could still see clearly the map with its crushed leaf pathways and crude approximation of the topography. He reached through the space beneath the trunk and scattered the drawing. A small, thin cloud of dust arose and drifted a few inches into the air.

The sun had crossed the afternoon sky, the shadows lengthening. Askon felt himself relax as they settled into their hiding place. And then, just as it had in the king's throne room, the eerie, unnatural calm fell upon him. He slipped the hood of his cloak over his head and risked a glance across the clearing.

Askon's half-elven eyes were far-seeing, but even he could not make out more than silhouettes as their pursuers emerged from the tree line several hundred feet away. Then, in his heightened state of awareness, he noticed something. One of the shapes moved deftly, almost effortlessly through the brush and branches. The movements betrayed a resolved determination, and under that, brutal anger. The shape wanted revenge. As clear as if he had called his own name aloud across the open space, Askon knew who it was. He lowered his head and turned to the others.

"Christopher," he whispered.

"What now?" asked Edward. However, it was not Askon who answered but Thomas.

"If the map was right, we are southeast of Shale, my village. If we can lose them in the forest again, we can cross the plain after nightfall. I know the area from the edge of the forest to my home," he said.

It was as good a plan as they were likely to find on little notice. Askon lifted a finger and indicated the trees behind them. Slowly, silently, they backed out of the clearing and into the depths of Ellmed again, crossing and recrossing trails, making blatant marks that led to dead ends, separating and reuniting in an effort to evade their pursuers. Christopher's woodcraft obviously exceeded that of the castle guards, but the three managed to gain on him bit by bit until afternoon descended into the blackness of night.

What was a slow and tedious process by the light of day became arduous under the nighttime shadows. In the darkness Askon could see more clearly than his companions, who now tripped and stumbled often as they followed a well-worn path toward the lilting trickle of a stream somewhere below. It had been quite some time since they had seen or heard anything from Christopher or the king's men, and even longer since they had encountered water clean enough to drink. At first the brush and terrain under the canopy of Ellmed had nearly been their undoing. Thomas fell behind, and Askon was forced to retrace his steps in order to set him right again. Twice, they had been within a long bowshot of their pursuers.

But they had not been captured, and it seemed that even Christopher had now lost the trail entirely or fallen so far behind that he would have little hope of regaining the lost ground. When they reached the stream, they cupped deep, gasping draughts into their hands, splashing the remains over their faces and onto their clothes. After taking his fill, Askon stepped into the swiftest part of the channel. Only a few inches deep, the water swirled around his boots, and his eyes could see the clear water become clouded with sediment where his friends saw only a glimmer on the water's shifting surface. Then in a few quick strides Askon moved a few yards upstream, where he waited for the others.

"Just get your feet wet and follow the water," he said softly to the others.

Thomas glanced at the water, then back to Askon. He produced an empty waterskin from a pouch along his belt. "'Always be prepared.' That's what they told me before I left home." His eyes fell again, and he knelt to fill the bottle. After a moment, he looked up once more. "What good are we doing by soaking our boots? The guards don't have any dogs."

Edward stood at the edge of the stream, hands on his hips and an expectant look on his face. The calm focus had lifted from Askon long before, but even without it he could read his friend's stance which seemed to say, 'You know he's right.'

Askon did know that Thomas was right. They were tired, hungry, and the darkness only made their progress more difficult. But he did not want to give Christopher any chance of following them once they had broken from the cover of the forest onto the open plain. "Indulge me," he said heavily.

A few minutes later, some way up the stream, the three sat, eating from the bits of nut and berry they had collected as they wound through the forest. Each selectively picked at his own meager supply and cupped handfuls of water from the stream.

"Alright," said Askon. "We're clear of any pursuit, but if they're still back there following—and they surely are—we need to keep moving. I know little about this territory, but we've gone much farther north than before the clearing. There, we were only a few miles from the castle. We've gone at least that far again, only straight north."

"Thomas," asked Edward, "how far north is your village from the castle?"

The younger man lowered the handful of nuts at which he had been nibbling and looked up. "Well, the plain actually slopes downhill from King's City to my village, and on clear nights you can usually see the outline of the turrets from the edge of town."

"Then we've overshot it." Askon sighed, annoyed. Doubling back to the south, even on the plains meant closing the distance between them and Christopher. He had hoped to leave the forest on a level, or as nearly so as possible, with Thomas's village.

"Don't lose your temper, Askon," said Edward smiling. "I wouldn't want to see Thomas slap you around again."

"Don't remind me," grumbled Askon.

After another few moments eating quietly, they rose and set out to the west. If Askon had judged it correctly, they had been moving in a straight line to the north but drifting gradually to the western edge of the forest. Little of the thick, slow brush remained between them and the plain. High above, Marten glided in huge arcs over the men. And under his watchful eye, only three shapes moved in the night.

Hours later, a bright moon shone over the Vladvir plain. Thin wisps of cloud filtered and shifted over the glowing orb, while a breeze rustled the stalks of thistle and twisted stems of sage. Birds and other creatures flitted from place to place, but their quiet movements stirred only the slightest sounds among the long-bladed grass. In the distance a herd of deer bedded down, languid shadows in the moonlight, and one antlered head lifted above the rest, a watchful guardian, silently listening.

Since leaving the forest, Askon and his friends noticed little that would arouse suspicion or doubt. Following more or less the path of the stream from which they had drunk at the onset of night, they made their way west and slightly south, observing Thomas's instructions. In so doing, they arrived without event at the outskirts of the village. By Askon's best guess, several hours still remained before sunrise. An attempt to enter the town at such a late hour would only attract unwanted attention, so the three friends chose a flattened hilltop for their camp. There, a wide vista allowed them some warning if anyone were to approach, and a few stunted trees provided cover from the wind and camouflage against keen, searching eyes.

Askon, tired and travel-worn as he was, elected to take the first watch. His friends had defended him when he most needed it, followed him unflaggingly through the maze of Ellmed, and in Thomas's case, offered sanctuary to known fugitives. Allowing them some time to rest, Askon decided easily, was the least that he could do in return. So it was that Edward and Thomas drifted into peaceful sleep.

Reaching for a nearby stick, and planting it vertically into the ground, Askon watched, by the light of the moon, a weak shadow appear over the ground. At the four major compass directions Askon made deep marks with his finger and then another, lighter yet precisely where the stick's shadow now lay. Listening to the slow deep breathing of his friends, Askon found himself matching the rhythm, and once again the quiet calm descended upon him.

There were seven trees beginning at the base of the small hill, each shorter than the one before it. Two had four main branches at the fork in the trunk, four had three, and the one under which Askon sat cross-legged had only two. The farthest tree housed a simmering beehive on its third main branch. The melon-sized hive stood smooth against the shadowed background of foliage. Even in the dark, Askon began to count the busy workers of the hive. They were inactive in the cool darkness, but each insect thrummed with anticipation for the morning's light. Finally Askon lost his count at nearly five-hundred. His eyes wandered, noting similar details amongst the branches of the other six trees: a bird's nest in one with more large debris than small, a non-venomous snake curling along a branch with two-hundred and sixty-two leaves from the point where the snake lay to the end, a half-starved squirrel moving from tree to tree, and many other nightly comings and goings.

When he felt that a great length of time had passed, he checked the shadow. It had not moved even in the slightest. There, at the tip of the blurry blackness, was the thin mark he had made in the dust. Based on his meandering thoughts, the process of counting five-hundred bees, and the analysis of each individual tree, he had expected to see the passage of an hour, at least.

The slow hours of a night-watch were no new experience for Askon. Upon enlisting in the king's army, it had been one of his first assignments to sit the initial watch several nights in a row. He knew the tricks for defeating boredom and the deceptively slow progress of time when all was quiet and uneventful; but this was different. It was as if time had stopped completely, or slowed so significantly that no perceptible change could be observed. Reaching into his shirt, Askon pulled the fragment of Alora's Tear into the open air. It pulsed soundlessly, and Askon stared into the depths of the gem. The green glow grew and shrank in hypnotic waves of light, now brighter, now darker.

Further relaxed by the fragment's light, Askon watched as it began to slow. At first the pulses were seconds apart, now they seemed minutes, now more, now stopped. When the light reached its dimmest, it held, shimmering in place. Complete silence fell on the hilltop. Askon stared at the gem. No rustling grasses intruded on his thoughts, no buzzing bees or flitting birds. Not only was it silent, but all around him, every leaf, branch, and creature was utterly still. Even the slow breathing of his companions had halted.

Something new entered his vision. It did not move. It made no sound; yet Askon knew that it was out of place in the scene. He tried to focus more closely on the new addition, straining his eyes toward the village where a torch cast the shadow of a man. But he did not belong there and had not been there when Askon first looked into the green stone.

The stillness shattered. With dizzying speed, everything in Askon's field of vision began to move. The gem pulsed, the trees waved in the wind, and Edward and Thomas began to breathe once more. And still, at the edge of the village, the shape that Askon knew to be Christopher stalked the shadows in and out of the torchlight.

Askon's reply came again in a whisper. "No. We've been followed." He reached out and grabbed Thomas by the shoulder, shaking him slightly. Unlike Edward, Thomas shot bolt upright, eyes wide.

"Whoa, easy Thomas." Askon's voice remained low and smooth, though louder than when he had awoken Edward. "Breathe. Just stay quiet."

Thomas did as he was told, and Askon gave them both a moment to gather their thoughts. Then, pointing across the hilltop, he motioned toward the tree under which he had taken his watch. The three stayed low to the ground, following Askon's lead. He settled onto the edge of a flat stone that lay buried in the grass. The others sat as well, and Askon pointed to the shadowy area where Christopher and the guards had first appeared.

Askon pushed back the hood of his cloak, leaned forward, and stared into the gray morning. The knuckles of his hand brushed back and forth across his upper lip, absently. One pointed ear lay exposed where the hood had pulled his hair aside. He flipped the ear and hair back into place. He said nothing.

The others watched as Askon had commanded, waiting for him to speak. The guards crouched, almost comically, in a shadow too small for their number. Who, or what they were hiding from was unclear. The men seemed disoriented, many of them looking from one side of the gathering to the other and back again. Askon knew that neither Thomas nor Edward would be able to identify Christopher as he had done. Only Askon's sharp sight and the fragment could somehow bring such clarity. If he was right, the others would see only a group of soldiers and their leader. It was enough though, even without the fragment. Edward turned to Askon.

"Christopher?"

"Yes," Askon replied without taking his eyes off the intruders. His hand moved to his face, and the knuckles brushed back and forth once again.

Thomas leaned in front of Edward, trying to get closer to Askon. "How do you know?" he whispered.

"I think it's the fragment," Askon said, his hand muffling the sound. "It happened first back in the throne room. I could tell that the king meant me harm long before it should have been clear. His face betrayed his intentions, as did Christopher's movements."

"Of course you could," said Thomas quietly. "He was the first to grab you."

Askon shook his head. "No. I knew before that, while the king was still treating me like a soldier rather than a prisoner. You were never undecided, Thomas. I saw that too."

Edward shifted uncomfortably. Askon smiled.

"And you had reason to weigh the situation, Edward. I hadn't told you everything. Had our places been reversed, I would have been equally suspicious," Askon said. "Then it happened a second time in the clearing. I knew it was Christopher by his movement and posture, or some other detail I shouldn't have been able to see at that distance."

"You're a half-elf, Askon," said Thomas. "Your eyes are much better than ours."

Askon shook his head again. "It's not that. I mean, you're right that I can see more clearly at a distance. But I couldn't see his face, certainly not here in the dark, where it happened a third time. No. It has to be the fragment. I…" He paused, trying to assemble the right words. "I notice things. The feeling is different than seeing. I know it as plain as if Christopher had spoken it to me himself."

Edward turned to face Askon. "Whatever it is, I'm glad it's happening. Otherwise we might have walked right into *that*." He pointed at the group of guards. The sunrise had brought some of the village to life. Here and there, people emerged from their homes and into the street. Christopher and the king's men approached them in turn. Several of the soldiers broke off from the main group and stood partially hidden where the worn dirt road passed the first buildings.

"We won't be getting into the village while Christopher still believes that we're headed this way," said Thomas.

Edward stood and brushed the back of his trousers. "Let's give them some time to decide that we're not coming," he said. "We can last a couple of days, frugal days, but if they aren't sure of our whereabouts, they may decide that we've gone around the village or taken an altogether different course."

Askon lowered his hand and licked his lips. "No," he said, without looking up. "The Norill could arrive at any moment. When they do, the villagers will be defenseless."

"Or they could be days away," Edward said, his voice rising. "If we go in now, Codard's men will be ready for us. We wouldn't even have the advantage of *boredom*. We should wait—"

"I will *not* wait!" Askon shouted, too loudly. The echo bounced through the trees and across the fields. Whether it reached the guards in the village, the three men on the hilltop could not tell.

"Quiet. You'll give us away," Edward hissed.

Askon gritted his teeth, his voice a smoldering growl. "I've seen one innocent village laid waste. I'll not see another." Quickly, too quickly, his friends moved away from him: Edward to the left side of the hill, Thomas to the right. In the blink of an eye they traveled several yards apiece. Askon sat seething, the flat stone cold against his backside. He looked around, and the passage of an hour slipped by in an instant. Thomas circled the top of the hill three times, stopping to kneel for what to Askon was only a second. Edward disappeared over the slope, then blinked in and out of the trees, finally reappearing on the opposite side of the camp.

Still angry, but beginning to feel the heat of his emotion subside, Askon rose from his seat and approached Thomas. If they were to save the village, or at the very least the villagers, they needed to act decisively and without delay.

Thomas sat amongst their meager packs. "Alright," said Askon slowly. "Why don't you tell me how you're doing all this?"

The younger man fumbled with the collection of supplies for a moment, then looked up. The half-elven eyes—one green and one blue—stared down at him icily. "I don't know what you mean. Edward and I left you nearly an hour ago, after the two of you disagreed. We all sat in silence for quite a while before I went to pack our gear and Edward left, as I assumed, to cool off."

Now it was Askon who stared back blankly. Then he reached for the fine silver chain at his neck and pulled the Time fragment from where it hung beneath his shirt. As always, the green gem pulsed with the same slow heartbeat rhythm. Askon cast his mind back to Tolarenz; he recalled the man hidden in his family's home. The soldier had been inhumanly agile. At the time Askon had attributed it to surprise, but now he was not so sure. And it had happened again in the throne room. The guards moved with blinding speed as he raged at Codard. It had happened a third time in the clearing with Thomas, when the younger, inexperienced man had batted Askon's hand down like a child at play. And the latest occurrence, the most unsettling to Askon, had left him exposed for what he now knew to be almost a full hour. In that time anything could have happened to him or to his friends, and it would all have been too fast for him to track.

An aged voice croaked out of memory, a voice from the town hall in Tolarenz, Morrowmen's voice:

"Caled carried the Time fragment. It has a more passive nature than the other fragments, though some qualities come and go as the pieces change hands."

And there was his answer, as blatant as a knock from Morrowmen's walking stick—and just as painful—not only in finally understanding but in realizing how obvious it all was.

"Askon?" Thomas moved his head to one side then turned, trying to see what Askon was seeing. He looked to the other side and raised an eyebrow at his unmoving commander.

Askon's fist and open palm came together with a *pop* as he emerged from his thoughts. "Edward!" he shouted. "Come here." He grabbed Thomas by the shirtsleeve, dragging him toward Edward. The prince met them halfway.

"What is it?" Edward asked irritably.

Askon smiled and placed a hand on Edward's shoulder, releasing Thomas who staggered a step before regaining his balance. "It's the fragment again. I'm sure of it now," said Askon. "On several occasions since Morrowmen gave it to me, I've been outmatched for sheer speed. Prior to a few days ago, I can't recall being bested in such a way more than a few times: my father when I was young, my trainer when I first began with Codard's army, and—of course—Caled."

"So you've always been fast. You're half-elf, Askon. It's almost like you've forgotten the most basic of facts. What's the matter with you?" asked Edward, his expression shifting from irritation to concern.

"Nothing is the matter," Askon said with a deep breath. He felt, if only slightly, what he had suspected to be true: the eerie stillness brought on by the Time fragment. Details emerged in his friends' faces, small things that no ordinary person could have noticed. "It's simple, Edward. The Time fragment is doing it all. Somehow, it changes the passage of time, or my perception of it. Back in Tolarenz, Iramov—" he paused, forcing the anger and sadness down. "He had to whip himself into a fury in order to make the Death fragment work. Mine apparently produces a similar effect when my emotions overtake me. His, it would seem, works to his benefit, while mine to my detriment. Time speeds up. I cannot react. And you all seem so incredibly fast."

"That could be a problem," Edward said, shifting his weight to one side. He and Thomas exchanged a knowing glance. "If it were true," Edward laughed, still looking at Thomas.

"Yeah, maybe you're just getting slow. You know, losing your edge." Thomas smiled.

"I'd say he's already lost it," added Edward.

Askon sighed. "I know what you're trying to do. It won't work."

"I'm not sure you know much of anything anymore, friend. Perhaps you should lie down," Edward suggested.

"The elders in my village used to take warm milk when they got this way." Thomas's voice had taken on the soft tones of a concerned caretaker. He lifted his hand to Askon's forehead. "No, sir, I really think you should lie down."

"That's enough," Askon barked.

Marten appeared, sweeping over the camp at high speed, circling, then landing at the edge of the scattered packs. The bird cocked his head to one side, fluttering his wings and tail feathers. Askon and the others stared at him closely. In a moment Askon had seen all that he needed. He lifted a finger to his lips and reached over to their gear. He unsheathed his sword, letting the scabbard fall lifelessly to the ground. With the polished blade gleaming in the sunlight, Askon indicated an area on the western side of the hill. Edward and Thomas gathered weapons of their own from where they lay near the bags. Below them a low, rumbling voice murmured quietly.

Moving silently to the edge of the hilltop, the three men gathered near a clump of twisted sage. Through the gaps in the stunted blue foliage they saw a man appear, walking leisurely from behind a tree at the bottom of the hill. A long gray beard spilled onto his chest and his balding head was bare save for a ring of white where the hair refused to fall away. His powerful stride betrayed one who has enjoyed a life of importance, and all the while they heard his song.

It was a song of working days and wondering nights, the melody rising and falling only moderately, with no piercing or thrilling highs, but with many lows which the old man sung with a vigor and robustness that calmed Askon and his friends as they watched and listened. When the man had meandered his way nearly half the hill's height, he stopped to stretch; the song continued. Then he began again, and after only a few additional steps, Thomas rose from the bushes. Both Edward and Askon reached up to pull the young man back into hiding, but they were too slow. Thomas bounded down the hill, stumbling once, but keeping his footing.

"Grandfather!" he shouted. Askon's keen eyes saw the old man's face brighten in a broad smile. His booming laughter echoed over the grasses as he raised a wide, strong hand in greeting.

CHAPTER SIX

Only What is Required

Askon pulled the hood of his cloak over his head and rose from behind the clump of bushes. Edward stood as well, and Marten landed with a flutter on Askon's shoulder. Their shadows stretched long and thin over the grasses on the hillside, angling toward Thomas and the man he had called Grandfather. Neither Edward nor Askon moved, however. They watched closely the edges of the trees as Thomas led the old man up the hill. Moments later, all four sat eyeing one another around the haphazard camp.

Thomas spoke first. "Grandfather," he said with a sweeping gesture, "this is Edward, son of Codard the king." Edward nodded slightly. "And Commander Askon of Tolarenz."

Askon stared open-mouthed at his young friend. They had traveled in secret, and now Thomas had revealed their identities without even a second thought. Askon tried to suppress the frustration, and with it the effects of the Time fragment, but the anger simmered beneath the surface.

Edward reached out and placed a heavy hand on Thomas's shoulder. "That will be introduction enough, Thomas," he said with the same dignity and lofty formality that he had used in the castle with his father. "I think perhaps Askon and I should know who we have the pleasure of meeting."

Thomas spluttered and stammered, embarrassed at the thought of having offended his superiors yet unaware of his mistake. The old man smiled again, broad and beaming. "I think I can manage that task myself," he rumbled. It was a warm, welcoming sound, and though Askon still felt the pangs of suspicion, they receded slowly as the man continued.

"The children, young men, and young women of the village call me Grandfather, but that hardly describes me in full." He chuckled to himself. "In fact, I am not and have never been a proper grandfather at all. The wife and I never did have any children of our own. She was always busy about town helping other families take care of theirs. Grandmother, they called her, obviously."

Thomas gasped and turned quickly toward the old man. "Called?" he asked. "What do you mean? Nothing has happened to her, has it?"

The old man laughed again, but this time Askon noticed a slight difference in tone. He waited for the calm of the fragment to show him more detail, but it did not. He was still annoyed that Thomas had revealed their real names. The old man's voice boomed on, and for the moment Askon ignored his suspicions.

"Oh, well, I didn't mean anything by it besides telling the story, Thomas. I think you should allow me to finish." He patted the young man on the back with his wide, flat hand. "Thomas here was one of our favorites, always very helpful, and we rewarded him often enough, I'd say."

Thomas's eyes lit up. "Grandmother's cakes are the best in the village," he proclaimed, grinning.

"Indeed they are, my boy," the old man continued. "Anyway, we've been at it so long, the village has taken to helping us out in return for our work with the children. And most every day, a young man or woman around Thomas's age will ask our advice on village business. They're so used to our input that sometimes I fancy we have more than a little influence on what happens around here."

Askon glared narrowly at Thomas, then turned his gaze on the Grandfather. "If you are so connected to the people of this village, then why do you allow the occupation of Codard's soldiers?"

"Allow?" The old man leaned back on the flat stone where he sat and folded his hands over his belly. "I said I had influence, not power, young man. There's a difference. And besides, whether I like armed men patrolling our village doesn't matter in the least. They're the king's men after all."

Askon said nothing, but Edward picked up where his friend had left off. "Indeed they are, Grandfather, and so too are they my men."

"As long as you really are the prince," said the Grandfather. "Of course, I have no reason *not* to believe Thomas here." He patted the young man again on the back.

"I am the prince," Edward said confidently. "But what, may I ask, are my father's—and my own—men doing in your village?"

The old man's laughter boomed again. "Shouldn't you be telling me that?" he asked. "It seems like something a prince ought to know."

Askon watched the conversation, listening closely for any missteps by the Grandfather, but he heard and saw none. He let the suspicions smolder.

"I have been on military assignment, *Grandfather*." This time Edward twisted the honorific like a knife, asserting his royal background and degrading the old man with an authority Askon had not seen his friend use before. "As a subject of this kingdom, especially one with, as you say, 'more than a little influence,' you are bound to tell me what my men are doing in this village."

The old man rubbed his head where the shining, bald skin met the white hairline. "You're right, Your Highness. I meant no offense. I should be able to tell you what they're doing. But the truth is that I myself don't know." He looked over the edge of the hilltop to the row of trees and the village beyond. "Appeared out of nowhere they did, last night. Can't say that I've ever seen anything like it. Then they started asking questions, wondering if we'd seen any half-elves around. No one had, of course. Folk of that sort haven't lived here since before the Scouring."

Askon perked up at the mention of his people and their troubled history. A series of pointed questions streamed through his mind, and the old anger bubbled inside him, but he did not speak. Revealing his background now might make an enemy out of an ally.

"But they stayed anyway," the Grandfather continued. "The soldiers, that is. Then, earlier today one of the children heard strange sounds out here on the hill, shouting or something. My ears aren't good enough for that sort of listening anymore, but the child was sure of it. So I came out to see what I would find. And I found you. That's all, Your Highness. I don't know anything else about your soldiers."

Edward looked out at the village, one hand moving about his temple. He curled the fingers into a fist and rested his chin on the knuckles. Thomas traced the edges of several clumps of grass with a sharp stick. Round and round it went. Across from them the Grandfather adjusted his long brown robe. He was uncomfortable; that, Askon could see easily. Once more he willed the fragment to bring on the calm clarity that would allow him to read the old man, but felt nothing.

"Well, should we tell him?" Edward broke the silence. Askon did not move. First Thomas had revealed who they were, now would Edward reveal why they had come? Askon would not allow it. He took a breath but found his voice much too late. Edward had already begun. The words floated by like debris in a swift stream. Askon could barely follow them.

"What I am about to tell you is of extreme import, Grandfather," Edward was saying. "No one, save the three of us and the king himself, knows of it as yet." Askon could not believe what he was hearing. He made another attempt to interrupt, but his thoughts felt sluggish, his speech slow.

"The defenses at Austgæta have fallen, and as we speak, a large Norill force is moving somewhere in the countryside north of here." Edward turned his gaze in the appropriate direction. "There are settlements between Austgæta and Shale, of course, but our men are unlikely to reach them before the Norill do. Considering the size of the enemy forces, those towns and villages stand little chance of defending themselves for long."

Askon breathed deep, relieved that Edward had chosen only to reveal a partial truth. Thomas's earlier mistake had made Askon second-guess his friends' judgment. His doubt concerning the Grandfather's motivations only compounded the unease.

Beneath the thick gray beard, a change came over the old man's face. Edward's information had come as a shock. "Should we not tell your soldiers then?" the old man asked.

Edward paused. He turned to Askon, who said nothing. "No," Edward replied. "No, we should not." Rising from his seat, the prince strode to the edge of the hilltop and faced the village. His shadow sprawled down the hill, making the cluster of thatched buildings seem small and insignificant before him. The others followed, and the four of them stood together, watching and listening.

"This division is on a separate mission. I see no reason to interrupt it," Edward said after a moment. "A handful of trained men would do little good in a battle against the oncoming Norill forces. My advice is that you collect anything precious that cannot be spared and leave now. When you do, so will the soldiers. Head south to King's City, or west across the river Estelle. If, for some reason, the Norill ignore your village, the people will have a chance to return. If you remain and the Norill come this way, none will survive their attack."

The Grandfather's face grew tight with concern. All of his good cheer evaporated almost instantly. Heavy wrinkles creased his eyes and cheeks, and a weight seemed to settle on his shoulders. Stooped and tired, he looked up from beneath heavy brows at Edward.

"Do not be afraid," the prince said. "We have arrived in time. Your people will be able to escape."

The old man grunted and stared at the village. Askon watched as the weight seemed to grow, pressing the Grandfather's shoulders ever nearer to the ground. Thomas embraced the shrinking man and lifted him back to his full height.

"We do need your help before you go, Grandfather," Edward said. "Our supplies have run short, and we have many villages like yours to reach before the enemy does. Is there some food or other goods that you could spare us? It is much to ask, I know, when you will be traveling soon also."

"We won't be able to carry all that we have stored, Your Highness," said the Grandfather slowly. "Come with me and I will share what I can."

"Thank you," said Thomas.

Edward placed a hand across the Grandfather's aged shoulder. "It would be best, I think, that we went unseen into the village. Our presence, plus that of my men might cause a panic amongst your people. Let us go quietly."

The old man nodded, his beard bobbing limply in the warm sun. They collected the scattered remains of the camp, Askon silent all the while. For now, he would trust the Grandfather, as it seemed they had little choice.

The four men wound a wide course about the southern side of the village, carefully staying as far or farther from the huddled buildings as they had been when camped on the hilltop. The majority of the day passed to the sound of Thomas's unending stream of questions for the Grandfather. How had his family gotten on since he set out with the king's army? Which crops were strongest? What repairs had been made to the house which had suffered a fire the previous fall? And on and on.

The day had been warm when they left the hilltop. But since then, a thick bank of clouds had rolled down from the north. When the dark band of gray first appeared, the Grandfather had stopped, staring in awe. He asked Edward if it was a portent of the coming Norill attack, and the prince shrugged off the notion. Askon recalled the darkness of the Death fragment, and hoped that Edward was right. There was no reason to believe that such a cloud could be produced by a fragment of the Tear, but the wonders Askon had seen were similarly farfetched. He shuddered at the thought.

When they had traversed the entire southern side of the village, stopping finally on the westernmost edge, the old man turned toward the nearest building. Quietly, they passed through the grasses and low shrubs to the rear door of the house. Marten descended and perched atop the ledge which overhung the door.

Inside, Askon was overwhelmed by a heavy musty odor. There was more to the smell than just a house kept by an older couple, it was in some way oppressive, even claustrophobic. On the walls hung various craft-works, some of exceedingly high quality and others shoddy, barely maintaining their shape. Some of the more eccentric pieces had notes hanging from beneath. Most of them read, "Thank you, Grandmother."

The rear entryway was a narrow hall wide enough only for one person. On either side was a bedroom, each with a bed and end table. The room on the right also had a small desk and chair, but the bed seemed as though it hadn't been used for many months. The frame was laid bare as many guest beds were in such villages, to keep off bugs or lice.

Through the entryway was a kitchen, and beyond that, a sitting room where a few simple chairs were collected around the stone fireplace. The Grandfather passed about the room, lighting several candles and lanterns. When he had finished, he rounded on Askon.

"Thomas says you're from Tolarenz, and I haven't heard word one out of you since we met on that hill this morning." Askon looked up from where he had knelt to adjust his bootlaces, the hood of his cloak casting a shadow over his forehead and eyes.

"And what would you know of me, Grandfather?" Askon said, finishing with the bootlace.

The booming voice returned, thrumming low through the gray strands of beard. "My village may be small and remote. I may seem a simple old man, but a fool I am not. I know what sort of people live in Tolarenz, *Commander*." And he twisted the word in much the same way as Edward had the Grandfather's title some hours before.

Askon's head snapped up again. "What sort, old man?"

The Grandfather smiled; on the surface, it was the same beaming smile as before, but it belied some scheme or alternate motivation. What it was, Askon could not say. The topic of Tolarenz and its people kept Askon from gaining any sort of focus or clarity. If anything, he struggled to follow the Grandfather's words at all.

"Elves," the old man said flatly, "or half-elves as I believe you all call yourselves these days." He stood straight, the weight that he carried on his conscience seeming suddenly to lift. Adjusting the belt of his robe, he took a heavy step toward Askon. "Your friend Edward's soldiers have occupied my village. They will not leave until they find a certain half-elf, by the name of Askon. Yes. Yes. They told me the name. But I ask myself why they are looking for you. Certainly not to tell you of the Norill invasion, as that is the news that you bear. Perhaps I should call them in?"

Askon leapt to his feet and reached for the old man, but his target had already eluded his grasp. Moving steadily, he unclasped the sheath at his hip and produced the long hunting knife. It glimmered in the candlelight. A chair clattered noisily, and the old man, arrested by Edward's grip, fell awkwardly into it. "Stand back Askon!" Edward said. It was a command, and Askon felt himself resist at first, then obey.

"Grandfather, why didn't you tell us this?" pleaded Thomas.

The old man said nothing. He only smiled.

Thomas tried again. "Please. I can't protect you from him." He indicated Askon, who had for the moment fallen back into the shadows of the kitchen. The drawn blade flickered, an unspoken threat.

"We are three and you are one," said Edward, still holding the man in the chair. "It would be unwise to resist."

Still the man smiled, but to Askon's surprise, his eyes began to fill with tears. The smile continued as he stared at some faraway point in the distance.

Tears spilled down the Grandfather's cheeks, and Askon turned to match the old man's gaze. There on the wall, hung a particularly well-crafted ornament. Its shape was that of two people, one man, one woman, with their hands joined together. Above it a wreath of flowers had been carefully arranged and dried. The figures stood over a crowd of other shapes that Askon did not initially recognize. The shapes were people but very small, children maybe, and only their upper-bodies showed in the artwork. The man and the woman both smiled contentedly.

"What is that?" Askon asked loudly.

The Grandfather said nothing.

"It's important to you, isn't it?" Askon lifted his sword to the delicate depiction on the wall. He angled the blade and knocked one of the dried flowers loose. It clicked lightly against artwork, then wall, then floor. The old man's smile vanished.

"Don't you touch that!" he shouted.

"Askon don't," said Thomas. He knelt before the chair in which Edward still held the Grandfather. "Where is she?" he asked. "Where is Grandmother?"

More tears rolled down, and the old man buried his face in his aged hands. "She's gone," he sobbed. "They've taken her."

For quite some time, the old man had difficulty regaining his composure. He cried, first softly into his hands, then louder and more openly until Askon feared he would draw the attention of Christopher's men. Thomas seemed content to comfort the Grandfather while Edward released his hold and backed away from the grief-stricken man. But Askon no longer trusted the Grandfather to be truthful, and every minute they spent in his presence only further proved it.

Finally, when Thomas offered to make a cup of tea for the Grandfather, Askon reached his limit. "That is enough!" he snapped. "This man had every intention of turning us over to the king's men. Now a few tears and an empty claim have you both waiting like lambs at the slaughter." He looked at Thomas and then Edward. "One of you should tell me why we continue to wait here. This man told us that he has more stores of supplies than could be carried out when they flee the Norill. Of that much, I believe he was truthful. We should take a share as payment for his deception and go."

Thin shadows played across Askon's tired face. It had been nearly three days since he had slept, and though his eyes gleamed like blue and green stars in a blackening sky, the candlelight betrayed the drooping brows and purpling circles beneath. He had sheathed the knife after it became clear that they were under no imminent threat. The clasp he left open, and it dangled loosely at his side. He pressed his fingertips into his eyes, awaiting a response.

But it did not come from Edward or Thomas.

"Don't you think I would've signaled the king's men by now if I meant you harm, boy?" the old voice boomed once again. "I've had a great many chances to betray you up to this point. I could have brought someone to the hill with me. I could have been more conspicuous as we circled the town. I could have alerted the guards as soon as we arrived—"

Askon's eyes narrowed with irritation. "Yes you could have done a lot of things. I understand."

The old man rose from the chair, and Edward, who had disappeared into the shadows, reemerged, wary now of the Grandfather. "But I didn't," said the old man. "And why? Because my wife has been taken. Your people, half-elf, are not the only ones the king treats poorly." He glanced at Edward. "His men needed leverage—and as I said—I have more than a little influence around here. They took what would give them the most power over me." He turned back to Askon. "What would you have done in my place?"

Askon took a seat in one of the chairs, leaning forward on his elbows. "You could have told us from the outset, when we met on the hilltop."

"I could have," the Grandfather replied. Then he paused, weighing his next point carefully. "But your purpose was unclear, and the king's men had declared you a fugitive. When Thomas introduced you," and at this he smiled halfheartedly, "I might've revealed everything to him, and you, on the strength of his character alone. But at the mention of your name, I allowed doubt to cloud my judgment. There I made the only mistake that I am willing to admit. I thought that I could postpone the decision until we arrived here. If I decided to call the soldiers, it would be easy for them to apprehend you inside my home. Should you somehow change my mind along the way, you would be relatively safe in this place as long as I kept quiet. For my mistake, I am sorry." He looked at Thomas. "I should have trusted you."

However, Askon was not yet satisfied. "This is all easy for you to say now that we have the upper hand."

"I am old," the Grandfather laughed. "If I cannot offer you up to the guards or rescue my wife in some other fashion, then you may do as you wish with me."

Now it was Askon's turn to laugh. "Some other fashion? You mean for us to do the work that you cannot. No, I don't think we will be doing that." He sat up in the chair, lifting his head and pulling back his shoulders. "I cannot tell you why they are chasing us. I cannot tell you where we are going. However, I *can* tell you one thing. Tolarenz *has* no people. Not anymore."

"Askon," Edward called from the shadows behind the Grandfather's seat.

Askon waved his friend off. Then he told the story—a version of it—to the Grandfather. Caled's death, the destruction of all the possessions, and the eradication of every last half-elf and human supporter; he included them all. The fragments and Morrowmen, he left out.

When he had finished, the old man spoke again. "I am sorry for the loss of your village, Commander. If I may ask, how does this explain why you are being pursued by the king's men, even as you travel with his son?"

"He is wanted for desertion," Edward broke in. "But we need to take him somewhere safe. He may very well be the last half-elf in all of Vladvir."

Askon had not taken the time to consider such a possibility before now. He knew that there were other half-elven settlements sprinkled throughout the kingdom, but none were as large or populous as Tolarenz. Some of his people lived in the large cities, though their lives were solitary and often reclusive. No, he decided, he was not the last.

"Oh I doubt he's the only one," the Grandfather grumbled. "Perhaps one of very few if Tolarenz is gone, but not the only one."

"Nevertheless, will you let us leave?" Edward asked.

"I will," said the old man softly. "Take what you need for the journey. You'll find there is plenty." He pointed to a pantry at the back of the kitchen.

Wide enough for two to stand comfortably, the small storage room held a great deal more than one might have guessed. They gathered several items from the shelves: dense bread, dried meat and fruit, roots and nuts. As they gathered, Thomas spoke.

"Sir," he said under his breath. The words were directed at them both, but Thomas's eyes were fixed on Askon. "I think we should help him."

"What? No. To reach the South Kingdom, we first have to escape Christopher. It would be impossible to keep up this chase for more than another couple of days."

Edward remained silent.

Thomas tried again. "All my life, this man has helped me. I probably spent more time, by choice, with the Grandmother than I did my own family."

"He lied to us, and led us into a trap."

"But he did not spring it," said Edward.

"Please," Thomas begged. "We won't be safe if we just leave him here. What reason would he have to keep our names secret then? But if we can rescue the Grandmother and then escape, we'll have made an ally."

The reasoning was sound. Even to himself, Askon had difficulty arguing. Yet, there was something about the old man that Askon still did not trust. He closed his eyes for a moment and felt exhaustion sweep over him.

"Thank you Lord Caled, but I do only what I feel is required of me."

It was his own voice, spoken what seemed a long time ago in the Tolarenz town hall. In truth it had been little more than a fortnight. He remembered too the list of accomplishments that Caled had recalled on that day, and how it had led to his selection as Caled's successor. But now there was nothing to inherit, just rows of empty houses and a pile of ash in the town square. Even so, he knew that his young friend was right, that they should help this man who had been to Thomas as Caled was to Askon.

"Alright, Thomas," Askon whispered with a sigh. "Before we leave, we rescue the Grandmother. I hope you have a plan in mind."

CHAPTER SEVEN

An Unwilling Accomplice

Dusk plunged deep into midnight while Askon peppered the Grandfather with questions, some relative to the rescue, some not. On the surface the situation seemed simple. Near the center of the settlement stood a small house, built in much the same fashion as the Grandfather's. There lived a woman, Ilsa, only five or ten years older than Askon. Tough and hale from a lifetime of hardship, she managed a scarce living on her own. When Christopher's men arrived in the village, he had declared her home his temporary center of operations, leaving her only two options: live with a houseful of strange men, or rely on the kindness of her fellow villagers while the soldiers put her out on the street. She had chosen the latter. Now she stayed comfortably with a generous family at the edge of town.

A great deal of their plan would depend upon this woman. Askon had, at first, responded poorly to the suggestion. "We might as well alert every villager on the row," he said irritably. "Edward, this type of operation is your specialty. Adding another mouth only encourages talk, does it not?"

Edward's response was noncommittal, but Thomas vouched for the woman. With Thomas's support, Edward seemed convinced that she would make a trustworthy ally. Askon continued to grumble and question, and doubt. After further debate, they settled on a plan of action.

First, the Grandfather, Thomas, and Ilsa would create a distraction, drawing most of the soldiers away from the Grandmother. Then, when only a few men remained, Askon and Edward would sneak into the house where she was being held and remove her, quietly if possible, by force if necessary. Meanwhile, the distraction would need to generate enough concern amongst Christopher's men to keep their attention while Askon and his friends escaped. Ideally, the Grandfather and Grandmother would then slip away to the remains of the hilltop camp. Only when all five were clear of the village would Christopher relent. He needed to understand that Askon had been there and gone.

Two weak points in the strategy nagged Askon, even after hours of heated argument, and they hinged on the displaced woman. First, for the plan to progress without incident, Ilsa would have to be brought into their confidence beforehand. This meant allowing the Grandfather to leave the house and bring her back. Thomas had expressed complete confidence in the Grandfather, but Askon remained doubtful. Second, once the woman had been informed of the plan, she would have to accept that she would be left behind, the leader of a small rebellion, possibly with blood on her hands. The

Grandfather and Thomas both agreed that there would be no better choice amongst the townspeople for such a task. Some of the men would have been better in a fight. But they, unlike Ilsa, had no immediate personal stake against Christopher or the soldiers.

Between the Grandfather, Ilsa, and a newly returned Thomas, they expected their cause to curry enough favor with the people to threaten the soldiers and convince them to leave. The villagers would outnumber the soldiers more than two-to-one. But if Christopher did not relent, Askon knew that a great many of Thomas's people would die, even in victory. And in the case of a fight, Askon would not be able to turn his back on them. However, if he, Edward, and Thomas were captured, their treatment would most likely be worse than the quick execution that Codard had commanded back in the throne room.

"I believe we have covered every foreseeable contingency," Edward said with finality. Askon's string of questions had grown increasingly disjointed and further from the plan in the course of the previous hour. They were tired—though Askon more so than the others—irritable, and anxious at the prospect of their carefully designed escape. Edward rubbed his face with one hand and stared into the fire. He spoke to the room at large: "Will it not suffice, Askon?"

For a moment Askon did not respond. He looked from Edward, who still refused to make eye contact, to Thomas, and finally to the Grandfather. Blinking heavily, he nodded his assent. There was no other way.

"Good," said Edward suddenly standing. "Grandfather, we place our trust in you. Prepare yourself, and retrieve this woman, Ilsa. I slept last night, if only briefly. I will take the first watch." He turned to Askon, who glared back, eyes ringed with red, the tired circles above his cheekbones nearly black in the wavering candlelight.

"We *will* bring her back, Grandfather," said Thomas earnestly.

The old man managed a mournful smile, yet said nothing.

Though Edward would take the first watch, Askon still did not trust the Grandfather. He sat up, resisting exhaustion. He considered following the old man, staying in the shadows, making sure that the mission was carried out according to the plan. However, he could not bring himself to stand. Instead, Askon watched the Grandfather cross the room, lift a cloak from a rack near the door, and fasten it at the neck of his robe. His worn boots, which he had removed several hours before, sat on the floor under the row of pegs from which he had taken the cloak. Kneeling slowly, he began to lace them: loop and cross, loop and cross. Askon felt his eyelids droop. Loop and cross, loop and cross. A long slow blink and the Grandfather had pulled on the second boot. Loop and cross, loop and...

"Askon?"

"Yes, Líana."

"Let's play the salamander game."

"The salamander game?"

"Yeah, the one that Father plays. Don't you remember?"

"No. Why don't you explain it to me again?"

"If I do, will you play it with me?"

"Yes."

"Ok. So, I sit on one side and you sit on the other. Right… there. Father says the game is about settling down. I think he does it when I'm too excited, but it's still fun."

"I think you're right."

"Well, you look at me, and I look at you, and we each choose something about the other. Like your nose or your shirt or a button. Then I go first. I say: 'Don't think of a—' and father always starts with a salamander, so we'll start with that too. Whoever thinks about one first—and you have to be honest—slaps the table. Then we do it again, only it's your turn to pick."

"Ok, Liana. Let's play, then."

"Don't think of a salamander!"

Slap.

"Askon… Askon, wake up." Edward's voice seemed muted, as if he were calling from several rooms away, or as if Askon had submerged his head in a tub of warm water.

"Sir. It is time." Now the voice was Thomas's, clearer, though still dampened and flat.

Slowly, Askon opened his eyes. Outside the window, opposite his seat at the table, the village was filled with gray images that betrayed the coming dawn. He had slept away the remainder of the night. Thomas and Edward stood near the front of the house, their traveling clothes and gear arranged neatly. Edward had no doubt made sure that Thomas's weapons were sharp while doing the same for his own.

Askon felt embarrassed that he had fallen asleep without completing the same evening ritual himself. He reached for his sword belt.

"We did it for you," Thomas said.

Askon shot the young man a glare and stomped across the room. He grabbed Thomas by the collar and pushed him up against the wall. The young man's eyes widened as his body seemed to shrink under Askon's grip.

"*I* did it for you," said Edward quickly, and Askon released Thomas, who fell awkwardly to the floor.

As a part of Askon's coming-of-age, he had sworn never, even in the greatest of need to allow another to handle the blade he would be given. It was to be protected, treated not as a cold, cruel instrument as many of the human trainers preached, but as an extension of one's self, even as a friend. Later he learned that, historically, the elves had made exceptions to this rule. Before the Scouring, when two friends had survived a great struggle or won victory against impossible odds, they would then sharpen the other's sword. It was a symbolic gesture that signified the bond shared by the two. As one helped the other in battle, so he did with the other's weapon when the battle had ended.

After Edward's rescue and their joint escape from Vestgæta, Askon and Edward had practiced this tradition, though to Askon's knowledge it had never been observed between human and elf. Since that first night, they had improved upon the original concept, adding a practicality that the elvish custom did not allow. On nights when one of them was required to keep watch and the other not, the watchman would sharpen both swords. Thus, if Askon were on watch for a group of soldiers and neither the second nor the third watchman would be

Edward, Askon would sharpen his own blade as well as his friend's. When the roles were reversed, Edward would do the same. Yet, amongst the members of Codard's army, many were the legends of Askon's wrath were anyone else to dare touch his sword. In this he remained traditional, like his father, and practical, like his mother.

Askon straightened his belt and glanced at Thomas. "I apologize for responding so harshly," he said. "After what happened at Tolarenz, the traditions—my father's traditions—seem somehow more important."

"I understand, sir. When Edward sharpened your weapon last night, I forgot that your people don't usually allow others to do that."

Askon turned his gaze on Edward. "Thank you," he said. "Now where is the Grandfather?"

"You're welcome," Edward replied, for the moment ignoring Askon's question. "I should have said something to Thomas about the sword. You seem to have found your speed again, though. I didn't notice any of the awkward sluggishness that you've been showing." Then he lowered his voice, whispering behind a cupped hand. "Are you still wearing the fragment?"

"I am."

"I thought you said it was slowing you down somehow. If that is the case, why were you able to grab Thomas so easily?"

Askon smiled. He cocked an eyebrow at Thomas. "I've had to teach recruits that lesson so many times before that it no longer truly upsets me. The anger is now more teaching tool than emotion. I still find it disrespectful, and with the fall of Tolarenz, offensive, but any real anger ceased long ago."

"Let's hope," said Edward, "that you can feel the same way about Christopher and his men if our rescue turns violent. We'll need every bit of your skill if it comes to a fight."

Behind them, the candle on the table went out. A thin wisp of smoke trailed up from the melted stub of wax. The interior darkened, and the oncoming light of morning glowed in the window glass. Without looking back, Askon flicked his hood into place and turned the doorlatch. "I have a theory that may allow me to resist the fragment, but I won't know for sure until we test it. Let's find the Grandfather."

On the other side of the door, Marten waited. Whether he had stayed there all night, Askon did not know. Fluttering his wings rapidly, the falcon hopped from the peak of the roof to one corner, and then from the lower eave to Askon's shoulder.

Rested and refreshed, Askon knew immediately where the old man would be waiting for them. They circled the small building and found the Grandfather vigorously explaining something to a tall slender woman. Without the light of day, Askon knew that neither of his friends would be able to see any details, but he could see that the woman had once been exceptionally attractive. Now her eyes were cold, calculating, her stark features angular and hawkish. Like a statue slowly worn by harsh winds, she had been eroded by the passing of years. And though she was tall—taller than Askon, yet shorter than Edward—her back bowed slightly, another sign of a difficult life. At her full height, Askon guessed, she would have easily looked down upon all of them.

"Ilsa," Askon heard the Grandfather say plaintively. "They will help us. They can rescue my wife. Please, let them."

The old man remained with his attention trained on the woman. He did not hear the others approach, but her eyes had already locked onto the shadowy forms that emerged from behind the house.

"This is our rescue?" she crooned, in feigned feminine distress. Her voice creaked with wear, like the hinge on an overused door. "An old man, a boy, and if this damn light isn't too dim, a half-sprite. One green eye, one blue? That hood fools me not at all, elf. Hiding something? Show your pointed ears if you want me to trust you." She looked back to the Grandfather. "That's a bad omen, Havard. A disguise is a lie, and liars make bad confederates."

Bristling at Ilsa's epithet, and unnerved by her perceptive observations, Askon felt the fragment's effect begin to take hold. The use of the Grandfather's real name caught Askon by surprise, and the woman's accusations showed that she would prove a powerful, if somewhat temperamental, ally. The world seemed to quicken, and Askon resisted the urge to clutch the fragment within his fist. Ilsa looked irritated, said something that Askon did not understand, and the old man responded in kind. They continued; Askon closed his eyes.

"Don't think of a salamander!"

Askon looked again at Ilsa. Now would be as good a time as any to test his theory. Below her left eye, just under the ridge of the cheekbone, a crooked scar marred her otherwise handsome face. It appeared old enough to have been there when the wrinkles of age had not, when she had been young and beautiful. Considering the possibilities, the difficulties of a woman marked in this way, Askon understood the abrasive tone and hurtful words. As he did so, her voice as well as the Grandfather's grew clearer. Their movements slowed, returning to normal. Askon continued staring at the scar.

"What are you looking at? A whole man would have the courage to ask instead of stare," Ilsa said without the feigned femininity. "Ah, but you're only half of one, aren't you?"

Askon reached out to grab her, but his friends were much too fast. Once again, the effect of the fragment returned. Edward grasped Askon's shoulder and Thomas his wrist before he could even begin his move toward her. He tried again.

"Don't think of a salamander!"

This time he picked something more innocuous than the scar. On the ground between Ilsa and the Grandfather lay the old man's satchel. Askon supposed it was filled with items that the Grandfather and the Grandmother would take with them to the hilltop campsite. Askon wondered if the Grandmother had made the bag herself. He examined each stitch, imagining an old woman's hand carefully threading the needle and sewing the seams. As he studied the bag, the quick speech and movement around him slowed once again. He tried to focus.

"You see that, Havard?" Ilsa said, again using the Grandfather's name, her voice self-righteous and hard. "I'd watch your belongings around that one. Thieves they are, skulking around in the night. Don't fool yourself. That green eye sees in the dark as well or better than we do in broad daylight."

Askon breathed deep, concentrating with all of his will on the satchel. The clasp was of fine craftsmanship, polished metal of some kind, rare in a village of this size and probably fashioned by hands different from those that had done the stitching. Women, especially old women, seldom learned the trade of metalworking anywhere in the kingdom. Askon lifted his eyes from the bag.

"The eye color does not determine the sight," he said. The response came level, though quavering near the end. If he were unable to hold a conversation, it was unlikely that a battle of any sort could be successful. Again he returned his eyes to the bag, choosing another detail in its design.

"What did you say, half-sprite?"

"His name is Askon, Ilsa," Thomas interjected. He had stepped forward so that he stood between his friend and their uncertain accomplice. "I have staked my freedom on his leadership. I led him here under the impression that we might find help, or support at the least. Instead we find contempt."

A smirk appeared on Ilsa's tired face, and the scar contorted with the movement, becoming more obvious even in the dimness. "You always were a fool, Thomas. They have silver tongues as well, I've heard. Beasts and birds obey their commands. Is that what you are, a beast beneath the yoke?"

Thomas took a step back, shrinking under the woman's withering words. His confidence shaken, he tried to reply. "I ... H-he ..."

"You see?" Ilsa said, lifting her open palm and jabbing it in Thomas's direction. "A fool."

Deep in his chest, Askon felt the old anger, biting and clawing, snarling to be released. He held it down as it struggled for the surface. Staring still at the bag on the ground between Ilsa and the Grandfather, he kept the anger at bay and the fragment dormant.

"That's enough!" Edward commanded.

Ilsa recoiled, genuine surprise on her face. She looked at the Grandfather. "And who is this?" she asked, eyes wide, like an animal ringed by hunters. She even seemed to crouch, ready for a spring.

The Grandfather looked perplexed. "I told you that there were three."

Ilsa did not move. "I saw only the elf and Thomas. You made the third. Then this one appears out of thin air."

"Ilsa," Thomas said. "He has been here the whole time."

Edward approached the woman slowly, both hands raised, palms up. "As part of my training, I've learned to remain unseen by even the most watchful of eyes. I stayed back in order to observe, and also to protect my friends were this some sort of trap."

"Not much of a plan, one protector against an ambush," said Ilsa skeptically.

The Grandfather moved quickly to Ilsa's side. He grabbed her shoulder, but she twisted away from his hand. "This is the prince, Edward," he said. "Be careful what you say."

A short, crackling laugh escaped Ilsa's tightlipped mouth. "Excuse me if I don't praise your lineage, Your *Highness*." She leaned back, resting her weight on one hip. "I'd offer you tea and cakes in my home, were it not in the custody of—oh wait—it's in *your* custody. Perhaps *you* should invite *me*."

With hands still raised, Edward stepped slowly toward her. As he drew nearer, he brought his hands to rest on the woman's thin shoulders. Upon contact she jerked her head and body away, trying to put space between them again. But Edward held fast, did not allow her to move. His face was calm, his expression warm. She scowled; he waited. Askon watched, wary that Ilsa might be armed, and unsure of what might happen if she produced a dagger or knife. In his mind, he continued to hold the image of the satchel: elegant stitching and finely wrought clasp, reinforced strap, faded wear marks, smooth on the inward-facing side.

Edward and Ilsa stared at one another: on one side a frozen, guarded expression, on the other, a warmth and power that Edward rarely allowed to show. And though they stood still as stone, behind each countenance a warrior fought a battle of will. Even so, a hard life filled with grief and loss on the plains of Vladvir could not contend with the will of kings, and that will shone brightly in Edward son of Codard. For only the slightest moment, the cold expression softened. To Askon's surprise, Edward then pulled Ilsa close, hugging her tightly.

Askon waited patiently to see how she would respond. Then he felt the fragment's calm, quiet focus. His senses heightened, and he tried to imagine the effect not falling upon him, but rather radiating outward, emanating from the glowing stone hidden beneath his clothes. He turned his attention back to Edward and Ilsa.

The span of time was brief by any measure. But both the Grandfather and Thomas remained motionless, so he assumed that it was exceedingly short. Ilsa, enfolded in Edward's arms, appeared at peace in a way that she would never have revealed by choice. Her eyes were closed, and the tiniest hint of a smile pushed the thin lips into a gentle curve. Her contentedness allowed Askon to see the truth. Behind the tightly closed eyes, Ilsa saw not Askon, not the Grandfather, not Thomas, nor even Edward who held her close. No, in her eyes was the man who was gone and the children who had survived only a few days more than he. In that moment, wrapped in the embrace of a prince, she was with them again, and her guarded, hardened, angry facade melted away. Askon smiled. With the help of the fragment, he understood her pain, and he saw it more clearly than Thomas, or even the Grandfather, both of whom had known Ilsa for years.

Then it was gone. Slowly, to Askon's eyes, she coiled her arms and shoved Edward away. With the twisted grimace that so contrasted the complete contentment of only moments before, she pushed away not just one man, but the whole world. Edward stumbled back, one step, then another, and looked expectantly toward Ilsa. She stood hunched, almost crouching, her expression guarded once again. But in her eyes, wounded and vulnerable, something had changed. Askon felt the effect of the fragment lessen, then dissipate.

"Alright," she said. "I'll do what you want, Havard. Just keep him," she indicated Edward, "away from me. And get me my house back."

The old man nodded. "Thank you," he said.

"But as long as that one's with us," and now she motioned toward Askon, "he stays where I can see him."

CHAPTER EIGHT
An Almost-Perfect Plan

Between a small house and a well-kept stable, where the creeping rays
of dawn had not yet ventured, two hooded forms crouched silently:
one black, one deepest green. Across from them, walking openly along
the gray path, a noisy group of villagers marched toward the center of
town. At their head were two men. The first was old, bald, with a long
gray beard. On his left walked the other: a youth, or so it seemed at
first, but his confidence and maturity grew with every determined step.
At the old man's opposite hand, a thin form strode proudly, almost
courtly, a woman whose carriage reflected both physical and mental
strength.

As the crowd approached their destination they found it surrounded by men in armor bearing the blue stag of King Codard.
Nodding slightly, the old man turned to the young who then fell to the

rear of the group, vanishing amidst the pitchforks, hatchets, and seldom-used swords. And still the hooded shadows watched.

Glancing toward the silent observers, the old man turned to face the heavily guarded house. The angry townspeople poured around the gate like batter in a mold, flowing slowly to press against the barrier until all the gaps were filled. At first the soldiers backed away, but after the initial shock they ventured forward, closer to the gate, weapon-points outward. At the back of the group, the young man rallied the most reluctant villagers. As he did so, a space opened around the old man and the woman, who now stood before the very entrance to the house, soldiers on either side. Then the Grandfather's thunderous voice boomed over the din.

"Captain Christopher!" he shouted. "You have taken up residence in a home not open to you. Your men are not wanted, and your captive is to be released. The people of our village have spoken. We ask only that you leave with your men immediately."

All eyes were fixed on the Grandfather at the gate. The door's creaking hinges screamed into the growing morning light. Christopher stepped onto the small raised porch; no one noticed the two hooded shadows pass around the stable, through the gardens, and behind the house.

"Grandfather," said Christopher as he glanced left, then right, surveying the number of townspeople and comparing it against his own. "As you know, I have the one that they call Grandmother in my keeping. I was unsure whether we had been too hasty in collecting her. But now I see that our fears were well-founded. We are here on official business, by order of the king. We've taken the Grandmother only as a precaution against just this sort of *rebellion*." The punishment for open opposition was well known in Vladvir. He let the word fall slowly, leaden and heavy in the ears of the villagers. "There need not be a conflict." He raised his voice to the level of the Grandfather's. "Surrender the half-elf Askon and his accomplices. When they are brought to me, I will release the Grandmother, this house, and the reward for turning in the fugitives." A surprised murmur rippled through the crowd.

"Rewards do not interest us, and no rebellion are we," thundered the Grandfather. "Vladvir is an alliance of free peoples. We serve the king when we are treated as allies, but not when we are invaded as enemies." The Grandfather gestured to the crowd. "These citizens have voiced their concerns and given their terms. You are not welcome, Captain Christopher. Release your prisoner and return the house to Ilsa, its rightful owner. Leave us." But Christopher had not yet finished, and the debate raged on.

The rear door, as Askon and Edward already knew, was guarded by two soldiers. Caught by surprise, it would be simple to overcome them. Askon had insisted upon the timing of their strike—precisely at daybreak. But as they slipped through the tall grass, ducking and hiding behind bushes, Askon saw not two but four of the king's men with weapons drawn at the back of the house. Askon guessed that no less than two additional men lurked somewhere out of sight.

Askon and Edward exchanged a quick glance. They were outnumbered, but probably not outmatched. Askon recalled his rescue of Edward at the battle of Vestgæta and their narrow escape. Granted the

Norill, though brutal and vicious, were no match one-to-one against a trained soldier; they were smaller and less well-armored. However, there had been dozens of Norill on that rainy night. Today there were only half as many of Codard's men.

A clamor arose from the front of the house. Christopher had finally pushed the townspeople too far. Voices shouted, some angry and some fearful. The guards at the rear door turned toward the noise, forgetting their post. As they did, Edward made a move to attack. Askon grabbed him and nodded behind them, to the east. The sun crept from its hidden place below the horizon, and the light of morning grew. Askon waited, turning his attention again to the house. Sunlight burst from behind the mountains, sweeping over the plains and bathing the door in brightness and color. With the light, Askon felt the unnatural calm and focus fall upon him. Again he tried to imagine it radiating from the fragment, rather than pressing down from above. He and Edward arose from the long blades of grass and rushed the entrance.

The guards heard their attackers before either could cross the full distance of the garden. Two of the men turned, bewildered and blinded by the sun's rays. Askon and Edward sprinted forward, then angled their paths sharply so that when they reached their opponents they had switched positions. The first two guards stood no chance. On Askon's side, the man had raised an arm to shield his eyes, but Askon's sword sliced through the tough leather hide of the man's armor and into the bone beneath before even the shadow had fallen.

Moving fluidly to his left, Askon angled the blade and thrust quickly, piercing the second guard before the man had a chance to turn around. Both guards remained standing, so Askon retracted the blade and cut again at the knees of the first man and in the same stroke opened the veins in the second man's neck. Still they stood, and again Askon cut. Twice more he struck the vital or weakened areas of his opponents. But they did not fall.

From the corner of his vision, Askon then saw the hidden guards that he had presumed Christopher would station in case of attack. Spinning away from the soldiers on the outside, Askon drew the long hunting knife. He passed through the door, driving first the knife into the man hidden on the right, and then the sword through the man on the left. To his surprise, they also remained standing, as did the two on the outside of the door. He pulled back his weapons and cut furiously at the two inner guards. With both hands, again and again he brought his weapons down upon the men: right, left, right left. They did not fall. Panic took him then.

He felt the calm focus of the fragment ripped away, like sleep after an unpleasant dream. He watched as the two men slumped to the ground—their faces unknowing, without even the surprise common in ambush victims. Outside against the blinding sunlight, Askon saw Edward pull his blade from his first victim and clash swords with the second. Dumbstruck Askon took two paces toward the door as Edward parried and drove a riposte into the second guard. Askon stared with wide eyes at the four defeated enemies of his own, and realization crashed down upon him. He had killed them all, mutilated them before the first had fallen to the ground, before Edward had even engaged his first man.

Edward approached Askon as he stood, gaping, in the doorway. "Four to two," said Edward panting. "I like the odds more even, personally." He turned, surveying the dead, then stopped, aghast. "Gods, Askon! These aren't Norill savages, they're men of the kingdom. What have you done to them?"

Askon looked up, speechless.

"Where is your honor? However angry you might be, show some respect. One day it might be us. You wouldn't have our enemies butcher us like so much meat, would you?" Edward turned away in disgust. "I don't know how you even managed it. I saw you standing there when I attacked the second soldier." He grabbed Askon's arm, shaking it. "Askon! What is the matter with you?"

Slowly, painfully aware of what he had done, Askon turned to Edward. Yet he said nothing.

"Come on. We don't have time for this now," hissed Edward. "We need to find the Grandmother."

Moving as quickly and warily as they could, Askon and Edward searched the entirety of the first floor. It was empty. The soldiers had helped themselves to everything in the kitchen and pantry, leaving behind piles of half-eaten food. The cupboards and drawers of the various furniture pieces had been rifled, their contents carelessly scattered. Outside, the diversion had turned violent. Askon hoped Thomas would be safe. Thirty villagers against what was now probably fifteen soldiers could still prove a difficult fight. After searching the bottom floor, Askon met Edward in the central room.

"Do these still seem like 'men of the kingdom' to you? Look what they've done to this house," Askon said in a low voice.

Edward glared, his heavy brows and lean face darkening. "Regardless, it does not justify your actions."

"I know. I think I can explain. When you—"

But Askon had no chance to finish. Through the window facing the street, he saw what had become of the villagers outside. Several lay dead, their bodies dangling over the fence posts near the gate. In the yard a soldier twisted and writhed, the ground reddening beneath him. All were pierced with thin black arrows. Neither Edward, nor Askon spoke another word. The Norill had come.

Leaping to the stairs, Askon bounded three-at-time to the top where he saw the Grandmother. In a small room at the end of the hall, the old woman sat tied and gagged in a rough wooden chair. She struggled weakly, her reddened wrists and fingers flexing against the bonds. The room appeared to be otherwise empty; Askon doubted that it was.

As he approached the door, fear grew in the old woman's eyes, but she wasn't looking at him. Askon burst through the doorway and jabbed to the left with his sword, Edward close behind. The blade slipped effortlessly through the air, meeting no resistance. But the strike had done enough. Askon's momentum carried him into the center of the room; he had missed the soldier who guarded the Grandmother by inches and was now dangerously out of position. Edward, however, did not miss. The soldier had not accounted for two men entering the room, and as he readied a blow for Askon, Edward's sword fell upon him. Two more quick cuts, and the man lay lifeless in a corner. Askon removed the Grandmother's gag and went to work on the ropes that secured her to the chair.

"Thank you," she choked.

Askon understood, then, why the Grandfather had nearly surrendered a friend for this woman. A woman who, in her time, would have been every bit as beautiful as any. But it was not beauty that made her worthy of such sacrifice. Even in the passing of many years, the Grandmother had kept a warmth and light in her clouded blue eyes. And those eyes seemed to know Askon at once, seemed to see what he wanted, to feel his pain, and to ease it. He could not speak. They were eyes like his mother's.

"Hurry," urged Edward. "Grandmother, we are here to rescue you, but you must follow my instructions."

The old woman looked from Edward to Askon. "Who are you?"

"It doesn't matter. Havard sent us. Right now he is outside and needs our help," Edward replied.

"One green eye, and one blue," the Grandmother stammered. "You're the one they were talking about: the fugitive."

"He is. But look how you've been treated. You have no other choice but to trust in us," Edward answered quickly, avoiding the chance she might continue as Ilsa had done.

She looked again at Askon, then to the crumpled soldier in the corner, and gave a weak nod.

Askon lifted her slowly from the chair, then released his hold. She stumbled, her legs stiff and sore. Her silver hair was matted and tangled, and streaks ran down her face where tears had run and dried. The two men helped to steady her balance.

"Grandmother," Edward said gently. "You must escape on your own. Go to the hill southeast of here. The one with the line of trees that climbs from bottom to top. There you will find the remains of a campsite. Havard will come to you there."

"How can you be sure?" The old woman's voice quavered with fear.

"If we go now and you escape," Askon answered, "I will make sure he reaches you, even if I die in the attempt." And with every word, he knew that he spoke the truth. This woman with his mother's eyes would see her husband again. Of that, he would make certain.

"I will go and trust you to keep your word," she said. "And if you do, I shall owe a great debt to your kind."

Edward took her hand and led her down the stairs. They moved quickly, and to Askon's surprise, the old woman kept up with seemingly little effort. When they reached the rear door, they quickly crossed the garden and passed behind the neighboring house. There, Edward indicated a suitable path for the Grandmother to follow on her way to the hilltop.

"Again, I thank you," she said to each of them. "Make sure that Havard returns. Goodbye." She vanished between the thatched buildings, each step taking her farther from the center of the village.

Askon and Edward took the opposite direction. They moved in short bursts: a sprint, then the outer wall of a house, another sprint to the cover of a barn, a few feet to an overturned cart. Staying low, the two friends made their way to the front of Ilsa's now vacant house. In the street, the clash and clangor of battle echoed through the churning dust. Ignoring the bodies, both Norill and human, Askon and Edward rushed to the opposite side of the street.

Evidently, the Norill had expended all of their arrows in the initial onset. A row of discarded bows lay in the dirt where the creatures had taken cover. Though the attackers had moved forward, their weapons remained. Shouldering one bow apiece, Askon and Edward went to work breaking the rest. If the enemy retreated to this position, they would have to continue fighting hand-to-hand.

When the bows were broken, Askon began gathering spent shafts. He avoided those that had found a mark in villagers or soldiers and instead plucked a large number from the ground where they had fallen. These Norill, though apparently few in number, a possible scouting party, were not excellent marksmen, even by the measure of their own kind. Using quivers lifted from the bodies of fallen Norill, Askon and Edward prepared to begin their part in the battle.

"We each take one side," Askon said quickly.

Edward nodded. "What about our escape?"

A black streak hurtled from behind a rooftop, angling toward them. They crouched and jumped clear. As he lifted himself from the ground, wary, watching the sky for incoming arrows, Askon saw that what had seemed to be an enemy shaft was instead the falcon, Marten. The bird skipped from the center of the street toward Askon, leaping to the shoulder guard. He paused for a moment, his head bobbing. Then, he shot back into the sky, circling toward the battle.

"Thomas and the Grandfather are at the rear of the group," Askon called across the street. "The soldiers are fighting at the front, defending the villagers. If we can turn the battle and push the Norill back, the four of us might slip away while Christopher's men pursue the scattering enemy."

Edward's voice dwindled as he ran along the street toward the battle, "What other choice do we have?"

Askon turned and jogged from one point of cover to the next, making his way to the position opposite Edward. When he arrived, he found that the battle had turned against the townspeople. Nearly twenty Norill still remained, though many had fallen since the initial attack. Christopher stood at the front of the fight, backed now by only five of his soldiers. Three large men, townsfolk by their clothing, seemed to be doing most of the offensive work. Each carried a long spear of the kind which had once been a fixture in battles across Vladvir, but with the kingship of Codard had fallen out of favor in military use. The wounds on many of the dead Norill proved the spears' continued effectiveness.

Most of the villagers remained standing. Christopher's men had died to protect many of them. But now, with so few soldiers left, the townspeople had begun taking casualties. At the rear of the group Thomas and the Grandfather fended off Norill attempts to flank what was left of Christopher's men. Next to them, Ilsa roared and slashed with two gleaming knives whenever one of the enemy approached. Askon waited for them to drive off a pair of Norill then whistled. Thomas heard the signal and hustled to the outbuilding where Askon leaned against one wall.

"The Grandmother is safe," Askon told him.

"Where is Edward?"

"He's on the other side of the street. We're going to push the No-rill back until they break and run. Christopher and his men will pursue. Tell the Grandfather to go to the hilltop, and try to convince Ilsa to move to the center of the column. When the Norill retreat, we make our escape."

Thomas looked worried. "But Askon, my family is here. They're safe for now, but what if the Norill come back?"

"If they attack again, the force will be much too large for us to defeat. You remember Austgæta."

"I do," said Thomas.

"Tell Ilsa to lead them south, toward King's City, or at least away from the village."

"Alright."

Through the swirling dust and noise of battle, Thomas made his way back into the fray. Askon then changed position, opting to get closer to the front, where Christopher and his men fought the main body of the enemy. As he did, he watched a Norill fall, unsuspecting, as a thin black arrow pierced its throat. Edward had hit his mark. Now it was Askon's turn. He aimed and loosed an arrow, felling another small Norill fighter. They continued in the same manner, changing positions every few shots, staying hidden all the while.

Slowly, the Norill began to lose their confidence, their heads twitching back and forth like frightened birds, searching for the source of the arrows. Another two fallen comrades and they broke outright. Wailing in their high pitched voices, the remaining Norill fled. And as Askon predicted, Christopher and his men followed, hunting them to the last. Askon and Edward dropped the bows and the quivers and ran toward the Grandfather's house to meet the others, hoping they would still be alive to escape.

✢ ✢ ✢

When they arrived at the Grandfather's home, Askon relaxed. Thomas helped the old man gather his traveling gear. Both had survived unharmed. Quickly, Askon and Edward shouldered their own packs. In the distance the sound of the battle died away as the soldiers and townspeople followed the remaining Norill to the northeast.

"Were you able to explain the plan to Ilsa?" Askon asked.

The Grandfather did not speak.

"I did," said Thomas. But his face was drawn and sad. "Though, she cannot lead the townspeople now. They killed her, Askon. She tackled one, cut him down, but another stabbed her in the back." He smiled, grimly. "Though it was his last. She rounded on him and drove her knives into his neck. But her wound was too great. In only a moment, she was dead."

Silently, they mourned her loss. Like so many others who had fallen, Ilsa would receive no proper burial. The day would pass too quickly and the Norill could return at any time. Askon hoped that she had gone to the place she had pictured while Edward held her close, hoped that she was at peace with the ones she loved.

The Grandfather broke the silence. "Her sacrifice will be well-known amongst our people, Thomas. Do not worry. All of today's sacrifices will be well-known." Looking up from his pack, the old man smiled. "Thank you, Commander, and you, Your Highness."

Edward extended a hand to the Grandfather and shook it firmly. "Where will you go?"

"I'm not sure, but my wife and I will lead the people away, hopefully somewhere safe. May we meet again, my friends."

The old man turned and began his march southeast, a hint of the old smile touching his eyes as they stared toward the hilltop. Askon, Edward, and Thomas hurried away into the tall grasses of the Vladvir plain. In turn, they too would make their way south, but not until they came to the great river Estelle. There, the king's patrols would be fewer and, Askon hoped, unaware of the hunt for him and his friends.

CHAPTER NINE

Along the Estelle

Evening approached on the second day after their escape from Shale. At first their pace had been nearly a dead-run, all whispering grass and well-worn paths. They angled southwest instead of following the streams and creeks that wound more directly toward the river. The second day had proved less frantic, a much needed change from the dash that had begun at King's City days earlier. Just after sunrise, they had begun their march, but the morning light revealed their location. Above them, on the opposite side of the river, loomed the Æsten Ridge.

Rising hundreds of feet above the surface of the water, the Ridge, as it was called by many travelers, was a place of worship for many people of the kingdom. It was said that on moonless nights, the faithful would ascend the sloping western side of the cliff and stand at its edge, calling to the gods. Those who were deemed worthy returned with pronouncements from their deities, while the unworthy were cast mercilessly into the churning waters of the river below. Thomas's family was one such group of worshippers, though none had attempted the climb. However, he had requested a few moments before the great stone to pray to his gods. Askon and Edward resisted at first, but relented after considering his sacrifice in leaving his people and family behind.

For most of the second day, the Æsten Ridge towered over them, until it slowly sank behind the horizon of sloping hills. In all the time on either day, there had been no sign of Christopher or a pursuit of any kind. Their plan—to make their way along the river until they reached the Greyarc—had one significant weakness. Despite the great bridge's reputation as the most reliable means of crossing the Estelle, it was also the most well-traveled. Their other option had been to angle northward from Shale, but that path led first in the direction of Tolarenz, then further on to Iramov's stronghold, and all the while the possibility of more Norill scouting parties. With little time to decide, Askon had chosen the southern route, hoping that Codard's efforts at capturing them were limited to the force he had sent to Thomas's village.

Now, as the heat of late afternoon pressed down upon them, bringing countless buzzing insects up from the river's dampened edges, the three men caught the first glimpse of their destination. The sun's rays ranged like fire across the wet grass, and Askon pictured the little river in Tolarenz. He saw the smooth curves it made as it flowed quietly through the valley. He heard its quiet clattering. He felt its cool water against his skin.

Then he remembered how different the Estelle was. In the spring it raged, every year crushing the bridges that were built to cross it, all except for one: the Greyarc. It was a marvel of human construction, built using thousands of pounds of stone. Each year, builders from King's City took the two-day journey out to the bridge and readied it for the high spring water, and each year it held back the Estelle and remained the only certain crossing for miles upon miles. Other crossings, like the one Codard's army had used in their march to Austgæta, were rebuilt or repaired according to the violence of the preceding spring runoff, but the Greyarc stood solid and unmovable even in the wettest of years.

Soaring above them, in what Edward and Thomas had remarked to be good spirits, was Marten. After his appearance in the battle, the bird had remained distant for several hours, returning to Askon's side only once briefly, just before sundown on the first day. Now he circled, as he had done for the rest of the journey, skimming the surface of the river or diving into the grass. With the bridge now in sight, he swept wide over the water and the massive stone structure spanning its banks.

Following a winding game trail, Askon and his friends snaked their way up a short rise. From where they stood at the top, all three could see the bridge in the distance, though only Askon could make out the shapes of the people treading its cobblestones.

"Well, there it is," said Thomas, wiping the sweat from his brow with a shirtsleeve.

Edward did the same. "Now we find out how well our luck holds."

"It's unlikely that your father would send a search party this way when we clearly headed north from the castle," said Askon. Even in the afternoon heat, he still wore the deep green cloak, though the hood lay piled loosely across his shoulders. Sweat beaded on his forehead.

"I know. We've been over it before," Edward said. He sounded tired. They all sounded tired. "Still, I think we should wait for nightfall. The cover of darkness might work to our advantage."

Thomas crouched in the long grass, then lowered himself to the ground where he sat with his arms wrapped around his knees. "Won't they still have guards posted, even at night?" he asked, swatting an insect from his exposed arm.

"They will, but in the dark Askon will look no different than any other traveler."

Thomas slapped another insect, this time at his neck. "And what if they recognize you?"

A half-smile appeared on Edward's face. "Well, then they recognize me. As long as they don't have orders, they'll suspect nothing."

"It's rare for a bridge-guard to interrogate a prince, Thomas," Askon added with a laugh.

Thomas swatted a third time, then flailed both arms, brushing several creatures off his clothes and skin. He paused a moment, then shook his head vigorously, his hair solid and unmoving. He ran his fingers back and forth across the scalp, a fine mist of sweat spreading above. He shook his head again.

"Just stand up," Askon said as he and Edward watched, laughing.

"I'm resting!" Thomas snapped.

The others continued their laughter. "Well, that doesn't look particularly restful."

Thomas folded his arms again, trying to appear relaxed. Before long, Askon could see hundreds of the tiny insects crawling over Thomas's clothes. Tiny red bumps appeared where they bit the skin at the base of his neck and along his forearms. Tension building, Thomas remained fixed. Askon glanced sidelong at Edward who lifted an open hand, each finger separated from the other. Without speaking, he counted in reverse. Five; he pulled in the thumb, four. Now the smallest finger. Three. Two. One.

"*Gah!*" Thomas spluttered. He jumped up, waving his hands furiously over his clothes and through his hair. "Gods…*bah*–Oh, fine!" He batted a few times more at his clothes. "Alright. You win."

Askon and Edward stared stoically at their younger friend. Then the three of them burst into laughter.

Hours later, dusk rolled heavily across the plain, subduing the insects on the damp riverbank. In their place, innumerable clicks, chirps, and buzzes rose from the reeds. The three friends, now seated atop the rise, gnawed at bits of dried meat and bread from the Grandfather's pantry. A ribbon of color laced the horizon in the west and wrapped its orange tendrils southward. There, where the failing light plunged below the edge of the world, lay the South Kingdom and Lord Apopsé. Askon wondered what he would find there: hope for revenge against Iramov, sanctuary from Codard's pursuit? Both seemed reasonable possibilities, but the thing he wanted most, peace and ease at the loss of Tolarenz, seemed unlikely.

Edward peered across their triangular seating arrangement. He dragged a hand over the soil, weaving in and out between tufts of grass. "Askon," he said sternly, "I think we should talk about what happened behind Ilsa's house."

Thomas looked confused, but he leaned in, waiting for Askon's response.

Askon, taken aback by Edward's directness in the face of his actions, felt like a cornered animal. There was no avoiding such a conversation. The explanation in his mind was simple, but the result nauseated him, as he knew it nauseated Edward and would Thomas as well.

Edward tried again, softer now. "We have followed you almost without question, my friend. I have done so against my own father, though I might've done that anyway." He laughed, a clipped snuffling amongst the clicks and chirrups. "And I intend to continue following you, as I believe you to be right. Yet, my conviction is less for not knowing what happened back there."

Reluctantly, and shaking his head slightly Askon attempted an explanation. "I don't know how it works," he said, lifting the glowing green fragment from its hiding place under his shirt. In the waning glow of the sunset, the silver chain glimmered faintly. "Just as the sun rose and blinded the guards, I felt a sort of calm and focus. I've felt it before, though never so prominently in battle. Usually when I feel it, I can see things that others might overlook: Christopher's gait in the clearing, allowing me to identify him, Codard's plan to arrest and execute me before his guards even made a move, things like that. Somehow, the same calm came on me before we struck, but I did not realize what it meant." He cast his eyes to the ground.

Thomas leaned in farther, now quite obviously drawn into the story.

"I attacked and fought just as I have been trained," Askon continued, "striking one man then moving to the next as quickly as possible. Neither had a chance to retaliate."

Thomas interrupted, "You're quick; we know this. It's one of the few myths about the elf-kind that is wholly true."

Askon smiled briefly, but then his amusement vanished. "They were still standing after two cuts, so I returned for another and another. And still they stood. Then I moved to the men inside the doorway, who had stayed hidden, and again they remained after multiple strokes. When I turned back to the outer guards, I think I understood."

Edward did not lift his eyes from the ground. His hand still traced tufts of grass. "And there I saw you. I had only defeated the first of my opponents while you had mutilated four."

Stung by Edward's powerful choice of word, Askon retreated inward. He reflexively lifted the hood, pulling it close around the sides of his head and stared blankly at a space in the center of the triangle.

"I'm sorry, Askon," Edward said after a moment. "But it is true. The fact is that you went too far. Those men should have been dead after the first wound. And if not the first, then certainly the second. When I—"

"I know," Askon replied from beneath the shadow of his hood. "It is inexcusable and won't happen again."

Thomas, who had leaned too far, toppled forward, catching himself with one hand. "You killed four before Edward could kill one?" he said with childlike wonder. "Wow."

Edward shot a glare at the young man. "Why did they stay standing? That is the question that still goes unanswered."

In the distance the waters of the Estelle roared against the Greyarc's stones. Beyond the bridge the dying sunlight faltered, faded, then disappeared. Askon turned to watch it go, then faced his friends again. "At first I thought they might be enchanted in some way, as the Norill were at Austgæta. But the darkness the Norill wield is too similar to Iramov's fragment to be a coincidence. I don't know the powers of each fragment, but I doubt that Codard's piece would keep men on their feet after an attack. "

"It's easy then." Both Askon and Edward turned sharply toward Thomas, who had spoken so matter-of-factly that they were taken off-guard. They waited. He continued, "Yours is the Time fragment, right?"

Askon nodded.

"Then it stands to reason that you might *influence* time with it." Thomas stood now, pacing with his chin resting on one hand. "Or, that time somehow influences *you*. If that is the case, your calmness might be a signal for it. Perhaps you were moving so fast that they didn't have the chance to fall to the ground before you had already rounded on them."

Askon's mouth fell agape, not at the explanation, for he had already guessed as much on his own. His surprise was rather at Thomas and his astute observations. So often the young man seemed clumsy, even incapable, but it appeared now that stupidity was not the source of his blundering.

Edward stood. "I easily defeated my first man with only one cut, a parry, and riposte. If it had been prolonged, I could imagine Askon felling two or three before me, but four trained soldiers would be nearly impossible."

"Unless his first attacks were before you even made contact," continued Thomas thoughtfully. "My guess is that, had he the chance to look in your direction, you would have appeared still as stone." Now the young man's eyes widened, his pace quickening. "And it would also explain why you are moving so incredibly slowly at times, Askon. Something is triggering the opposite of what happened in the battle. And it has to do with time; I'm sure of it."

Askon, still crouching under his hood, gazed up at the others. "So I am slow at times and fast at times. Perhaps Morrowmen will be able to explain, if we get the chance to see him again."

"I should like to meet this Morrowmen," said Thomas lightly. "It would be interesting to test my theory and to learn more about the properties of each fragment. He probably knows a great deal of their history as well. Do you think he'd explain it to me, Askon?"

Askon smiled. "I think he would, but he has little patience for idle questions and even less for poorly considered assumptions." Then, rocking back on his haunches, Askon moved to stand at his place in the triangle. He stopped as Edward approached.

Slowly, with his palm open, Edward reached down to Askon. In the prince's face, Askon saw that he had been forgiven. He clasped his own hand around Edward's forearm and pulled himself up.

"If Thomas is right," said Edward. "There was no way for you to know about the fragment's effect. Now that we understand it, maybe Morrowmen can help you control it instead of it controlling you."

"Maybe," said Askon dusting himself off. "I hope so." He dropped the fragment back under his shirt where it pressed coolly against his chest. As it touched the skin, Askon thought he could feel its glow growing and fading. And he wondered if it really could make time ebb and flow.

CHAPTER TEN

The Greyarc Bridge

An hour later they found themselves approaching the bridge. Their descent from the nearby hill-crest had been slow. Both Askon and Edward tried to assess the situation at the Greyarc with little luck. A thick blanket of fog had drifted along the churning waters of the Estelle, settling fixedly around the bridge. From the river's eastern bank, even Askon could see only as far as the halfway point to the other side.

As they entered into the dim torchlight, they knew that the east bank had been reinforced, not a good sign if they were to pass unnoticed. Askon counted eight guards and one captain serving as leader. At about half the distance between the hilltop and the bridge, Askon tried to bring on the calming sensation which would allow him to interpret the situation more effectively, but to no effect. The others coaxed him and offered suggestions, but these only further frustrated his efforts.

With his hood drawn and eyes downcast he walked two steps behind Edward, side-by-side with Thomas, and opposite the lead guardsman. Thick smoke mingled with the fog, and the rushing water boomed. Long, faint shadows stretched across the stones, a faded pantomime of the night's events.

"Evenin'," grumbled the guard.

"Good evening," Edward replied, halting. He stretched and faked a yawn.

"Aye, indeed it's late to be on the road, 'specially this far out in the plain," said the guard.

Edward blinked slowly. "Yes, sir. You don't have to tell me about it. All day we've been walking, but I'll tell you right now, dark and cool is an improvement over this afternoon's heat. I'll stay up late any night to get out of that blistering sun. How about you? You prefer the nightshift to the day?"

The guard looked past Edward and cocked his head to one side. "Oh, I'm a right night-owl anyway," he said, peering through the torchlight at Askon and Thomas. "New to the post here though. Can't say I've enjoyed the noise an' the damp. The leatherwork gets a film goin' on it, an' that brings the mold. Course, the metal's worse; rusts in a couple days, it does."

"I'm sure it does," Edward said calmly, still feigning sleepiness. "However, the heat is not our only cause for being on the road tonight. We're in a bit of a hurry."

"Oh?" said the guard, suddenly looking suspicious. He eyed Thomas and Askon warily. "Mind if I ask what the rush is? It's part o' the job y'know."

Edward motioned toward Thomas, "Well, my brother and I are heading south with our friend here, looking for a traveling group that probably passed through early today or late yesterday."

"What sort of group would that be?"

"Oh, just folk like anybody, but women and men both."

"And who are they? Where were they headed?"

Edward shook his head. "It's a long story, that one, but I'll tell you the short version. My brother, you see, he had this idea that we could make a good deal of coin if we sold supplies to travelers passing through our village. Right, little brother?"

Thomas hesitated, "Y-yeah. I did."

"He's pretty ashamed about it now," said Edward quickly. "And he ought to be. His plan was to raise the prices dependent on the look of the group and their apparent need."

"Well that's a bit dishonest, now," said the guard.

"I told him so, but he managed to get the whole village on board. He'd raise the price so high, you'd think no one would pay, but the other shops were the key; they would go even higher. Then he'd share the profits between all the merchants after the sale."

"A clever plan," the guard said, his round face puzzling between admiration at the genius of the scam and disapproval toward its moral implications.

Edward began again. "It was, until the kid suckered a bunch of wealthy looking types for more than he should have."

"What happened?"

"Well, it turns out that they were rich-looking and on the road for a reason."

"Highwaymen?"

Edward nodded. "You guess right, sir. And these highwaymen didn't like being beaten at their own game. They came back and burned every shop in the village, vowing to spread word about the pricing trick."

The guard looked confused. "You still haven't said what brings you to the road."

"When the rest of the villagers heard what had caused the burnings, they ran all the merchants and their families out of town. The three of us stayed behind to help clean up some of the mess from the burnings. My friend here," he looked at Askon, "had it the worst. His wife was still at home when the highwaymen came. They didn't find her, but the fire did. He doesn't say much since then."

The guard shook his head. "Well, a dishonest man is dealt a dishonest hand, my mother always said."

"Perhaps," said Edward softly. "Anyway, that's what brings us out here. We've all got some family or friend who left town already. Now we're trying catch them up."

"I can't say I like your story very much. Probably would've been on the highwaymen's side of it all. But you seem to have learned your lesson."

All three nodded.

"Go on through and get back to your families." The guard stepped to the side and waved off the others who stood nearby.

Across the wide cobblestone surface of the bridge, several men on horseback could ride alongside one another. Askon felt small as they passed onto the gray stones, and oddly vulnerable. For the moment, eight guards backed them and an unknown number would be waiting on the other side. He tried to imagine how Edward's invented man would act in the situation. All the while, the Estelle roared against the bridge.

They kept on at a slow pace, taking several minutes to cover the distance between the eastern guards and the center of the bridge. The fog swirled around them, thickening until neither bank was visible. Somewhere above them, Askon knew, Marten would be watching, but even the falcon's sharp eyes would be useless in the combination of darkness and murk. After a number of yards, Askon felt the slope of the cobblestones begin to descend toward the western bank. The feeling was subtle, but clear. Arches made for stronger structures than did flat surfaces, but only the most accomplished builders were able to construct them. Landmark projects, like the Greyarc or Codard's palace, were among their number.

Shortly after the change in slope, two tiny points of light appeared in the fog. Around the points, wide, perfectly circular rings stretched into the misty air. As Askon and his friends drew nearer, the rings grew larger, and wavering flames emerged from the points at the center. Askon watched as the ribbons of orange danced and curled. The rings of light then became so wide that they dissipated at the edges of his vision, and he found himself standing inside their glow. Only a few yards in front of him, the blurred forms of the western guard station came into view. The three stopped, and Askon tried to listen, but heard only the constant blaring of water on stone.

Thomas tugged at the edge of Askon's cloak, trying to whisper and yet be audible over the rushing river at the same time. "Where are the guards?" he said.

Askon and Edward scanned the clump of wooden structures before them. The guard station on the western bank was deserted. Askon peered back into the fog toward the eastern bank. A chill prickled its way along his spine, and a sudden gust of wind pushed the fog briefly aside. In that moment a glimmer shone through the darkness, a flashing blade catching the reflection of the guttering western torches. Askon stood stick straight.

"Run!" he ordered.

Thomas did not hesitate. He was already two steps in the lead when Askon and Edward turned to sprint for the opposing riverbank. In short order they overtook him, and all three ran side-by-side, the empty guard station moving closer and closer. Behind them, Askon heard shouting somewhere beneath the din, and still they ran. Askon loosened the scabbard in his sword belt while Edward's sword, already released from its sheath, flickered in the torchlight. Less than twenty feet remained as they closed on the west bank. The fog clung to their clothes until all the edges were damp. Five more feet and the shouting became suddenly clearer. Thomas stopped, looking back, and the others turned to pull him along. But behind them, they saw nothing, only the swirling fog.

"Come on, Thomas. We're almost there," Edward commanded. But when they turned again toward the western bank, they found that the trap had already been sprung.

Now, at the brink of sight and fog, armed men appeared one by one. A thicket of sword points gleamed, the reflections from the torches climbing the length of the upraised blades then sliding down to the hilts. The formation tightened, and more soldiers appeared, twice the number that they had met on the eastern side. Several more appeared and the noose continued to close. Back-to-back the three friends now stood, weapons ready. The trio retreated to the east, but the remaining guards emerged with the round-faced man in the lead.

"Not a bad story, for a pampered princeling. 'Course, maybe I shouldn't be so surprised, considerin' your traitorous ways lately," he said.

Edward did not respond, nor did Thomas. Against his back, Askon could feel their rapid breathing. Something would have to be done, and quickly. They could rush the smaller force behind them, but that would leave them on the wrong side of the river. And if this crossing was blocked, it stood to reason the successive bridges would be as well. If they charged the western bank, they would almost surely lose the conflict, but if they did win—or merely break through—they would be free to make a mad dash in the direction of the South Kingdom. Whatever they did, they were running out of time as the two groups of soldiers moved ever closer.

"We're here to apprehend a traitor," said a commanding voice.

Askon's mind ground to a halt. The voice was new and came from somewhere within the press of soldiers on the western side.

"A prince. A soldier of the kingdom. An ex-commander. It doesn't matter. A fitting story for three fugitives," said the voice.

Briefly, the western line parted and a figure strode between them. He stepped into the torchlight, and even without the calming effect of the fragment, Askon recognized his haughty posture and confident stride. Somehow, faster than they could cover the distance from Thomas's village to the Greyarc, Christopher had overleaped them and had time to set a trap. By Askon's current count, it seemed Christopher had acquired another twenty men of his own in addition to the regular bridge guards.

Frustration and a tingle of the old rage curdled in Askon's heart as the torches illuminated Christopher's face. This was not the man who had taken Tolarenz from him, but Christopher supported that man, and the mere thought of Iramov's deeds brought the anger to a boil. Now the scene moved swiftly, and once again Askon found himself bewildered by the conversation, as though the world itself had accelerated.

"For the death of Patrick of King's City," Christopher said with relish, "the betrayal of the king and his lands, for the destruction of several small villages beginning at the edge of Ellmed and ending at the river Estelle, I hereby place these men under arrest by order of King Codard."

The words flooded by like the river, and Askon struggled to swim against the current. Had Christopher suggested that the three of them destroyed several villages? Did that mean that the Norill had done so and that Christopher was aware of it?

"—that stands in the way of this arrest," Christopher continued, while Askon sluggishly pondered the implications, "is hereby considered an enemy of the king."

From behind them, three of the eastern guards latched onto Askon and his friends. Thomas tried to attack, but the guard easily parried the wild slash. Edward seemed resigned to his fate, and Askon, still swimming against the world's swirling torrent, had no time to react.

Christopher leaned in close and flipped the hood from Askon's head, "I win, half-man," he murmured.

Askon roared back, a guttural, inarticulate sound that died in the heavy air. Deep inside the rage clawed and scrabbled wildly, rending, tearing, screeching for purchase, but the scene only accelerated further. The eastern bridge guard held him fast.

"Put this animal in irons," Christopher crowed with a short laugh. Lifting a gloved hand, he struck Askon with the backside of his fist. "Down!" he shouted, and laughter rippled idly through the crowd of soldiers. Askon tried to fight, but the guard's grip held strong. Where were Thomas and Edward? Still beside him, or had they been dragged away?

Thunk!

The sound seemed to somehow loosen his captor's grip. Askon twisted against it. When he looked up, Christopher was gone.

Thunk!

Not gone, just moved to the side and hunkering with his back against the wall at the side of the bridge. Askon wondered why.

Thunk! Thunk!

This time the captor let go. Askon was loose. Inside, the rage dug in and thrust its bulk to the surface. Another moment and he was upon his enemy.

Thunk!

The strange, rhythmic punctuation continued. Askon stood toe-to-toe with Christopher. Their blades clashed against one another, Askon's face a wild grimace of green and blue. Then the resistance from Christopher's blade fell away. The rage bellowed its victory, trumpeting the death of its victim even before Askon's sword struck home.

Thunk! Thunk! Thunk!

He was falling, had overextended himself in the fight. He struck the cobblestones. He was on his back now, staring up into the fog. A star glimmered beyond the mist, lonely but bright. Where had the soldiers gone? And why was he on his back? Then, gleaming before his eyes, a blade blotted out the star. Christopher's heaving outline, black against the burning torches, cast a shadow over Askon's vision. Slowly the blade turned until it hovered point downwards.

And then it was gone.

Askon came to his senses with his back against the cold, wet stones. Somehow he had come to rest against the sidewall of the bridge. The swirl of fog and arrhythmic peppering of *thunks* continued. For every one of the dull sounds, an arrow buried itself in a target or went clattering across the bridge, and Askon understood the strange sounds. While Christopher had attempted to arrest them, archers had begun firing upon the bridge.

Looking from one side to the other, Askon discovered that he was but one in a number of presumably dead bodies, each with its arms and legs splayed awkwardly against the wall. Thick arrow shafts, tufted with bright feathers, sprouted from the twisted forms, a gruesome field of flowers blooming red and yellow in the night. But he was not dead, and the bridge was not empty.

In the glow of the torches, two figures danced to the eerie percussion of arrows. Their swords flashed and flickered, and Askon thought he could hear their shouts, but neither seemed to heed the danger of the hidden archers. Then the rain of arrows stopped.

Askon pulled himself to his feet but stayed low, in case the shooting began again. Across the width of the bridge, a man lay writhing on his back. Collecting his own sword where it had fallen lifelessly next to him, Askon crossed the distance swiftly. No arrow protruded anywhere from the man on the ground, and Askon approached with caution. But before he had achieved half the distance, the man's identity became clear. It was Thomas.

Ignoring the concealed bowmen, Askon skidded to a halt, kneeling at Thomas's side. He lifted the young man's head gently, looking up and down for an arrow or sword wound.

"Thomas?" he said, worry straining his voice.

But Thomas did not speak.

"Thomas!" Askon shouted, heedless of the possible threat.

For a moment, the young man continued to squirm, groaning and mumbling incoherently. But it seemed that he had suffered no mortal harm. Askon dragged him to the side of the bridge, under the shelter of the opposite wall. The clash and clatter of the dancing swordsmen continued, and Askon knew who they would be.

Sidling along the wall, Askon closed the gap between Thomas and the two shadowy dancers. Where the other soldiers had gone, he was unsure. Many lay dead upon the Greyarc, but not all. As he drew nearer to the duel, he realized that he could not reach them in time. Both fighters, panting and heaving, hefted their swords as if some force greater than simple weight pulled the points to the earth. One swept high into the torchlight, and the other met it. A clang rang out against the rushing river. Sparks erupted from between the blades, and both swordsmen recoiled at the tiny flecks of light and the shock of impact. The blades raised again, would meet again, but this time one halted in midair, twisting gracefully before stabbing forward into the body of its enemy.

Askon squinted through the haze of smoke and fog, but could not see clearly which man remained standing. The winner rose, drawing himself up into a stance of confident superiority. With head held high, the shadow-man panted into the mist. Askon's heart sank. No rage fought within him, only sick, heavy sorrow.

And then, through the fog and smoke, into the glowering torches stepped Edward, prince of Vladvir.

Askon breathed deeply and a weight lifted from his frame. Behind him, he felt the presence of Thomas, who had come to his senses and joined Askon on the western side of the bridge. The three rounded the wooden barricade, entering one of the sheltered spaces that made up the four corners of the bridge. One guard, it seemed, had come to the same conclusion, but too late. He lay dead on the floor of the narrow room, another of the brightly feathered arrows in his back.

"Christopher is dead," Edward said flatly, still panting.

Askon sighed. "He was once a good man. I chose him for the Norogæta mission myself. You know, just now, I thought the result was the opposite."

Edward scoffed. "That he had defeated me, you mean?"

"Yes."

Shaking his head, Edward slapped Askon on the back three times in rapid succession. "You were worried." Edward smiled. "You underestimate me, friend. You're not *that* much better."

Thomas grabbed them both by the shoulder, shaking them vigorously. "If you haven't forgotten, we are not alone!" he said. "Whose arrows are these? And where have the rest of the soldiers gone?"

Askon cocked an eyebrow and looked from Thomas back to Edward. "I don't think we'd be alive if the arrows were meant for us. It seems we're at the mercy of these marksmen. I think they'll decide when to show themselves."

"I, for one, will thank them when they do," said Edward. "Without them, we would be in chains on our way back to the castle."

Askon nodded. "You may be right. We shall see."

CHAPTER ELEVEN

A Marksman and his Mark

For a long time, nothing happened. Had it not been for the pounding of the Estelle against the Greyarc, all would have been completely silent. The heavy fog hovered for a few more minutes, then wafted along with the current of the river. Above the bloodied bridge stones, the moon shone and stars sparkled in a deep black sky. Mist rose from the churning water to glint in the moonlight. Inside the tiny room on the western bank, Thomas rummaged through a cabinet. After an excited scrabble, he extracted a small, tightly wrapped bundle of salted meat. With their own packs scattered and nothing to do but wait, Thomas shared his discovery with Askon and Edward.

More time passed, and Thomas began to nod, slightly at first, then more obviously. His head dipped and bounced as he woke himself again and again. Edward leaned in, slapped Thomas lightly on the shoulder and ventured a whisper.

"Do you think they've left the guards for dead?" The question was directed at Askon.

"I don't think so," Askon replied, shaking his head slightly and rubbing one side of his face where a black smudge streaked across the skin. He looked disgustedly at the residue on his fingers and wiped away the rest with his shirtsleeve.

Thomas blinked slowly. "They wouldn't leave," he said through a yawn. "Whoever shot all these guards, and not us, must have had some purpose. Traps like that don't happen by accident."

A crooked half-smile curled across Askon's face. As he had on the hill at sunset, Thomas spoke in the same clear, analytical tone that so contrasted his usual blundering. Again, the observations were rather obvious, but in his amusement, Askon resisted the urge to comment.

"They saw us here on the bridge and let us live," Thomas continued. "My guess is that they've been gone, hunting down the remaining soldiers. When they come back—"

"They'll know we're here," said Edward.

Askon considered their options again. If they stayed, he and his friends would be at the mercy of the mysterious marksmen. During the fight, the archers had let them live, but would they now? On the other hand, if they tried to escape and the bowmen had left guards of their own—which they most certainly had—Askon and the others could be shot down easily. Their escape during the battle might have been a fluke. Fate decided for him.

"Come outta there!" growled a husky voice.

None of them moved. Then the voice came again, louder against the rush of the water.

"I said, come out!"

Askon peered sidelong through one of the narrow slits above Edward and Thomas. On the western bank of the river, five bowmen stood, evenly spaced around the tiny guardhouse. Three had their bows drawn and ready to fire, the other two waited with arrows knocked loosely against the string. From the center came the husky voice again.

"Aye, count 'em all ya want. There's more than five of us out here."

Still Askon said nothing. Peering into the distance, he tried to guess how many bows were aimed at them and whether they could make a break for cover.

"You 'scaped our shots in the dark, but ya won't now," said the husky voice. "This bridge was a trap, if ever I saw one. Waitin' for somebody, you were. If you've got him in there with ya, I mean to see him."

Once again, the three remained silent. It seemed to Askon that this man thought he had trapped some of Christopher's soldiers, as well as their prisoners.

"Yer leader's dead. Saw one of the prisoners cut him down. You're outta choices. Come out."

Askon watched as the man at the center of the five bowmen sig-naled the rest to move forward before he spoke again.

"What are ya in there, some kinda chickenheart?"

Like thunderheads looming on the horizon's edge that roil and glower only to be cast aside by the wind, a broad smile stole across Askon's face. And though he tried to suppress it, a triumphant laugh burst from deep within him. Puzzled, Thomas and Edward looked first to one another, then back to Askon. In his eyes, two silver beads welled, and spilled down his face. When he spoke again, his voice came hoarse and thick through the din.

"And what of it?" he choked. "I've got a dozen silver coins that say the only chickenheart here is you!" His smile beamed on.

"What was that?" said the man outside.

"And another purseful that says if you fought for yourself you'd be laid up before you could call me that again!" Askon shouted.

Edward and Thomas crouched, mouths gaping as Askon rounded the corner of the guardhouse and stepped, still smiling, into the open air.

"I thought you weren't a bettin' man?" asked the husky voice. With one hand he gestured to his bowmen. They lowered their weapons.

"Well, around here it seems I'm not thought of as any kind of man. A traitor, yes, a half-elf, yes, but not a man. And it looks like I'm not the only traitor." He shook his head and relief surged through him. He had guessed it only moments after hearing the voice, but now, even in the dim mingling of moon and torchlight, he was absolutely certain. Askon turned and waved toward the guardhouse, a signal to the others that all was clear. When he turned back, standing before him, smiling wolfishly in return, was John.

Edward and Thomas crept warily from their hiding place in the guardhouse. Recognizing John, Edward rose up to his full height, no longer concerned for his safety.

"I wondered when you would put the contents of that thick skull to work," he said.

For a moment, John stared, eyes narrow, his rugged face a mixture of absent carelessness and annoyance. "Say Askon, does a person have to honor a prince if he's considered a traitor to the crown?"

Askon shrugged his shoulders, a small gesture, but it was enough.

"That's what I thought," said John grinning. "In that case," he turned back to Edward, "there's more brains behind the left eye of this thick skull than a slack-jawed, house-bound, crown-hook like you has in his whole head!"

Edward laughed. "Crown-hook? That's the best you can do? Your copious intellect astounds, as usual."

John pointed to the bowman on his left. It was the round-faced guard from the eastern bank of the bridge. "Well, 'cording to him your copulous intellect could use some work."

"Copious, John, not copulous," Askon corrected.

"Ah, what the hell does it matter, anyway? Fat lot 'o good it did for ya in any case, eh Edward?" John straightened his posture and thrust his chest forward, his head bobbling pompously. "Our permanent dwelling arrangement came to be inhospitable to our persons," John drawled in mock nobility. "Thus," and here he flipped a hand and gave a short bow, "my compatriots and I come before you, our mercantile efforts in disarray, at the mercy of these—What do you call them?—Ah, men of the high-way."

Edward crossed his arms, rocking back on one hip. "I don't talk like that."

John slapped one knee, laughing at his own joke. "Hey, I'm just repeatin' my man's report. Gotta get the facts right, ya know."

Thomas stepped cautiously through the dimness. He eyed John and the other archers as the two friends bantered back and forth.

"You stood against us in the throne room," Thomas said, and the accusation killed the mirth instantly, like a bucket of water on a campfire. "Edward had to knock you out of the way." The young man's eyes burned. Though Askon and Edward accepted John's help, with Thomas it would not be so easy.

Askon reached out and put a hand across Thomas's chest, holding him away from John and the bowmen. Then he looked to his old friend. "Thomas has a point," he said. "Back at the castle, you didn't help us."

John shook his head and kicked at a loose stone. "Ah, well I didn't hurt ya either," he said. Then weakly, "What? You think Edward could knock me over so easy?"

Placing his other hand on John's shoulder, Askon smiled. "You say that now, but I don't think you had decided yet. The things you said, about the battle at Austgæta and my leaving Thomas and Christopher, you were right, and you knew it."

John kicked the stone again. It clattered a few feet and spun on one edge before falling to the ground. "It wouldn't be the first time."

"Be serious, just this once," Askon said. "What changed your mind?"

Stepping back, John pushed Askon's hand gently from his shoulder. He looked out over the river into the darkness. "There was so much to take in," he said slowly. "You were talkin' about Tolarenz being wiped out, an' I'd just seen the General's forces routed and Austgæta burned. Those Norill are comin' for the whole of Vladvir, and I needed to do what the king paid me to do: defend the kingdom. So, by the time you even get there, he's told me that we're allies with Iramov. And I says we've always been that. But when you told your story, I didn't know how to take it. It didn't seem real, all this talk of Alora's Tear and magic and such."

At this, Thomas interrupted. "You felt the darkness in the cavern and saw what it could do at the Norill city."

"Yeah, and what of it!" John barked.

Askon pushed Thomas slowly away from John, then lowered his hand. "Why don't we just hear what John has to say, eh Thomas?"

John continued. "Like I said, I didn't know how to take it. I picked the wrong side, alright? You three bolted, and Codard sent Christopher after you. He told me to stay, but by then I already knew I had made the wrong call." He looked at Edward, "Must be the thick skull, I guess." He smiled again. "But if mine's thick, Codard's might be thicker."

"Why do you say that?" Edward asked, and Askon saw the sting of criticism pass over his friend's face.

"Well," said John, "I got him to tell me the plan. You're not the only one who can slap together a story to get your way."

Smirking, Edward patted John on the back. "Oh yes, you've always been quite the charmer."

John nodded, considering the possibility. "It was enough this time. And I'll tell ya, when I heard it, it was all I could do not to give him a piece o' my mind right there." Now he turned to Askon. "It's not just Iramov that he wants to join up with. He's got it in his head that Apopsé's going to make a run for the western plains and Grafmark and even your valley, Askon. His new partner's convinced him that he needs another ally until Apopsé's out of the picture."

"Who?" asked Thomas. "There's no one else, unless he plans to venture beyond Ellmed."

"The Norill."

Edward crossed the space quickly, so quickly that Askon stood motionless with surprise. But this was no effect of the Time fragment. The prince was now inches from John's nose, one hand at his shirt collar the other cocked back into a fist. "Take it back," Edward snarled.

To Askon's further surprise, John, who was almost always quick to a fight, stared meekly at the upraised fist. "I wish I could, Edward," he said. "But your father's so afraid of what could happen that he's willing to fight alongside 'em for now. Iramov says it's temporary, that he and your father can turn on the Norill when they defeat Apopsé. To tell ya the truth, I think it's gonna go the other way. It'll be Codard against Iramov, the Norill, and that darkness we saw at Austgæta."

"And that I saw in Tolarenz," murmured Askon.

"When I heard all that, my mind was made up," John continued. "My men and I were ordered to guard a bridge up north in case you came that way, and we were supposed to tell people that we were there to protect them against the Norill, even to fight and kill any Norill that attacked. The main Norill force is somewhere in Ellmed for now. As soon as we were clear of the city, I told my men everything. Needless to say, we didn't follow the orders. Most of 'em, I sent to a safe place.

The rest came here with me or went north to watch the other bridge. We figured the crossings were our best bets to find you, because with Tolarenz gone you'd have nowhere left to go but the South King-dom." John leaned in conspiratorially. From whom he was hiding his message, Askon was unsure. "There's more too, Askon, but I don't want to talk about it here or waste any more time waitin' around. We need to go, before more of Codard's men show up."

"Alright," said Askon. "Thomas, are you satisfied with John's an-swer?"

"I suppose."

"Good. Then I have one request, John. Christopher, at least, should receive a proper burial."

John seemed dubious on this point, but he nodded. "I'll have a few men remain here to build a pyre. I've got a couple who can pass for servants of the king." He motioned toward the round-faced man. "Us though, we're gettin' gone as quick as we can. They're lookin' for you, Askon. Iramov and Codard, I mean. Codard wants that jewel you've got, and he wants it bad. Like I said, I've got a safe place, but we can't be followed. It's only safe 'cause it's secret. Let's go."

They left the bridge under a silver sheen of moonlight and star-light bright enough to illuminate the rustling grasses of the plain. Even John spoke little as the Greyarc grew ever smaller behind them, finally disappearing into the folds of Vladvir's tumbling hills. Askon was unsure of the destination, though he had deduced that John's hiding place must be somewhere in the forest of Grafmark, as it was the only sure cover west of the river. Far to the northwest lay Iramov's strong-hold and the valley of Tolarenz. Southward, of course, was Apopsé's kingdom and Askon's eventual goal. There he would find Morrowmen and hopefully some clearer answers to his questions about the Time fragment.

CHAPTER TWELVE

The Gates of Grafmark

When the first glow of morning stretched to meet the fleeing stars, the land began to change. The soft swish of grass gave way to crunching flecks of mica and crumbling granite. Patches of dirt, spongy with the decay of scattered leaves and needles dampened their footsteps between the grit of the rocks. Tall clattering shrubs replaced the grass, a few at first, then so many that the travelers were forced to bend and slide through a noisy wall of green. With care, they wound their way through the brush, cautiously moving the branches, never breaking them. Any trace of the company's passing might lead to their discovery. And so, under warm morning sunlight, their progress slowed.

Soon, amid the rattling shrubs, trees began to appear: a pine here, a spruce there, even an elm or an oak for good measure. Then, at the top of a rise, Askon saw it, stretching before him like the battlements of an enormous, ivy-bound castle. It was the forest of Grafmark, a mixture of trees and moss and brush so dark that night was black as pitch and noontime only a dingy gray-green.

Askon had seen the forest before. While in the employ of the king's army, he had passed its borders multiple times, though much farther north. He had even entered into the forest, once, at the battle of Vestgæta, though it was so far north as to be nearly a different place altogether. There, the conifers reigned and the weather was cold. Here, the forest seemed to exude a clammy warmth, like a hall crowded until its occupants have room only to stand. "The Forest of the Dead" it was called by those who named it, long before Askon of Tolarenz or Edward, son of Codard passed under its grim canopy.

Even then, as Askon stood wondering at its nearly impenetrable border, he remembered the stories told by the elders of Tolarenz. Some said that inside its gloomy depths, the trees devoured children who wandered haplessly into the twisting thickets. Others said that the dead tended the forest for a garden, and that anyone stepping inside would be forced to labor in the same enterprise. Nearly every family, it seemed, had a story concerning Grafmark: men who changed into beasts by the light of the moon, spirits that inhabited the trunks of trees or that floated on the mists, creatures unspeakable that breathed the screams of frightened travelers and drank the blood of those who died in fear. The list went on and on.

Years ago, a much younger Askon scoffed at these stories. A soldier in training had no place being afraid of a forest. However, the same younger version of himself had also mocked the idea of Alora's Tear. Now, it was all too obvious that the Tear and its power would in some way help to shape the future of two kingdoms. So, it was with trepidation and a respect for the unknown that Askon followed his friends into the folds of Grafmark, Forest of the Dead.

Not long after they had entered, John called a halt. He gave several quick orders to individuals within the group. From the time that John had led them safely away from the bridge, Askon had watched the count in their company gradually increase as they collected scouts and watchmen along the way. Those with orders now fanned out and investigated the edges of a wide green space. It was indeed dim under the forest canopy, but here a glowing shaft of light bathed the center of the clearing with warmth and color. When the men returned, reporting what they had found, John called to Askon and his friends.

"Don't know about you, but I could use a good sleep," he said. "It's been a full day since I've had any rest, an' that was only a short bit while we waited to see if you'd show up at the Greyarc." He stretched his long arms and released a noisy yawn, his wide mouth gaping cavernously.

Thomas looked around the clearing. "Sleep. Here? In the forest of Grafmark. You're certainly joking."

John was not. Since they had entered the forest, Askon had felt the lack of sleep begin to catch up with him. Though in their travels from Thomas's village to the Greyarc they had been able to rest, his sum total of hours slept to hours awake in the last week was woefully in favor of the latter. Dark circles hung beneath Edward's eyes, and even his stride, usually proud and tall, had sunk with exhaustion. Thomas however, had slept—if only for a short time—while they waited in the Greyarc guardhouse. He looked little the better for it. Upon entering Grafmark and all the while, he had been even more nervous and shaky than usual, often tripping on fallen branches or trunks, frantically regaining his footing only to stumble over the next obstacle. At first, Askon found it comical. But now he realized, under the shadow of Grafmark, Thomas would be getting little sleep indeed.

John appointed a watch. Thomas volunteered to be among their number, then flopped onto a flat mossy space near the base of a thick cedar tree. From beneath the shade of his own ancient cedar, Askon watched for a moment as his friends made themselves comfortable in the green glow of the trees. The thick air pressed upon him, slowly collecting beads of moisture, and he fell heavily into sleep.

"Askon!"

"Yes, Líana."

"I'm afraid."

"What's the matter?"

"It burns. I think I'm on fire. Will it ever go away?"

"It's just a fever, go back to bed."

"But… I'm scared."

"Of what?"

"Of the monster."

"Líana, there are no monsters here. You're safe. Go to sleep."

"No. He's here. I can smell him. I hear him breathing. He's right there."

"There are no monst—"

"Askon!"

When he awoke the creatures were already upon him. Askon jumped up, slipping as the moss tore loose revealing slick, dark mud.

He fell, sprawling back to the ground as they battered his face and chest. It was too late. They had taken him in his sleep. He fumbled for his sword belt, but the blade was pinned awkwardly beneath him. Giving up the sword, he went for the long hunting knife at the opposite hip. It too remained jammed in the sheath.

Now, he felt true panic overtake his senses, and the familiar feeling that time was slipping away from him, everything moving too fast. The creatures continued their assault, and Askon's panic rose even further. Where were the others? Why could he not hear them? Had they been taken silently while he slept? The thought stirred the rage deep inside and it rushed with splayed talons and screeching violence, to the surface. Askon screamed, yanking with all of his might on the jammed hunting knife. It came free.

Now, the anger from within had taken control. If his friends were dead, gone like those he had lost in Tolarenz, Askon would be sure to take as many of their killers as he could, and no amount of bloodshed or pain would satiate his hunger for revenge. He screamed again and flailed in a wide arc trying to slice through the vile fingers of the creatures that groped and strangled. He spun, slashed, kicked, screamed a third time. But the creatures only danced away, laughing, each one a chittering shadow. They were so fast.

Askon slipped again and fell back into the mud; stinging pain lanced along the length of his hip where the hilt of his sword had been driven into the muscle and bone. He released a final scream and felt the fingers tighten like the cold, grim touch of the Norill prisoner at Austgæta. And he heard the voice, the same booming voice, like death itself inside the private spaces of his mind.

"Askon!" it thundered. The grasp tightened, and the darkness settled in like the fog over the Greyarc bridge. Askon writhed under its weight. Then, with all of the strength he could marshal, he pulled against the grip. But it held fast. All he managed were four tortured words.

"I'll kill you all!"

"Askon, wake up."

Bleary-eyed and panting, Askon awoke, his fingers twisted tightly into the collar of Thomas's shirt. Beads of sweat poured down Askon's face, and he threw the young man aside. Thomas stumbled, then caught his balance a few steps away. As he moved, the sun came beaming through. Askon shielded his eyes. The light was followed instantly by the stinging slap of cedar branches against his face. Askon batted them away only to be assaulted again. He sat up, still heaving, and looked around.

Over the grass and leaves of the clearing, the green glow had deepened, the bands of light cast down from the canopy slanting steeply as afternoon pressed itself against evening. Here and there John's men lay against trees and fallen logs. Many of them were already awake, though not yet on their feet. A few, like Thomas, wandered from tree to tree, rousing those who still slept. Under a large cedar, John snored noisily, his mouth the wide "O" of a minstrel mid-song.

Abruptly, and with some surprise, Askon turned. There, still only inches away, knelt Thomas. With a start, Askon scooted to one side, his eyes narrowing in annoyance. He stretched, arms wide, and allowed a long yawn to escape. Leaning back on one elbow, he reached up and snapped the cedar branch that dangled in his face. He cast it aside angrily. But instead of whistling satisfyingly through the air and slapping against the ground as he had intended, the branch wafted softly along, looping and floating on its light green foliage like a lazy butterfly. The branch whispered its scorn as it flew, then alighted a mere yard or two from where Askon lay. Now even more annoyed, he again regarded Thomas who remained in place.

"What are you waiting for?" Askon said, allowing a bit too much of his irritation to come through in his voice. He recognized it immediately. Like a scolded dog, Thomas cowered, casting his eyes to the ground. As he did, a hand reached down from above, roughly slapping the young man aside.

"Fool boy. Give the man some space. Can't ya see he's got somethin' on his mind?" John proffered a hand to Thomas, who now lay awkwardly on the mossy ground. With a tug and a smirk, John yanked Thomas to his feet, but the force was too great. Carried by the momentum, Thomas continued on past John and into a fallen tree. The young man stumbled, but caught himself on the prostrate trunk. Now it was Thomas's turn to be annoyed. He glared back at John.

"Oh, don't get yer garter belt in a knot, now. Let's get a little to eat while Askon comes around." And he stepped lightly away from Askon. He gave Thomas a few quick, overly forceful slaps and led—almost dragged—the young man to the other side of the clearing where a smokeless, white-hot fire burned, and men stood tending pieces of roasting meat and pungent herbs.

Askon rocked back on the other elbow and cast his eyes up into the canopy. High above in the branches of the tallest trees, Marten hopped and fluttered from one side of the clearing to the other, scanning, as usual, for any creatures unwise enough to move beneath his watchful gaze. As he observed the bird, Askon's mind drifted back to the dream. Until earlier that day, his desire to find and eliminate Iramov had been motivated solely by his personal loss at Tolarenz. Askon thought of Líana, whose voice he heard so often in his dreams now. Hers was not the only life cut short by the hatred of one man. How many children like her had been in Tolarenz that day? How many adults?

Askon's personal revenge drove him to begin, still drove him to continue, but John's story had crystalized his resolve. If Iramov had his way, how many in the kingdom would fall under the smothering blackness brought on by the Death fragment? And for what reason would they pass from the world: greed, power, hatred?

But then another thought occurred to Askon. The men, women, and children of the kingdom were not likely to be treated as were those in Tolarenz. Subjugated perhaps, imprisoned maybe, but Askon's people were gone for a different reason. And that same reason would not apply to Codard's other subjects. Perhaps in the most dangerous of cases, Edward for instance, or rebels like John would be subjected to the Death fragment's power. But the people of Vladvir would go on largely oblivious, with a new, albeit more dangerous and unstable ruler.

The people of Codard's kingdom had cast out Askon's ancestors, had forced them to find and build a place where they could live without harassment or scorn. John would feel it was his duty to protect the kingdom's citizens, as he had done in Codard's army for years. To Edward, these were his very people. He could no easier turn his back on them than Askon could on Roland, the smith, or Halan, the falconer. And though Edward might oppose his own father, perhaps even fight against him, he would not do so easily. However, if John's information proved true, they would have to do exactly that: defeat not only Iramov and the Norill, enemies that they could all agree upon, but also Codard and the army of Vladvir.

Silently, and without Askon's knowledge, a shadow grew alongside him. Dusk had begun to settle on Grafmark, and the livid greens warmed to orange and pink as the beams of light in the clearing faded. The shadow continued to increase until Askon's eye caught a subtle movement. He glanced over his shoulder.

"Do you have something to say, Edward?" he asked.

Unruffled as Askon knew he would be, Edward leaned a shoulder against the rough bark of the cedar. He too looked up into the canopy where Marten perched sullenly, unable to acquire a meal. "Something is troubling you. Something beyond the obvious," he said. "I was already awake when you had your dream. We could hear you shouting. I told the others to disperse, to look away. But something about the way you twisted and turned made it all seem more than a simple nightmare."

"I think it was," Askon said. "It's Líana. When I go to sleep, I hear her voice. She and the others like her are the true tragedy of Tolarenz. They will never see the world or have a chance to change it. They are gone."

Edward stepped around the trunk of the tree and slid down next to Askon. Pulling his knees up to his chest, Edward continued to stare into the treetops. "Nothing that we do, be it rebellion, revenge, or otherwise, will bring them back to you. When my mother passed from this world, I too wanted revenge, though mine was silly and childish. The sickness that took her was an opponent I could not fight. I vowed that I would find a cure, and as only a young boy can, I studied and discussed with my father's greatest physicians what might be the solution. But the destruction of this foe was beyond my power, is still beyond it." He sighed heavily and turned his dark eyes, a king's eyes, to his friend. "It's not Iramov that you're most worried about," he said somberly. "It's me."

Askon turned away from the depths of those eyes. He meant to say all that had been on his mind, to reveal the doubts he had about John, the same that he had about Edward when the time finally came to challenge Codard. But all Askon could manage was a hypnotic nod: up, down, up down.

Edward's eyes released him and wandered back to the latticework of branches above them. "I do not know either," he said with an honesty that came as both a surprise to Askon and as the most predictable of responses. "My father is," and here the prince hesitated, "difficult." Edward stood and offered a hand to Askon. "We shall see what I decide, in time. My next choice comes not until we reach the South Kingdom. There, I will speak with Apopsé, attempt to know his mind and if he indeed intends on attacking Vladvir. By then, it is my hope that we will have found this Morrowmen. From your description he seems to be uncannily wise and aware of the moving pieces in our land. Perhaps he can settle my choice, or help me in the process of so doing."

Askon nodded again, the same hypnotic, wordless rhythm. Marten swooped down, landing with a flutter on his shoulder. The bird's cold, hunter's eyes locked onto Edward, and the two stared at one another momentarily. But not even the eyes of a king could win this contest. Marten stared on; Edward looked slowly away.

CHAPTER THIRTEEN

The Grafmark Norill

The cooking fires had been extinguished, the supplies collected. All that had once been emerald green, paled now and faded to gray or darkest purple. To Thomas, the idea of traveling within Grafmark after sundown was anathema. He worried and fretted, asking Edward to stop the proceedings. When the prince had deferred to John, the company's true leader now, Thomas had merely hung his head. Yet he held fast to his request. Sure enough, John reacted as any of them might have predicted.

"Scared by a lot o' ghost stories. How'd you even stick with Askon for so long, spineless as ya are?" John blared, so that all the men might hear him. "I'll tell ya what, Thomas. You stay here and hide from your spooks. Maybe you can catch us up in the morning."

Defeated, Thomas turned and walked slowly away. He shook violently from head to toe, and his skin had turned as pale as the silver shafts of moonlight that blinked in and out of the trees. What specifically he feared, none of them knew, but even Askon felt some of that same irrational terror deep down. John, in his attempt at decisive leadership, merely masked the same dread that every man in the company tried to ignore.

After pressing through the clattering underbrush for nearly an hour, the bracken suddenly gave way. In the gloom and smoke of the burning brands, Askon saw the trunks of massive trees whose lowest branches spread widely somewhere above, beyond the reach of the meager lights. Row upon row, like the enormous pillars of a giant's hall, the trunks faded into the blackness. Askon waved his torch from right to left to little avail. On every side, into the deepest distance the great hall of trees stretched on.

"Ha!" John barked, a broad smile spreading over his face. "I knew we were close. Up till now, you've been standin' at the doorstep. Now our lady mistress has let us in. Good news always, that."

"What's good news?" asked Thomas shakily.

John laughed, "Bein' let in by a lady mistress!"

Nervous laughter rippled through the company, but no one allowed himself much mirth. Though the sounds seemed to leap loudly out of one's mouth at first, they soon died amongst the trees.

Askon approached Thomas, who smiled awkwardly, but had not laughed. "He's saying that we have now entered the heart of Grafmark, the true forest, if you will."

"Aye, that's what I'm sayin'," John said with a sniff. Then, "If you were afraid before, you best steel yourself for what comes next. This is where the stories come from."

Edward glared. "Stop torturing him, John. Can't you see he's having enough trouble as it is?"

"I think I know what's true in my own forest!" John roared back at the prince. "You may weave a tale and a lie and a scheme with the best, but we're not in the king's court anymore. Your vocabulation does not one lick o' good out here. And though I don't hold to ghost stories, like our boy Thomas, there's dangers enough for all in the heart of Grafmark."

Edward nodded and stepped slowly away, this time ignoring the mispronounced words and misguided attack on Thomas. They were too far into the forest to escape or even find their way back, so Edward deferred to the new leader. It seemed that the berating of Thomas was a price to be paid under John's authority.

On they went through Grafmark's great, pillared hall. Earlier in the day, Askon had felt as though they fought unnecessarily against the forest when they could have been moving south. Now Grafmark did indeed seem to welcome them in, or beckon them on to some unknown threat. Either way, they would be sufficiently hidden from any pursuit that might have trailed them from the Greyarc.

After they had passed in silence for some time through the trees, Thomas approached Askon. Marten still perched on his shoulder, and the bird's piercing eyes stared, unflinching, at Thomas.

"Sir," Thomas began. "Back there, when we left the underbrush, John called this *his* forest." He sidled from left to right as they walked, moving his head back and forth, trying to avoid the gaze of the falcon. "What did he mean by that?"

Askon watched with a smirk as Thomas bobbed and swayed under Marten's glare. Shrugging his shoulder quickly, he dislodged the bird, who flapped up into the lowest level of branches. "He might be overstating it a bit, to call the whole forest *his*. Though it has been quite a number of years since he enlisted in Codard's army—longer than myself by a significant margin—John's home was here, somewhere in Grafmark. We all knew that he came from the Forest of the Dead, but no one talked much about it. Most said that when asked, he would merely shrug and change the subject if the questioner was of equal or higher rank and viciously attack them if they ranked lower. He once told me that he joined the army to escape his home, though it seemed more for wanting freedom than fearing something from this forest."

Thomas nodded lightly, thoughtfully, then lowered his head. Askon was sure that the young man was trying to understand why John was so determined to harass him. But the connection between that and the myths of Grafmark did not seem clear.

"My advice is to simply avoid John for now, and if you must be nearby, stay quiet."

Thomas nodded again, but Askon did not see it. On the periphery of his vision, amid the darkness and faintest outlines of the towering trees, a shape moved noiselessly. Askon stopped. Thomas did not, and nearly ran his torch into Askon's back. Without moving his eyes, Askon swung his own torch behind him. Thomas plucked it from his hand without a word.

With the light behind him, the shapes of the trees at the edge of sight became clearer. What had been a smudged blur, was now the stark, gray outline of a thick cedar trunk. He peered into the black, waiting to again see movement in the distance. It did not come.

Thomas took a step forward, but Askon waved him away, allowing his eyes to do the work that the torches could not. A creeping dread looped its talons around Askon, and he wondered if the stories were true. It could, he thought nervously, have merely been some forest animal ranging in the night. But if the old wives and grandfathers of Tolarenz spoke true, then a ranging animal at night could mean anything. In his mind, Askon pictured a pack of wolves circling the company, closing in like a rising tide around the last point of high ground. He imagined them twisting, convulsing brutally, as wolf became man. He envisioned them plotting together in gruff voices that barked and whined. Then he felt it: the feeling that time had begun to slip away. Thomas, though standing still, rocked back and forth unnaturally, like the accelerated pendulum of a clock wound too tightly. Askon tried to focus, but now he thought he saw more shapes at all sides of the company.

"Don't think of a salamander."

In his mind, the small voice, Líana's voice, drifted through the fearful imaginings. Breathing deeply, Askon reached under his shirt and pulled out the glowing fragment of Alora's Tear. He pushed away the stories and myths of the forest, trying only to see the many smooth facets of the jewel or the loops and twisting curls that made up its silver setting. He breathed again and stared as the pulsing slowed, gradually at first. Then, like a twig bent double upon itself that suddenly snaps, the light inside the fragment went out.

Askon looked up. All around him the world was completely still. He no longer remembered what had been troubling him, what had made him so afraid. Whatever it was, it had affected Thomas even more. On the young man's motionless, unblinking face, Askon read the deepest terror. Then it came back to him: the movement in the trees. Askon redirected his gaze to the space in the distance where he had seen the blurred shape. This recollection seemed to jar something loose in the stillness brought on by the Time fragment, and the scene before his eyes began to move again. He looked back down at the gem. It had resumed its steady-heartbeat pulsing, but the change from dark to light was very slow. Trying to focus on the metal of the setting or the facets of the gem left the rhythm unaffected. Whatever he had done to halt the scene completely seemed unlikely to return, so he looked again to the trees.

It was still dark, and though the power of the fragment—and his own half-elven eyes—allowed him to see further into the towering pillars of Grafmark, the distance was much less than it would have been under daylight, even the muted light in the Forest of the Dead. Directly before him, peering around one of the largest trunks, was the shape. It swayed like an underwater plant, revealing itself, then passing back into hiding. It stood only a few feet from the ground, and Askon knew instantly that it was not human, nor elven. For a moment, the shape stayed hidden, unaware that it had been detected. The rest of the company trudged sluggishly onward through the forest. Only Askon and Thomas had stopped.

Scanning the trees, Askon saw that the creature wasn't a single shape, but many. They hunkered behind rocks or lurked in the brush around the bases of trees. One crouched menacingly atop a low branch, its eyes wide and glaring. In his mind Askon began a count, but as the number grew higher, he realized that there were far more shapes than men. With each increment, the scene before his eyes became more fluid, the power of the fragment receding. Askon clung to the feeling, trying to stay focused, but it slipped away bit by bit. Just before the motion around him returned to normal, one of the shapes moved.

It crossed from its hidden position behind the large cedar to a neighboring tree. As it walked, Askon recognized the lanky, loping stride. Other details became clear: large round eyes, greasy strands of black hair, skin pale-gray like boiled meat, arms too long for the body. Without doubt, this could be only one type of creature. Many times Askon had observed that staggering gait and crooked stance. The shapes in the distance were Norill. And now, in the pitch-black of Grafmark, they gathered in a silent, ominous ring.

As the realization struck him, Askon felt the power of the fragment dissipate. He turned to Thomas, and spoke in a whisper. "We are being watched. Go now, and tell John. There are Norill in the trees all around us. I will find Edward. Speak nothing to the others, and try to avoid looking suspicious. They have not attacked us yet, but even the slightest sign of our awareness might provoke them!"

Thomas did as he was told. He carried both torches away, moving across the line of John's men. Soon, the torches were merely points of light, and Askon stood alone in the darkness. He flipped the hood of his cloak over his head, a thoughtless reflex. At first, the night seemed to grow darker, but before Thomas had overtaken more than a few of the other torchbearers, Askon's eyes had adjusted and the trees all around became clearer than ever. He no longer had any assistance from the fragment, nor did he need it. Now that he knew where the watchers were posted, it was impossible not to see them. His hands slipped to his side where he loosened the clasp on his scabbard. He tugged the hilt slightly, to be sure it would come free if the Norill made the first move. Then he waited to see if any of the shapes would shift their positions. When they did not, Askon quickly found Edward and fell into step beside him. Lifting a finger to his own lips, he leaned in close, whispering.

"Norill. In the trees. They're all around us."

Edward nodded, his eyes darting left and right as he searched for the watchers. "I thought you might say that. I've noticed movement in the shadows, but I assumed they were animals of some kind."

"As did I. Thomas is looking for John. I told him to avoid alerting anyone else."

Edward loosened his sword.

Shortly thereafter, Thomas reappeared, now with John in tow. Each carried a torch, but they both passed them off to others along the line. They approached Askon and Edward, the latter carrying the only light.

"We could set a false camp," John said without preamble. "That might bring 'em in close."

Askon shook his head. "By my count, they outnumber us."

John chuckled to himself. "Norill's a half a man at the scales, two at the smell, and a quarter in a fight—"

"I think you'd find them quite capable with the tactical advantage," Edward hissed.

"What, so it'd be better to bull-rush 'em, ya think?"

"No, I'd say not."

Edward and John glared at one another through the flickering shadows of the torchlight while the rest of the company moved on through the forest.

It was a long time before any of them spoke again. When they did, Thomas broke the silence. "We've been walking for a while now," he said quietly, "since Askon noticed them. They haven't attacked us yet. Perhaps they mean not to?"

"Oh, and *perhaps* they've set up a surprise party for us with cakes and a tea table," John whined in his best imitation of a courtly lady.

Askon sighed. "That's enough John. I know this is your expedition now, but Thomas has taken enough abuse. Let him be."

John emitted a grunt, but did not indicate whether or not he would relent. Regardless, his plans seemed unnecessary as they continued on through the night.

After a miles-long march, the Norill had still not chosen to harm them. At intervals, Askon had seen both greater numbers and fewer, but they never came closer than they had been when he first realized that they were there. In fact, as he and his friends plunged deeper into the forest, the Norill had actually backed gradually away from the company. One by one, mile by mile, the watchers disappeared. When only a few remained, Askon turned to John.

"There are hardly any Norill left. I would have suspected that their number would grow as we went further," Askon said.

John smiled. "They might just be dead."

"What do you mean?"

"Well, that'll be the Darts of Grafmark takin' their share," John replied, the smile spreading slyly across his face.

"I don't like the look of that smile," Askon said. "Where are you taking us?"

John sniffed. "Home, o' course. And the first sign o' that is the Darts, my friend. These boys around us, they're just the new batch. When a person lives in the middle of a forest like this one, they gotta have somebody to defend 'em. I figure we passed into the Darts' watches about an hour ago. Anybody who ain't from this forest'll be in their sights. Lucky though, you've got me. Better hope I'm recognizable after all this time, else we might find ourselves sproutin' arrow fletchings."

Whether John's mysterious Darts had managed to kill the Norill watchers or they had merely dispersed of their own accord, it took less than an hour before Askon saw the last one vanish into the depths of the forest. Despite John's claims, the only living creatures they had seen since nightfall were the Norill. If the Darts of Grafmark lurked somewhere in the trees, Askon of Tolarenz could not see them—even with his half-elven sight. Shortly after the last Norill disappeared, Askon felt the soft spongy earth angle upward. The company seemed to be climbing a rise. Normally Askon and the others would have been able to see such a slope coming from miles away, but the darkness as well as the thick canopy above had hidden it from view.

Up the hill they went, still passing through rank after rank of towering cedar and pine or beech and oak. Such a mix of trees Askon had never before observed, and he thought of his father tending his diminutive versions on the workbench behind their home. Had his father seen a forest like this? It occurred to Askon that they had never discussed Grafmark. In those days, the Forest of the Dead seemed a distant fairytale, like that of the Tear. But now it was all too clear how real a child's story could become. A wish grew within Askon, to have asked his father about this place. If anyone would have known a version of the truth, it would have been him.

Askon stood now at the top of the rise. Half of the company stood with him, waiting for the others to catch up. Among those at the top were Edward and John, while Thomas straggled behind not with the second group, but at its rear. In a few places, the climb had been too steep, and the thick layer of leaves and needles tore loose, revealing slimy black mud. Thomas twice had fallen and rolled several yards back down the hill. He came up looking like a wallowed pig, dark streaks covering one side or the other.

When the last of the stragglers had gained the crest of the hill, a strange glow rose from the east. Suddenly they could see farther into the trees, and silver-black became gray-green. Somewhere, far beyond the sight of anyone in John's company, the sun had broken the horizon, calling forth the dim twilight-daytime of Grafmark. Askon watched as Marten hopped from tree to tree, gliding and landing, gliding and landing. The bird disappeared into the canopy and perhaps flew above it. Then in a flash of feathers, like an arrow or soaring spearhead, Marten came streaking back through the branches. With the air whistling as he passed, the falcon circled Askon once then splayed his wings and landed hard on the shoulder guard. The impact drove Askon forward, and he stutter-stepped to keep his balance while Marten flapped his wings in an effort to do the same. When the two came to rest, Marten stared fixedly west, leaning forward as though hunting.

Falcons in Tolarenz, and anywhere the elves lived, were trained very differently from those raised by humans. The birds were not tied or hooded, nor were they forced to work as servants to their keepers. Elven falconry relied on trust and companionship between falcon and falconer. Most human keepers were servants themselves and the true owners of the birds usually nobility of some sort. The owner would have rarely had the patience to bond with a bird, let alone multiple birds. An elven falconer would often lose many candidates, sometimes on the order of ten-to-one, before he found a falcon that would return of its own volition. However, when they did, the birds made for more than just living weapons in the hunt. They became companions and friends whose sight and mobility extended that of even the purest of elven blood. It had taken the greater part of a year for Marten to become acquainted with Askon after being raised under Halan's care, and in the years since their bond had grown strong indeed. Now, at the top of the ridge, deep in the heart of Grafmark, Marten meant to communicate with his friend. Ignoring the others, Askon bolted into the trees. Marten clung to the shoulder guard at first, but after a few yards he leapt into the air. Askon sprinted along behind, keeping pace as best he could.

A feather here, a flash of color there, Askon ducked and weaved, all the while keeping his eyes trained on Marten who slipped between the trees like thread through a needle. On they went, a hundred feet, over a fallen tree whose trunk was as thick as Askon was tall, another hundred and the ridge line broke, the terrain descending gently. A light grew somewhere ahead of them, but Marten flew onward. The ground flattened into a wide plateau and Askon ran another hundred feet, and then another. Then Marten spread his wings to their full width, fanning the feathers wide. Askon took the gesture as a signal that he should stop.

He skidded to a halt, needles and leaves pushing up into small piles around his boots, the black mud beneath the decomposing top layer exposed in streaks behind him. He leaned heavily against the nearest tree and panted. When he lifted his head, an unexpected sight met his eyes.

Ten yards before him, the plateau ended, but it did not roll gradually down into more ranks of huge trees. It disappeared completely. Askon was standing at the edge of a sheer cliff. Its ragged gray face dropped many hundreds of feet before it was swallowed by the treetops that reached up to meet it. In the furthest distance, a jagged mountain range rose above the valley to the height at which Askon stood and then beyond, a third again higher. Its looming bulk reminded Askon of the mountain that towered above Austgæta so many miles behind them. Between the cliff face and the mountain, the verdant green of the treetops rolled like a soft carpet in all directions. But this green was not the muted, sickly color of Grafmark as they had seen it for the last day-and-a-half, the trees in the valley were bathed in warm, pure sunlight.

To the west, near the mountain's base, a wide space had been cleared. There, thin tendrils of smoke rose from a large cluster of buildings. North of the town, the clearing continued and the sunlight glinted off a small pond and stream. All around the water, the distinct crisscross patchwork of sown fields lay open to the sun's rays. Above, beyond the tree line at the edge of the cliff, the blue sky stretched endlessly, interrupted only by puffs of downy clouds. Askon gazed unmoving into the sun-gilded valley. He felt Marten land at his shoulder, but his eyes did not turn from the sight before him.

"And that, friend o' mine'd be Dalstone. What'dya think of her?" It was John's voice, harsh and gravelly in the beautiful quiet above the valley. At first Askon tried to ignore him, not out of disrespect, but in hopes that he could cling to the scene below for just a moment longer. "No answer means one o' two things, I always say. One, that I was right, and two, the guy's too dumb to answer."

Askon ignored him and continued to take in the sight. "It's beautiful, John," he said quietly.

John slapped Askon on the back and Marten flapped uncomfortably. "It is, until ya live there your whole life. Stay if ya want, but talk to me in a few years and we'll see how much ya like living in that hole in the ground."

Edward and Thomas, as well as most of the other company members, had caught up. Their gear rattled along with their heavy steps. Edward approached with Thomas a few steps behind. "Well who would have known," Edward began.

"I would have," John interjected. "That, right there, is the whole point of stumbling through this blasted forest."

Askon was still in awe. "It's so isolated," he said.

John shook his head and pointed north. "It is. But not as much as you might think. The river that runs along the base of the mountains comes down from alongside your man Iramov's stronghold near Vestgæta. It's every bit as vulnerable as Tolarenz was, if that's what you're thinking. Though it does have one advantage. Hardly anybody knows it's here."

Askon turned away from the sight, a pained look buried just beneath the superficial smile on his face. "That certainly would have been an advantage," he said.

For a few minutes more, they stood on the brink and looked into the valley. Askon wondered if John was right. It didn't matter. Had Tolarenz been built in the depths of the forest, somehow Iramov would have eventually come. An army would have been of little help to the attackers in Tolarenz, as it would have here in Dalstone. With only a few men and the Death fragment, Dalstone could be wiped out just as easily as any village. With an effort, Askon drove away the images of silent, empty buildings, and household goods piled in a burning heap. The images went, but the anger welled up in their place. And if only a little, Askon saw his friends moving ever so slightly quicker than they should have. He thought of his own fragment, of its power over him, of its possible uses against Iramov, but they seemed small and weak in comparison to the damage the Death fragment could wreak in only a few moments. However, in the warm sun above Dalstone, Askon swore again to stop at nothing—whatever Morrowmen had to say when they reached the South Kingdom—until Iramov had been defeated. What he would do with the Death fragment if they were able to eliminate Iramov, Askon was not yet sure, but he hoped that if he couldn't find the answer, Morrowmen would know it.

The anger passed, and time returned to its normal pace. John led them south along the cliff's edge until they came to a narrow path. Wide enough for two men to walk abreast, the thin pathway wound crazily down the sheer rock face until it vanished into the trees far below. Thomas balked at the trailhead, but John, in his cruel unfeeling way, goaded the young man on until Thomas realized that they had gone too far to turn back. They passed then into the trees and across the valley floor. By noon they drew near the edge of the forest and Dalstone itself.

CHAPTER FOURTEEN

Dalstone

At the gate a gnarled old man frowned and squinted at them: John in the lead, backed by Askon, Edward, and Thomas. Gathered at the tree line were the remainder of what John was now calling "The New Darts." As instructed, they laid down any and all weapons. Through the frown, the gatekeeper seemed pleased. Contrary to John's assertions, the old man had not recognized him, but had quickly sent for John's father, who lived on the northern edge of town.

The gate itself, a contraption of crude but clever construction, had been designed to fall on top of an opposing force. Edward said that in his father's castle, designers had deployed similar measures, though much smaller, to dispatch the mice and rats that sometimes escaped the several cats and small dogs kept within the palace. Whatever mouse the people of Dalstone hoped to catch with their gate would be fearsome indeed. Around the mousetrap gate, a wall much like the fortress of Austgæta had been built. Narrow pointed poles made up the majority of the wall, a perfect line of giant wooden spears. At the base, the townspeople had dug a deep ditch and lined it with hundreds of overlapping spikes poking at angles through the soft, silted earth. These spikes appeared to be made from the same trees as the wall itself, though the ones chosen for the ditch were thinner and sharper.

While the company waited, the gatekeeper allowed them to sit and eat what food they might have carried along. All were well supplied. The three fugitives had recovered the stores taken from the Grandfather back in Shale while John and his men remained comfortable on their provisions from the king. In the warm sun they relaxed, though they stayed outside the reach of the gate.

"Might even have to miss a place like this," John said through a mouthful. "'Course I'll have the twitch and the jitter to get outta here before a couple days are done."

Thomas, who had calmed significantly since putting the winding cliff trail behind them, seemed to be enjoying himself. He leaned back, taking in the unfiltered sunlight. "I don't see why. We've been through the whole of Grafmark and—"

"Ha!" John's laugh thundered across the clearing. "Oh *have* we? Here's this tremblin', shakin'-like-a-leaf half-a-child tellin' us we've been through Grafmark." John laughed again, and bits of food landed lightly on his shirt. He wiped them away absently. "You hear that river, boy?"

Thomas nodded.

"You see that mountain?"

Again, a nod.

"Well *that's* still part of Grafmark, my friend. And I'll tell ya what. If you think you've seen it all, comin' into Dalstone, you'll have to have a rethink. 'Cause the stories you heard? They come from that side o' the river."

Thomas craned his neck to the top of the mountain, his smile fading again into uncertainty. After a moment of thought, he looked away. "Whatever is over there, it isn't here now. The town seems to be relatively well-defended, and you've forgotten your confidence in the Darts of Grafmark, John. I think we're as safe here as anywhere."

John grunted one of those grunts that Askon knew to mean, 'I don't have anything appropriately scathing to say at this moment, so I'm going to let that slide.' Thomas, it seemed, had overcome his fear of the forest and now sat happily basking in the sun, eating a handful of dried fruit and nuts from the Grandfather's stores.

An hour passed, yet the gatekeeper did not return. After consuming their rations, the New Darts had taken to dozing. Some sat with their backs to large stones and fallen trees, chatting or playing cards or dice to pass the time. Others painstakingly honed the edges of their weapons. Askon, engaged in the latter, ran the whetstone along his sword in long rhythmic strokes. As part of his daily ritual, the process had become one of routine more than need. In the last two days they had seen no combat, though he had crossed blades briefly with Christopher on the Greyarc. Still, he proceeded without thinking. Before long, battle would find them. The ritual nature of the sharpening simply assured that Askon would be ready.

Meanwhile, John had grown impatient. He ranged up and down the wall grumbling to himself. At times he turned and shouted at groups of men in the company. For a moment they would stand at attention, but when John had passed, they went back to their diversions. And so the day wore on with Askon and his friends once again waiting to be admitted by the wary.

If John seemed irritated at the wait, so did the citizens of Dalstone. On the opposite side of the wall, a crowd gathered. Men, women, and children peered through the small gaps between the poles. A murmur grew, and Askon felt that more than a few of the words spoken inside Dalstone were of apprehension and worry, if not outright protest at the company's arrival. Amid the noise of the crowd, Askon overheard a few of the louder voices.

"I count at least forty," said a man.

"Maybe, but you never could count very well," said another.

Askon laughed at that.

"Isn't that Mark's boy, leading them?" asked the first man.

"He's got the jawline, that one," said the second.

"They don't all look like they're from Dalstone," a woman's voice commented.

"Yeah, 'specially *that* one," a young boy agreed.

Askon flipped the hood over his head, then turned away, feeling the cool shadow fall over his face.

"Indeed m'boy," the first man answered. "That one there does look different. I'll betcha he's nobility or some-such. Got the posture, he does."

"Not to mention he's wearing the king's crest," said the woman.

Askon sat up. He certainly wasn't wearing Codard's stag, hadn't since his first days in the king's service. Casting his eyes from one man to the next, he saw that in fact, none of them were still wearing the crest. Apparently, after they had left the city, the New Darts had fashioned emblems for themselves. Upon closer inspection, the armor had only needed slight alterations. The cloaks that the New Darts wore were the same that had been issued them by the king. However, they had cleverly inverted the fabric so that Codard's blue stag lay hidden. On the outside—which had until recently been the inside—they had hastily drawn what Askon assumed to be a tree, or several trees. The dull gray, probably a soft clay or mud of some kind, was visible enough against the black fabric. Askon thought he could see a large arrow piercing the foliage of the tree from left to right on some of the uniforms. Whether this emblem was entirely new or based on the existing Darts' design, Askon did not know. But it was not the gray-on-black emblem that had caught the attention of the townspeople. It was the bright blue stag of King Codard.

At first, Askon did not see the symbol anywhere. His instinct had been that Thomas still wore the unaltered uniform. In this, Askon was wrong. A few feet away, Thomas sat talking with one of John's men, the cloak around his back inverted, though without the muddy gray emblem of the New Darts. Then it became obvious. Without looking, Askon knew who would be wearing the king's symbol, knew it for a certainty. Beside John, another few yards farther from where Thomas sat, strode Edward. Had John not been the one to approach the gate, Edward would clearly have looked like the leader. He stood tall, with a posture only trained in the houses of nobility, his dark eyes surveying the men with a detached sense of authority and responsibility. And though he would smile from time to time, even laugh aloud at John's jokes, he seemed somehow more stern and solemn. That, combined with his meticulously well-kept appearance and the brilliant blue stag blazoned on his back, made him difficult to overlook, and impossible to ignore.

Before the crowd had any more time for questions, the murmur died away. Stepping to one side or the other, the people bowed their heads and allowed a wide path to open at the center of the group. Through it walked the hunkering gatekeeper and a thick man with a long, full beard black as night and flecked with strands of silver. As the large man passed, the onlookers bowed even lower, causing a ripple that made his passing like a wave rolling slowly onto the shore. Here and there, he nodded, reaching out with an open hand. The members of the crowd would rise, but kept their faces downcast. Shuffling alongside him, the gatekeeper seemed to enjoy the respect-by-proximity; he smiled a twisted smile each time the people bent low.

Carefully, thoughtfully, Askon examined the large man. A short cloak hung from his shoulders in a style similar to those worn by the king's courtiers. It had no hood, and the man's thick black hair lay plaited in a heavy braid down his back. His robes were dyed rich purple, though not so shadow-deep as the robes Morrowmen wore. Down the center, starting just below the man's chest and continuing to length, hung a wide strip of gray. A thick yellow-gold rope cinched the robe about his waist and his girth rolled over the cord like bread over the sides of its pan. Askon thought he looked more than a little like a younger, more opulent Grandfather.

"John of Dalstone," the large man boomed. Yet it was not a voice thick and full like the Grandfather's. It was every bit as loud, but the sound was thin and reedy. "Come forth!"

Askon observed how a fair number of John's men stood up at the sound of this voice. They stood at attention, though their faces were bowed like those of the townsfolk inside the gate. John, with a leisurely stride, even for him, detached himself from his conversation with Edward and ambled slowly over to the gate. Edward continued without so much as a glance in John's direction. He and Thomas then sat next to Askon, who continued to watch the exchange between John and the large man at the gate.

"Men of Dalstone," the large man said, even louder this time. "Gather around, for there is much I would ask of you."

Quickly, the men whose heads had been bowed only seconds before, came leaping across the wide clearing. They encircled the gate but remained several steps behind John. Again they lowered their faces. John did not.

At the same moment, small movements rustled the branches and low shrubs at the edge of the tree line all around the clearing. With no time to rise, Askon instead crouched low, scanning the perimeter. Instantly his sword came free of the scabbard. Edward had taken the same position not because he saw the movement in the trees, but on his friend's reaction. Thomas fumbled with his own sword belt, trying to stay as low to the ground as the others.

At the tree line, the rustling continued until John's company was surrounded. Grim-faced men with cold eyes emerged from hiding, their hands at the strings of long bows curved crookedly in two directions rather than the usual single arc to which Askon was accustomed. He had seen this type of bow before. Some of the men in Codard's army would use no other. Askon found them to be unwieldy and inelegant, though archery had never been his strongest talent.

With those cold eyes unblinking, the men stalked forward. At the edges of the clearing, the scattered members of John's company backed away from the new arrivals, compressing the group into an ever smaller space. When the men from the forest had squeezed the company into a tight circle, they stopped. Lowering their weapons so that the arrows still rested on the string, the men waited. In the silence, Askon could hear John and the large man as they continued their conversation.

John was livid. "Here we come, through that blasted forest, men to bolster the Darts. Hell, I've even got 'em wearing the tree and quarrel. Now what? You got us penned like chickens for the block."

If John's was the voice of anger, the large man's was calm and smooth in equal measure. "Son," and at this Askon nodded to Edward. They had both anticipated as much. "As you well know, Dalstone must be quite careful in watching its borders. The dangers of Grafmark are many, and not all of them come from west of the river."

"Then where were your boys when the Norill had us surrounded in the dark, eh?" John demanded. "I told mine there was no need for worry, 'Oh, the Darts'll be on 'em sure as sure,' I said. Was I wrong?"

"We did see the Norill that followed you—"

"We? Meaning you crawled out of your temple to check on us yourself?"

The large man's tone changed instantly. Any warmth that had been there, was gone. An icy malice replaced it. "The wisdom from that temple keeps *you* alive. I choose the Darts' directives based on the voices of the gods. All of Dalstone is in their debt." And here Askon noted a subtle change in tone. "Even a coward, a deserter, who cried 'Mommy' at the nightstand while the others his age learned to be men. Even one so spineless as he owes his life to the gods."

Immediately, Askon understood the dynamic between John and Thomas, why every time the younger man spoke even the slightest contradicting remark, John came down on him as though it were the greatest of offenses. Askon expected that with such a scathing tirade, John's inevitable retort would be spectacular. It never came. Only silence. Confused, Askon pushed through the crowd of New Darts, who stood or knelt before the father-son discussion. When he could finally see his friend, the scene surprised him. Kneeling before the large man, was John. There were tears in his eyes.

"I beg pardon, Mark, priest of the temple, guardian of Dalstone. I have misspoken," John said, flawlessly. It was enough to turn Askon's stomach.

"Am I not also your father? Show a son's respect in your acknowledgement."

"Father," John said, and bowed low, until his face nearly touched the ground.

After a moment in which the priest gazed down imperiously at his son, he knelt as well. He grabbed John solidly by the shoulders and lifted him from the ground. "The gods allow to live those who learn from their mistakes. Even fools who make many," he said with only a touch of the earlier coldness. "Now, what brings a fool back to his home after so many years gone?"

John pulled away from his father's grip. "We came, because there's nowhere else for us. Codard's decided to set himself up with friends who'd destroy or control the lands of free men—" here he hesitated and looked back toward the crowd. Askon knew who he was looking for. "—and other folk as well. I could say more about 'em, but the king's got spies all over these days, might even have some all the way out here in Dalstone."

Mark's eye swept a broad arc which covered the whole of the company as well as the Darts proper who surrounded them. "Foolish reasoning again!" he snapped. "If the king's spies are here, then you have already been defeated."

"Sir, if I may," Edward offered. He had approached in his familiar almost-invisible way and now stood just inside the circle.

"You may not!" came the response in the same icy voice Mark had used with John earlier. "Who is this man, John? Shouldn't your followers address you when they speak? What kind of leader are you?"

John looked quickly to Edward, but did not issue a command. "The kind o' leader who knows when to respect his men for what they are," John said flatly. "This is the prince, Edward son of Codard. He follows me, indeed he does. But I don't make it my responsibility to command him, 'cept when I have a mind to, and I don't right this minute. 'Course that doesn't mean he'd listen if he had a mind not to. Got his own followers, this one, and rightly so I'd—"

"Though as a man rescued by the commander, your son, I would respect his orders were he to give them," Edward interjected.

A short, choked laugh escaped John's mouth. Mark stood silent.

"And while I'm at it," John added. "We've got Askon of Tolarenz, former commander, and good friend o' mine."

Mark stepped away as if John had just lit himself on fire. The large man lifted his hands and turned them, palms out, toward Askon's position at the edge of the inner circle. "O-of w-where? T-Tolarenz?"

"Yes," said John as his father continued to back away.

"Why did you not say so?" Mark asked.

John raised an eyebrow. "Why would I? It's him we're hiding. Codard's new friends went after Tolarenz first. Askon's the only one left."

"Not the only one," Askon said, his voice like the whisper of a ghost from beneath the deep green hood. "There was another."

John looked annoyed. "At any rate, we haven't been in the habit of letting everyone know he's with us."

Mark glared at John as if his son had just forgotten to introduce him to an important dignitary at some political function. Askon glanced at Edward, who simply shrugged. A moment passed in silence.

"My sincerest apologies, Askon," Mark said. Now it was he who bowed low. As he did, the crowd of townspeople gathered behind him kneeled as well. Askon felt awkward and uncomfortable towering over the lowered heads, most of which almost touched the ground. Thomas stooped to do the same, but Edward slapped him briskly on the back of the head and pulled him to his feet.

When Mark arose, he stepped hastily across the open space to where Askon stood. Again he knelt, then grabbed Askon's right hand and kissed it. Askon resisted the urge to pull away.

Had I known," Mark said softly. "I would have had the entirety of the Darts at your back from the moment you entered Grafmark." He stood and raised his voice. "Men of Dalstone, Darts of Grafmark, and others here gathered. We have today a great and fortunate occurrence. One that Dalstone has not seen for many a year. Not since I was a young boy has such a guest graced our halls." He waved away the men who stood or knelt near Askon, including Edward, Thomas, and John. Slowly, Mark led Askon to the center of the ring, just in front of the gate.

"We have here with us today, one of the elven blood." He paused, and Askon heard gasps and murmurs in the crowd. "Yes, you heard me true. The nearest to the gods of all the peoples walking these latter-day lands. Tonight, we prepare, and in the morning we begin. I declare now, a great celebration! I will confer with our guest, and we can hope that much will be gained in the knowledge we share. May the gods smile upon Dalstone!"

At this the crowd burst into applause. Mark raised Askon's arm into the air, and the crowd cheered. Then, as quickly as it had come, the moment passed. Later, Askon recalled Mark having begged his pardon while he began preparations and that the crowd had been commanded to make ready as well. But in the moment, Askon merely stood, bewildered as the throng of villagers milled about and dispersed.

Edward slapped him hard on the back. "Well, that's not something that you see every day, now is it?"

Askon said nothing and continued to stare at the busy townspeople.

"John, why didn't you tell us that elves, even half-elves like Askon were so revered in Dalstone?"

John kicked a loose stone with the tip of his boot. "It's new to me, it is, Edward. It's new to me."

From somewhere behind them, they heard Thomas's voice come drifting over the din. "Historically, the elves were well thought of, I'm sure Askon knows that, but not for quite a number of years, many more than any of our lifetimes or those of our great grandparents even. Indeed, there was once a time, just after the Knight of Vladvir discovered the Waterside Parchment and ended the great darkness—"

"Oh, shut up!" John said sulkily. "What kinda fairytales ya been readin' at bedtime, eh? Talkin' bout knights and such."

This time, Thomas stood his ground. "It's true," he said, though still somewhat shakily. "In the years after the first reported contact with the elves, the people of Vladvir practically worshipped them, until they grew distrustful, that is. It began mostly amongst the nobility. No offense, Edward."

"None taken," Edward said smiling.

"They didn't like the power that the elves seemed uniquely able to wield, so they began cultivating rumors of conspiracy and evil intent," Thomas continued. "Of course, the elves hid no actual ill-will. After that, certain parts of Vladvir never trusted them or their descendants again. Others continued to worship, or at least revere, them in secret."

Askon sighed and watched the townspeople scuttling about. Now and then one of them would bend to the ground or bow respectfully as they passed. Askon looked over his shoulder at his friends. "That all ended with the Scouring, Thomas. Anyone who supported, let alone worshipped, the elves was either captured or killed a very long time ago."

"Not to mention I ain't kissin' your boots anytime soon," said John with a look of mild disgust. "When I left, weren't nobody around here'd say a half-elf was any better or worse than anybody else. Seems like things change fast."

Askon turned away from the preparations that went on dutifully behind them. "Well," he said. "At least it's a warm welcome. I think we'll have to wait and see what your father has to say, John. Maybe he can explain our reception. It's been years since you left. Who knows what spiritual decisions they might have made since then."

John grinned, then shoved Askon hard. "Oh yeah, enjoy it while ya can there Askon. Be the big celebrity. We'll see how ya like it after about four or five hours o' him jawin' you about the gods and the spirits and whatnot. You'll be beggin' for me to take you back to the Greyarc before nightfall tomorrow. Just you wait."

With that, he stormed off. His parting words sounded like a joke, but Askon wondered if the others had noticed the subtle difference. Dalstone made John uncomfortable. And his discomfort was amplified whenever Mark came near. The celebration and strange reverence for Askon was a tiny pebble on top of a great mountain of larger stones that John carried concerning his home.

CHAPTER FIFTEEN

Unkept Secrets

Hours later, long after the sun had fallen behind the mountain that loomed across the river, Askon sat at the edge of a simple bed, the first that he had slept in for quite some time. Its four bedposts had been roughly hewn so that the tops resembled the head of some kind of dog. Awkwardly, these carvings faced the inside of the bed as if watching the sleeper. The bedding, soft and freshly placed, reminded him not of home, where his family had been more fortunate than others and his bed more comfortable, but of the many bunkhouses where he had slept during his time in Codard's army: Vestgæta, Norogæta, Austgæta, and the training facilities inside King's City. All of them had bunks with similar accommodations. An end-table of similar workmanship sat next to the bed, and a heavy trunk had been placed at the foot. In the trunk, Askon left his sword and the contents of his pack. On the table a thin, pale candle burned above a brass plate with a finger-loop on one side. Around him the same scene repeated thrice more: once for each, John, Edward, and Thomas.

The look of the four friends had been much altered since their arrival at Dalstone. Each had bathed and tidied his appearance, trimming the beard (as John had done) or shaving the stubble (as had Askon and Edward). On Thomas's face no beard yet grew, nor would it. John, of course had made this another point upon which to prey and had enjoyed no end of amusement as they readied for the meeting with Mark and the celebration to follow.

Their weather-beaten clothes had been exchanged for well-fitting gifts from the people of Dalstone, as Mark had commanded; and though Askon tried to refuse the gesture, Edward accepted on his behalf, ever the politician. Aside from their cloaks—Askon's deep green and Edward's black with the bright stag blazoned in the center—their boots were the only articles of clothing they wore that were still their own. John's cloak had been replaced with proper Darts of Grafmark slate-gray, as had Thomas's. Now they sat quietly at the four corners of the dimly lit room, Askon looking anxious and John sullen. Edward and Thomas seemed pleased and excited for the commencement of the feast, respectively.

Across town, in another collection of bunkhouses meant for the Darts, the rest of the company lodged. Their amenities were similar to the four friends, though a few had pitched tents or spread bedrolls in the grass surrounding the buildings. All around, the townspeople teemed with energy, even many hours after the newcomers had arrived. While the New Darts, Askon, and his friends made themselves at home, men, women, and not a few children walked briskly from house to house, gathering food of all kinds. Others carried decorative objects: a wreath or a banner, candlesticks, tablecloths, fresh flowers.

Earlier, from the wide porch of the bunkhouse, Askon had watched as Dalstone's people went about their work. Like the current of a slack-water stream, they drifted ever onward toward the large hall on the north side of town. There was no placid lake, the streets were wider, the buildings less lovingly crafted, and the gardens almost nonexistent, but in spite of these, Askon could not help recalling Tolarenz. These people, of course, carried their belongings to a celebration rather than a burning that would destroy everything. It was then that Askon turned away, opened the flimsy door, and stepped back into the candlelight.

That had been nearly an hour ago. Now sitting at the edge of the bed, dreading the upcoming feast, he wondered if they couldn't simply escape into the darkness and follow the river in hopes that it would lead them nearer to the South Kingdom. His right hand wandered to his belt, where the long, thin hunting knife lay in its sheath. Without a thought or care, he popped the thin metal button in and out through the strip of leather which kept the knife from working loose on long rides.

"Wear the button out that way, you will, worryin' it like that," said John. He sat at the edge of his bed, hands on his chin, elbows on his knees.

Askon retracted his hand. "Old nervous habit, I guess." And so it was, for around the slit of the button hole, the leather had been polished and worn so thin that the clasp seemed almost decorative rather than functional. In the time since he had last replaced the fastening strip, the habit had become so unconscious that he rarely noticed his hand falling to the knife-side of his belt, the fingers flipping the button back into place.

Edward spoke next, his tone authoritative, stern. "Alright. I'm looking forward to this celebration for a number of reasons, not the least of which is to see John and Askon squirm a little." He looked around at the three others, John frowning, Askon staring, Thomas's eyes bright with excitement. Then, realizing that he was making a speech, he sat back down on his bed. "However, this is not where we—and by 'we' I mean Askon, Thomas and I—intended to go after we left Thomas's village."

John perked up. "The way I remember it, your plan had you captured and dragged back to King's City. Better here than there, I'd say."

Nodding in agreement, Edward went on. "Of course, of course. Without your help, it all would have ended at the bridge. Still, we had—we have—a destination. Part of the reason I stayed with Askon is to see this man Morrowmen and hear what he has to say concerning Iramov, my father, and—" he lowered his voice, "Alora's Tear."

Askon's eyes widened, and he nodded almost imperceptibly toward John. Edward understood his mistake, but the beat in between went on too long.

"Aye. Now's as good a time as any, for that," John said, as though the topic were as benign as the weather.

"Wait," said Askon. "You knew?"

"O' course I knew. Whaddya got running in that mind o' yours?" He reached over and rapped his knuckles on Askon's forehead. "I was in the throne room when your piece came tumbling out on the chain.

And you yourself told us all about the Death fragment that Iramov used in Tolarenz and somehow at Austgæta at the same time."

"I have a theory about that," said Thomas, but Askon waved him off for the moment.

"Alright John," Askon said. "You say you want to talk about the Tear. Why?"

John kicked his feet up and lay back on the pillow of his bed. He crossed his ankles over the footboard and stared up at the ceiling. "Well," he began, "remember how I told you that there was more to say after I explained Codard's new friends? Ya know, when Edward nearly took my head off?"

"Yes," Askon replied. Edward looked wary, as though he were afraid John might attack his father again.

"This is it," John continued. "I know all about the three fragments of Alora's Tear. The king's got one for sure, and I know how it works."

Across the room, Edward stared silently, his eyes distant, his breathing slow.

John went on. "If I recall proper, Askon, you were shoutin' about a Time fragment just before Codard's boys closed in on ya."

Askon remembered the moment vividly, the heavy thump against the back of his head as the king's appointed executioner closed in. John had stood by, indecisive and angry over Askon's decisions at Austgæta.

"Do I recall proper?" John asked.

"You do," said Askon.

At the foot of the bed, John lifted one leg and slid the other underneath, recrossing his feet. "So that's one. The second is the Death fragment that Iramov used against us at Austgæta and against your people in Tolarenz," he said. "The third is the king's, and though it won't be wiping any cities off the map, it's a storyteller at least."

Thomas cocked his head to one side, his eyes pinching almost to slits. "What's a 'storyteller'?" he asked quietly.

"Speak up when ya got a question!" John growled.

Edward stirred from his reverie. "It's slang for something that merits telling a story. In most uses it almost exclusively relates to women, which comes as no surprise considering *our* storyteller."

"Anyway," John said, clearly irritated by the interruption, "if I had to hazard a guess, I'd call the third piece the, 'Wait, Where-the-Hell-Did-That-Thing-Go?'" fragment.

Askon laughed. "Kind of an unwieldy name, don't you think?"

John wasn't joking. Askon watched his expression change slightly. Perhaps he was searching for an alternate name. "No. It's about the only name I can think of at the moment," John said. "And I'm tellin' ya, this one's important, so shut yer faces and hear what I got to say." He adjusted the pillow and cleared his throat loudly for effect. "Codard uses the 'Wait, Where-the-Hell-Did-That-Thing-Go?' fragment to move people and things around."

"How?" asked Thomas.

John hardly skipped a beat. "Didn't I tell you to shut up? I thought I did. So here's how it works based on what I've seen." The others leaned in close, and John dropped his voice almost to a whisper. "He gets a group gathered, usually guardsmen or some others he thinks he can trust. Then he swears them to secrecy, to never speak of what they're about to do. Sometimes he tells the story of the Gods and the Flying Boy, but not always. He brings in a couple o' priests, I think mostly for show, as Iramov doesn't seem to need any help usin' his fragment. They start chanting some nonsense about the gods, while the king leaves the room. I can't say exactly what happens after, but when the chanting's done, the lot o' soldiers who were in the room? They're gone."

"That's perfect!" Thomas exclaimed, unable to control the outburst. The others looked on curiously. Even John seemed interested. "If that's how the king's fragment works, then my theory is correct." Thomas stood and began the absent pacing that Askon had come to associate with the young man's bouts of surprising intellect. "Iramov used the Death fragment at or near Austgæta and the Norill colony. Nothing else could produce the darkness we felt in the caverns and nothing else could have given the Norill the advantage they needed to rout the General and Victor before we arrived." He paused, thinking for a moment, his eyes cast upward and his face downturned as though he were trying to look into his own brain. "Assuming that the king and Iramov were already working together, Codard could have transported his ally to Tolarenz instantly after the battle was over."

John sat up. "That would make sense," he said. "We never felt or saw the darkness again after the caverns. The battle that the Norill brought to Austgæta was all numbers. Ours were too small and theirs were too great."

Askon gestured to Thomas, indicating that he should finish his theory.

"And there are other instances where people have appeared where they shouldn't have been, considering the amount of time: Christopher, most notably. He was behind us all throughout Ellmed, yet ahead of us by the time we reached my village. There we outran him again, only to be headed off at the Greyarc."

Rubbing the newly smooth skin on his face with both hands, Askon nodded slowly. "I think Thomas is right," he said. "You told me about the battle at Iramov's stronghold and how you were strangely transported back to the city. What if you and your men were the king's last effort to stop Iramov?"

Edward's eyes showed not affirmation, but deep sadness. "Or maybe we were sent as decoys, knowingly, to lose the battle and cover any suspicion that the two might be allied."

Thomas sat down next to Edward. "That may be. But he also used his fragment to return you from the danger."

"He didn't return the men who died in that ambush!" Edward said, sounding more like John than his usual, collected self.

"Thomas has a point," said Askon. "However, I'm afraid that Edward's story makes too much sense to ignore. If the king has been turned and is fully allied with Iramov and the Norill, he would need to keep up the opposite appearance."

"Something doesn't fit, though," Thomas said, resuming his pacing. "If Codard could recall Edward before, why not now? Couldn't he just bring us all back to the castle?"

John was ready with an answer. "I'll tell ya what else I know," he said. "Usin' that thing takes somethin' outta him. Wears him out. Hard to say, but it seems the more people he moves and the more often, the harder it is on him. Maybe all this movin's just got him too tired."

Askon listened intently as his friends continued the debate. He knew already that the 'Wait, Where-the-Hell-Did-That-Thing-Go?' fragment was in fact the Space fragment as described by Morrowmen back in the Tolarenz town hall. The others, Sight and Life, were with Apopsé and Morrowmen himself. However, in neither his explanation in the throne room, nor in his discussions with his friends had he revealed the names of the Tear's pieces or the properties he suspected they possessed. But now that they had followed him so far and through so much danger, Askon felt it unfair to keep his remaining information secret. Morrowmen, he assumed, would have chided him (perhaps even used the stick) suggesting that he wait to tell his friends. Another lesson in patience. Askon ignored it. He was resolved. Their fates had somehow become bound. His information would be theirs. As he returned his attention to the conversation, he found Thomas mid-theory.

"—the possibility that the king has to know where we are before he can bring us back?" Thomas asked the group.

"I s'pose," mumbled John. "It would explain why you're all still here."

Without further consideration Askon plunged ahead. "Alright," he said. "No more secrets. John, I thank you for telling us what you saw in the king's presence. I'm almost certain we passed by the room where he keeps his fragment on our way out the back of the castle."

Edward went white. "Askon, if I had known. I'm sorry. I dragged you away from it."

"Don't worry about it," Askon replied, shaking his head. "What's done is done. It is out of our reach now." He paused, looking at the faces of each of his friends. "Like I said, no more secrets between us."

John laughed, "You know me, I don't have any secrets most times. These seemed more important, though, so I kept 'em to myself."

"True," Askon replied. "You have proven yourself already. But now I have something I'd like to tell you all before we go to this celebration. First off, your impractically named piece of the Tear is actually called the Space fragment."

"Oh," John grunted. "I guess that's simpler. Like my name better though."

Askon went on. "It is one of five fragments of Alora's Tear. Long ago the Tear was divided in order to protect the kingdom and to settle political disputes over who should possess it. The other two are the Life and Sight fragments. Morrowmen, of whom I know little more than you, keeps the Life fragment. He has been its keeper for many generations. In fact, he claims to have been alive not only for the separation of the Tear, but for the coming of the elves and the great darkness."

"Ha!" John cackled. "An' you believed him? Well, if you believe that, then I got a story for ya—"

"Save it," Askon said coolly. "He also says that Caled's age was approximately the same as his own, but that doesn't matter now. Caled's gone." Briefly, Askon felt that the emotion would overtake him, that by speaking Caled's name he would bring back the memories of Tolarenz, silent and empty. They did not return. "The final fragment, Sight, is in Lord Apopsé's possession. Neither he, nor Iramov are the original keepers of their fragments, just as the king is not.

"What capabilities each of these fragments have, I do not know in full. The Life fragment keeps Morrowmen alive and has incredible healing powers. I watched a wound disappear almost instantly after Morrowmen simply waved the gem over my face. I think it's clear that regardless of Norill alliances or burned villages or what happened at Tolarenz, the fragments are the true driving force. Iramov wanted Caled's fragment, but he and Morrowmen had already made their decision. Codard is probably just a pawn for Iramov at this point. If I had to guess, I'd say that Iramov intends to use Codard to get to Apopsé's Sight fragment. Then with the combined power of Death and Sight, he will conquer the king, taking a third of the five. That leaves only me and Morrowmen, if he doesn't somehow find one or both of us at some point along the way."

All sound in the small bunkhouse ceased. No one spoke. Between the Tear and Askon's speculation as to Iramov's plan, they found their position to be worse than they might have imagined. Outside, footsteps approached. Soft scuffling filtered through the door, then the telltale *thump, thump, thump* of a closed fist on wooden paneling.

CHAPTER SIXTEEN

Uninvited Guests

The front facade of the Dalstone meeting hall was a wonder. A large pinewood porch spilled onto the lawn in three tiers, each level as wide as the sleeping quarters in the bunkhouse. Thick wooden pillars supported a heavy stone-tile roof, the like of which Askon had never seen. At each of the four corners, the gables of the roof dipped and hooked toward the sunset sky. At the center of the third and highest tier, the pine-slab door waited, blood red with rough angular cross hatching engraved in its surface.

Askon and the others followed a scrawny young man of no more than fifteen summers from the bunkhouse door, through the town, to the entrance of the meeting hall. In the streets, eyes watched their every step, but not with suspicion; no, these were looks of reverence and awe. Some turned sharply away if Askon tried to make eye contact, others continued to stare. One woman, obviously in the throes of some religious awakening, shoved her newborn son into Askon's face.

"Kiss 'is face, o ye of the elvish blood! A brave blessing to give to him."

Stumbling slightly as he recoiled from the screaming child and its mother, Askon tried to speak. He couldn't give any sort of blessing to a baby. And it was not in his nature to lie. For a moment he stood, dumb and silent. John came to his rescue.

"Move on along there. There ain't no blessings to be had from this one. He's given 'em all out already. See'm again tomorrow, an' maybe he'll kiss the little bastard."

Now the woman recoiled. She opened her mouth, a pool of invective bubbling up behind her eyes, but something silenced her. Pulling in the baby, she pivoted on a heel and shuffled back down the street.

Edward eyed John, his upper lip curling in disgust. "Was all of that really necessary? Would it not have been sufficient to just tell her to leave? Questioning the legitimacy of her baby seemed a bit, well, rude."

"Ha!" John laughed, his shoulders shuddering with the force. "Yeah, maybe you're right, but it's more fun my way." He chuckled again, more to himself than out loud this time. "Wouldn't you say, Thomas?"

Thomas managed only a weak snuffle, but no more. John's face soured almost instantly.

"Fine," he grumbled. "See if I help anybody next time."

They crossed the remaining length of town and stopped at the foot of the meeting hall's sprawling porch. Climbing the steps, Askon listened as the wooden boards groaned with the weight of the four men and their escort. The boy raised both hands to them, palms up. Then he rotated one hand and pushed firmly; the heavy panel swung slowly open.

Inside, torches, braziers, and a roaring fire at the far end of the chamber bathed the meeting hall in orange light. Along each side of the enormous room, benches and tables had been arrayed and laden with celebratory bread, wine, mead, and meat of many kinds. A great number of townsfolk had already gathered and found their seats. Workers milled about busily, hopping from table to table, attending to the final preparations.

"Askon half-elven, of Tolarenz!" called the boy who had led them from the bunkhouse. The announcement startled Askon and turned the attention of all those seated in the main chamber. A cheer roared forth and Askon's face reddened. After a too-long moment, the sound died away as the boy waited to announce the others.

"Edward, Prince of Vladvir," he said, with much less vigor, "as well as Thomas, newly dubbed Dart of Grafmark, and John of Dalstone." No cheers this time. John frowned, and Thomas looked characteristically awkward. Edward, on the other hand, smiled broadly and bowed.

"Thank you for the warm welcome," he said in his smoothest politician's voice. "I am sure I speak for my friend Askon when I say, Dalstone's accommodations and hospitality are of the very finest."

At this, a mild applause rippled over the assembly. Then the boy led Askon and the others on a winding way through the tables. As they passed, men held out their hands, waiting for Askon's acknowledgement. He grasped the first in the way Edward was wont to do, both hands, one over the other. After the first two, Askon realized that it would take an incredible amount of time to shake each hand in such a fashion. Instead of doing so, he began bowing to each of the men and women with his palms pressed against each other. He hoped that such a simple nod would not offend them.

It did not. When they reached their seats near the fire, the boy pulled out a high-backed chair for each Askon and Edward. John and Thomas had individual chairs as well, but the craft was of a lesser quality, the backs not quite so high. John wrenched his into place and flopped down.

John's father, Mark, sat at one end of the head table. On the other was a withered old man. There was more to this person than it at first seemed. Askon was reminding himself to return to that thought later, when Edward placed a hand on his shoulder.

"Just relax," he said.

But Askon had already relaxed. Here in the warm fire-lit hall, his worries melted away like a tallow candle burning low. All around the chamber, the guests—or hosts, he was unsure which to call them—sat with upturned faces, awaiting some gesture or recognition from the head table. Askon waved a hand and the crowd erupted again into raucous applause. He smiled awkwardly. And though he felt uncomfortable, no threat or doubt entered his mind. On the periphery of his vision, Mark, the night's true host, collected himself and spread his arms wide.

"People of Dalstone," he said with authority, "on behalf of Thane Eldred, I hereby begin our feast and celebration." Thomas began to clap, but the thin slaps of his palms were the only sound in the hall. He stopped. Mark continued. "As you know, the gods have seen fit to bless us with the presence of a special guest. Earlier today…"

Mark's voice faded, became a braying drone in the back of Askon's mind. He felt the eerie sensation of time slowing down. The candle wax of his worries flooded away; the fragment had taken over. And then he thought that perhaps it was time that more resembled wax: congealing, hardening until it trickled and stopped altogether.

To his left sat Edward, arms folded, listening attentively to Mark's speech. The speaker heaved like a slow ocean wave. In that proud face, mouth half open as it drew breath for the next piece of oration, Askon read an immense and dangerous pride. The gods would serve the ambitions of John's father; he would force them if he had to. Looking deeper, Askon felt the machinations that clicked and whirred behind Mark's flushed face, a clockwork curiosity clattering toward his eventual goal. If anything were to happen to Dalstone's thane, Eldred, Mark would be the one to take his place. Under the effect of the Time fragment, everything about John's father screamed for power, for control, for adoration.

With an effort, Askon looked away from Mark, expecting the fragment's power to fade, to return time to its natural state. Instead, the feeling intensified and the subtle movements of the guests became even clearer. Almost as though the firelight had selected certain individuals, Askon saw the thane's supporters, their faces shining, eyes focused not on Mark but on the old man seated to Askon's right. In the shadows scattered throughout the hall, he saw darkened visages and the glittering eyes of those who stood to gain from the thane's fall. Their attention was on Mark. Askon blinked. In John's absence Dalstone had divided itself almost equally: one faction for Mark, another for Eldred.

Now Askon turned to the thane. Thinning silver strands of hair tumbled from his age-spotted scalp, the faded white curls spilling onto sharp shoulders. Below them a rich red robe adorned in golden tracework hung loosely. A twisting braid of beard rested on his chest, small beads hanging from two strands on each side, and a large wooden ring binding the tip of the larger braid in the center. When Askon entered the hall, he saw only a hunkering shell of a man past his prime. But the fragment's power showed him the truth. Behind the age, under years of idleness, the ironwood strength of a mighty leader still grew, knobbly and old, but still hale and razor sharp. The old man smiled: a grim, wicked, and powerful gesture. Askon had no doubts; Eldred intended to take his people back from Mark's clutches, an old lion lying in wait.

Askon shuddered at the cold, calculating eyes, but felt more than a little admiration. Eldred could have given up long ago, but for some reason, he bided his time, allowing his opponent to grow fat and overconfident. Soon the conflict would come to a head and the men in the light of the fire would confront those in the shadows. A chill crept over Askon, and he hoped that he and his friends would be long away before the fight began. Then the fragment's power receded.

"… this momentous occasion," Mark was saying as Askon's senses returned to normal. "I give you, Askon of Tolarenz!" Cheers erupted, though they now felt somehow hollow and void of any real praise. Askon remembered the faces in light and in darkness. He nodded an acknowledgement to the assembly. Mark slammed his fists onto the surface of the thick table. Askon anticipated a great boom, but the clenched hands managed only a dull, meaty *thud*. The crowd roared anyway. "Let us begin!" Mark shouted and flopped into his seat.

No luxury had been spared in preparation for the feast. Course after course of delicious food swept across the tables. As soon as one plate had been emptied, it was swiftly removed and replaced with a different dish. Askon tasted several local fish from the western stream, chicken and wildfowl, savory beef, and a bit of pork and lamb. By the time the servants rounded the heavy tables with dessert pastries, Askon felt leaden with food. At first he had not accepted the wine or mead. His suspicions after seeing the two opposing factions were too great.

As the night went on, however, he found himself slowly consumed by drink as well as food. The forms in the hall became blurred slightly at the edges and warmth churned in his belly. He had indulged in this way before—either with his friends in the king's army when rations had been particularly fruitful (on account of Edward being in the company) or in Tolarenz during harvests of great plenty; but it was only now that he realized how similar his drunkenness, to whatever degree, was to the Time fragment's effect. Time felt slower, people's voices were muddled and distant, and he felt an isolation from those around him. The difference of course, was the lack of clarity. While earlier he had seen exactly what Eldred and Mark meant to gain through this celebration, now he saw only a blur of mirth between old friends.

After hours of food and drink, the urge to relieve himself became too great, and Askon rose from his seat. He wobbled and would have fallen, but the high-backed chair caught him, and he steadied himself. The crowd quieted. With an effort, he forced his eyes to focus and turned to Mark.

"Tell them that I'll be back," Askon said, but *them* sounded like a strange snake hissing in the grass and *back* became *mack* through the screen of drink. He started away and found his balance lacking. To his right foot, the floor rushed up more quickly than he expected, but he stayed upright. Swinging his left leg out from the chair more carefully, he made his way toward the nearest doorway, the toes of his boots shuffling or bumping the floorboards as he went. He did not see his friends rise from the table and follow closely behind.

Through the haze of smoke and alcohol, Askon emerged from a side-exit onto a smaller version of the three-tiered front porch. Behind him, the mumble of celebration inside the hall churned and clattered. Inhaling deeply, Askon felt the air, clear and cold, fill his nose and lungs. It was nothing like the stifling humidity of the rest of Grafmark; it reminded him of home. Several yards away, beyond the rear corner of the building, clusters of shrubs grew like furry black animals in the darkness. He started toward them, but forgot the porch stair. The world swept out from beneath his feet and he tumbled into the open space. A steel grip closed around his arm, arresting him before his face could collide with the pine boards.

"The only thing worse than a fool, is a drunken fool."

Askon tried to turn and face the voice, but the near miss had scrambled his balance. "Wh—what? Morrowmen?" The word tumbled out of his mouth as *Murmalin.* How could the old man find him here, so far into Grafmark? Askon waited for the reply or the whistle and crack of Morrowmen's walking stick. But it did not come.

"No, ya lush. Think maybe you had enough in there yet? Gotta pace yerself an' watch that ya get enough food between the drinks. Some o' that mead's a hell of a lot more powerful than any o' that fruity swill ya got back in Tolarenz." The voice did not belong to Morrowmen.

"Ugh," Askon groaned. "It's called wine."

"I know what it's called," John replied, "cause I've tested it myself. Like just about ever' drink Vladvir has to offer. I'll tell ya what, my friend. Practice makes perfect. See, that's why you were 'bout to chew on the porch boards, and I'm standin' here right as right." Then, without warning he turned convulsively and vomited over the handrail.

A grimace of revulsion crawled over Askon's lips and face, and he tried not to be sick himself. "Practice makes perfect, eh?" he laughed.

"It's all part o' the process, my friend. Purgin' the toxin," he wiped his mouth with his shirtsleeve. "You'd know that if ya had the practice."

"Oh, what a sorry sight this is." Askon looked past John to see Edward, standing with arms crossed, shaking his head. "The professional and novitiate, both an utter mess." His voice came clear and strong through the cold night air.

Askon frowned and pulled himself upright along the porch-rail. "I saw you drinking as much as anyone. How are you so—so…"

"Not drunk?" Edward asked. "You saw what I wanted you to see. Not to mention what I wanted the townspeople to see."

"Oh yeah," John grumbled. "The princeling's been trained since birth. He—" but John didn't finish. His face paled, and a sickly green cast washed over it. He turned again, hanging his head over the rail, gagging.

Edward chuckled. "Yes, oh practiced drinker, I have been trained. Nobility are forced to attend such gatherings constantly. If I did what you two have done at each of them, I'd never recover. Just because I appeared to match you glass for glass, doesn't mean that I actually did."

"Well, bravo for you," John gurgled.

Now it was Thomas who came through the door. Without warning he burst onto the porch. "John!" he hooted. "Dalstone is great! Who knew that deep in the forest—" He didn't finish. As he waved his arms in exuberance, the first tier of the porch caught him as it had Askon. But there was no one to save Thomas. He crashed into the second tier in a heap, his chin bouncing heavily as he landed. Rolling over slowly, while the others watched with worried eyes, he burst into cackling laughter. "I f—f—fell. Ha!" The laugh sounded like a bark followed by a howling series of squeals and finally silent clicking spasms. Edward sighed while Askon, John, and Thomas went on laughing uncontrollably.

When the shrieks of laughter had run their course, the four men fanned out into the bushes. John and Thomas attempted to negotiate the remaining steps with caution, while Edward hopped down them easily. Askon leaned against the handrail, his head still swimming, and chuckled again to himself as John and Thomas toppled over one another. Instead of following them, Askon made his way to the opposite side of the porch and another clump of low brush.

He stood there for a moment, looking up through the sparse needles on the edge of the forest at the distant stars. The tiny points of light seemed to pulse, less on account of the stars themselves and more on account of the drink working its way through Askon's system. He identified a few constellations and thought of how each appeared slightly different than it would have from behind his house in Tolarenz. Then he counted, wondering if it would ever be possible to know how many stars there were, but his clouded mind lost count. When he had finished and cinched his belt again around his waist, he turned back to the porch. But the others had not yet returned from the edge of the trees on the opposite side.

For a moment, Askon waited, wondering if perhaps he should just return to the hall. While he was busy counting the stars, it was possible that Edward, John, and Thomas had already gone back inside. Then a sound came through the trees.

In the alcohol-haze, Askon found it difficult to make out the noises clearly. Laughing? No. Shouting. Then the clear ringing of weapons. But he and his friends had come unarmed to the party. None of the four wore a sword, though Edward and Askon had both carried knives in their belts. Again the clatter rang out.

"Askon!" It was Edward. Something had gone wrong in the bushes. Askon thought he could see shapes in the shadows, but the darkness was too deep and his own senses too impaired.

Askon drew his knife from its sheath and bolted toward the blurred movement. He covered a few yards before his balance failed him. With a jolt he tipped to one side and would have fallen into brush had he not caught himself with an outstretched hand. He continued forward with heavy, swerving steps. Plunging into the trees, a thin limb reached out, scraping his face. He batted it away, squinting to see where his friends had gone. Then, from the corner of his eye, he detected movement in the shadows. Another limb lashed his face, and then he could see them, but only barely. They were moving away too quickly. Terror built up inside him.

Not now. Stop it! I have to find them. His thoughts were directed at the Tear fragment, but if it could hear them, it showed no sign. All around him, time seemed to speed along, and though he struggled desperately to control it, the drink made it impossible. He bounced roughly off of a thick tree trunk, and peered into the forest.

At the edge of his sight, he found them. Four large figures with long, drooping arms carried John and Edward into the trees. John's eyes were closed and his head hung awkwardly to one side. Edward's eyes were open, but they stared, eerily unfocused and empty. His body rolled to one side, and the carriers turned to collect him again. As they did, Askon's fears were affirmed. Somehow, a group of Norill had managed to gather in the trees outside the hall, surprising his unarmed friends. Two smaller Norill, with bent backs and shuffling steps, dragged a squirming, thrashing Thomas, who was now bound and gagged. Then came the rage.

So powerful was the emotion Askon felt as his only remaining friends were carried off into the night, that though every particle of his body desired it, he could not even scream at the vile creatures who vanished quickly into the trees. He surged forward, teeth clenched, his jaw so tight that it burned with the strain. But with every step, no matter the energy he expended, the Norill moved farther away.

"Don't think of a salamander."

Askon ignored the memory and again drove his feet into the hard earth. Still, no amount of effort could propel him fast enough. With every step he felt more and more sluggish. They were beyond his sight now, though he followed another ten yards into the thickening brush. Then, like a trap set carefully by a watchful hunter, a twisting strand of ivy hooked the tip of Askon's boot and he slammed, face first, into the dirt. The shadows became blackness as he lost consciousness.

When Askon first opened his eyes, searing pain blasted his senses. His mouth felt like it had been stuffed with straw or the tufts of summer dandelions. A piercing light lanced into his brain, stabbing viciously at all the soft places. And all around a voice shouted, rising in volume until it seemed his skull would split from the strain. He brought his palms to his face and pressed them heavily into his eyes and forehead. The voice went on.

"Askon! What are you doing out here? We've been searching everywhere since you left the celebration late last night." The voice sounded concerned, even worried, but it was not a voice which Askon recognized.

Askon willed his swollen tongue and mouth into words, but they were soft and inarticulate: "Thomas and the others. Norill. Where are they? Last night—"

"Sir," said the voice, once again battering his ear-drums with its force, "You aren't making sense. I should get you some water and perhaps a healer. They have herbs and mixtures for this sort of thing."

"No," Askon coughed. And he mastered himself, pulling the thoughts and words together like a rope stretched tight around a heavy bundle. "My friends. They were taken last night by Norill. I followed them, but—" He paused, embarrassed. "I was too drunk to keep up or catch them."

Lowering his hands and squeezing his eyelids together, Askon rose unsteadily from where he had fallen in pursuit of the others. His limbs ached and his head throbbed, but he concentrated on the voice, bringing the young man slowly into focus. It was the boy who had led them into the hall the night before.

"I'll take you to Mark. He will know what to do about this," the boy said, a bit quieter now. "From time to time this happens around here."

"What?"

With his own arm around Askon's for extra support, the boy started toward the meeting hall. "Living in Dalstone," he said, "and more importantly, in the heart of Grafmark, you get used to strange events. Once in a while, the Norill come down from the mountains and capture people of the village. They've become so clever about it that sometimes, given the right target, people don't notice for days, not even the Darts."

"That's terrible," Askon snapped, and felt his own hoarse voice pound against his senses. "Why doesn't the thane assemble a militia, or order the Darts to pursue them?"

The boy nodded. "I think the thane would do so of his own accord, but Mark has advised him against it. Mark says—and the Darts confirm—that the colony is not far to the northwest of Dalstone, across the river. However, both also claim that the approach is riddled with traps and many Norill scouts. The Darts now refuse to search. Instead, they defend our borders and hope to catch any Norill raiding parties before they enter."

Askon recalled the night spent in the gloom of Grafmark and the Norill who had shadowed their steps. "On our way to Dalstone, my friends and I were watched by Norill. They stayed out of human sight, but I was able to see them several times, lurking in the trees. They did not attack us, though. We thought they might be—" Askon stopped to consider how much he should say, trying to think what his father would advise, or Morrowmen, or Caled. "We thought they might be different Norill. Part of a group we fought against at Austgæta."

The boy interrupted him. "No, they were Grafmark Norill. As long as Dalstone has been here, the Norill have lived in the forest. Probably, the Norill were here first."

With a curt nod, Askon followed the boy to the meeting hall where Mark had spent the remainder of the night and some of the morning. Askon had many questions concerning the Grafmark Norill and the location of his friends, but he decided it better to leave them for Mark or the thane. Askon's head pounded and he resolved to first find water and a place to sit before he spoke with either leader. He did not know what had happened to his friends, but there was little he could do without first discovering where they had gone or how he would find them. He and the boy stepped through the thick doorway, and Askon found a seat at one of the only remaining clean tables. Disappearing into the kitchens, the boy retrieved a large vessel and a clean cup. He poured clear water from the jug and handed it to Askon.

"I'll go find Mark," he said.

Though the night had been mostly a blur, in the harsh light of morning Askon remembered one thing clearer than all the rest—even clearer than his friends' abduction: the faces in the firelight. There was tension in Dalstone, and the faces which aligned themselves with Mark were not those with which Askon would align himself. Even in his current state, he knew it would be a huge mistake to ignore what the fragment's clarity had revealed. As quickly as his muddled mind would allow, he called out to the boy.

"And bring Thane Eldred as well."

CHAPTER SEVENTEEN

Into the Trap

It took longer than Askon expected to rouse and retrieve the thane. For the first hour, the water and the quiet of the meeting hall chamber had been welcome, soothing to his sensitive eyes and ears. The second hour was not so welcome. With a clearer mind, he rehearsed the words he would use to convince Dalstone's most powerful men that they should help rescue his friends. Halfway through the third hour, he began to worry. His friends were out there somewhere in the hands of the Norill, and he could do nothing but sit and wait. At the end of the third hour, the servants appeared. The clanking plates jabbed like pins, and the anger started to build. Where were they?

When the sun climbed above the hall, Dalstone's two leaders finally burst into the main chamber. Mark came first, his face a carnival mask plastered with worry. Then came Thane Eldred, who walked more slowly, the pronounced shamble of the old, equally as false.

Askon thought of his friends, and the torments they might this very moment be forced to endure.

"Where have you been?" Askon demanded with a shudder. Mark's worried facade contorted into simpering surprise at the broken decorum. "It must have been at least three hours! Mark, this is your son we're talking about. And Eldred. What takes a thane so long to rise from his bed? In Tolarenz our leaders are—were—first to awaken. Is it not so in Dalstone?"

A sly smile crept over Eldred's face, but he said nothing. Mark, on the other hand, was all words and worry again.

"Oh, my son. I wish there was something we could do. These creatures, they harass our borders and capture our women, but seeking them out is folly. Gods! Why punish your loyal servant so?" He fell to his knees.

Askon stood, now fully in command of his body again, wrenching the much larger man from the ground and up to his face. "Stop groveling and use your wits." He felt himself growing angrier with each word.

"Don't think of a salamander."

Mark fell back to the floor with a thud, and a snuffling laugh escaped through Eldred's nose. Askon heeded his sister's voice from the past and looked away from Mark's sniveling face. Behind them, an ornate candlestick sat alone on one of the tables. Wrapping his mind around each curve and notch, considering the gleam in the gold and the streaks of gray that signaled it to be as false as Mark's whining pleas, Askon felt himself relax. If these leaders could not control themselves, he would.

Gazing at the candlestick, the world seemed to slow, and the intentions of the two leaders became clear. Behind Eldred's clever smirk, the machinery of his mind worked steadily. Mark's puling supplications only emboldened Eldred, but Askon's plight and that of his friends did not appear to be of much concern the thane. If it would benefit his return to power, he might help, but he had no desire to sacrifice even a single man to the cause.

Mark, whose cries were blatantly disingenuous even without the fragment, appeared to Askon in his true form. He seemed to shrink and whither. His body, much larger than Askon's, seemed little more than that of a petulant child beating his hands against the floor. He would cry and gnash his teeth, but in the end would no more send a man to help Askon than would Eldred, and for the same reason. Trouble had been brewing in Dalstone for too long, and a false move by either party could set a battle in motion.

The streaks on the candlestick seemed to thicken and spread across the whole of the object. Askon turned away from it, disgusted at its corruption, disgusted that neither man would assist in finding his friends. With that, the fragment's power lifted. Anger rushed in to fill its place.

"You whining, spineless, cowering fools!" Askon shouted. Mark stepped back in feigned surprise while Eldred hardly moved and still said nothing. The anger continued to grow until Askon felt the fragment's presence once again, only now his words grew slow and labored, the thoughts of the two leaders hidden. He ignored it and pressed on. "Stay here if you will. Lend no man to my cause. Mark, you wouldn't even save your own son."

"And why should I?" Mark snarled. His attitude twisting just as quickly as Askon's. "That insolent waste can rot for all I care. He's an adult. In fact, he left Dalstone happily years ago. There are larger matters to which a priest must attend."

Askon clenched his teeth. The whole debate, if it could even be called that, was just wasted time and energy. "Fine then. Have your politics! I'll go myself. All I need to know is the location of the Grafmark Norill colony."

With eyes half-lidded and darting from Askon to Mark, Eldred, Thane of Dalstone, uttered the first words Askon had heard him speak. "I will send ya three."

"What?" The response came from both Askon and Mark, simultaneously.

"I said that the thane sends three men, an' one of 'em from my personal guard even."

In his anger, and under the power of the fragment, Askon did not detect Eldred's intentions. The thane cared no more for Edward and the others now than he had when Askon had been able to read him clearly, but sending men now gave him a political advantage. It was a calculated risk.

"Thank you," Askon replied, his anger cooling. "Where is the colony?" He followed Eldred past a gaping and indecisive Mark until they reached a small door at the opposite end of the main chamber. Inside, Eldred swiftly collected a map and torn piece of parchment. He traced a rough copy of the original, marked the path with a thick line and drew a five-pointed star over one of the mountain's lower sides. He thrust the parchment toward Askon. "This is the best I can do. The men I'm sendin' know the local terrain, but they won't do much to help findin' the colony. We don't send people that way, as ya well know."

"Any help you can provide is greatly appreciated," Askon replied. "But I must leave soon if there is to be any hope of bringing back my friends."

While the thane had drawn and discussed the map, Mark made his way across the chamber and into the small side-room. He looked at the map, then at Eldred. "It seems that I can spare two men for this mission. The Darts have recently grown significantly, and the new recruits follow my son."

Askon rounded on Mark, "Then why not send them all?"

But Mark had since found his self-control. He replied coolly. "For all that we know, the Norill could be planning a larger attack. Their surveillance of your movements in the forest suggests that they might be planning something. Also, I think their chosen targets may not be a coincidence. It's safest for Dalstone if the Darts—even the New Darts—stay and guard the village."

Askon accepted Mark's contribution. With six men, himself included, they stood a chance of entering the Norill colony undetected. Any more and they would be better off bringing an army. A few men could hide or sneak; for ten or fifteen, the same task was much more difficult.

"Thank you," Askon said.

Mark smiled a thin, veiled smile. "Oh, you're welcome. I'm glad I was able to arrange it. I'll send the boy to rouse my men and Eldred's."

The thane turned decisively from the parchment. "No you won't. It'll be my orders to my men. You just let me tend to 'em, an' you worry 'bout yer own."

Mark stood, nonplussed, and nodded sagely. "Alright then. We gather here in one hour—"

"No!" Askon shouted, and the word echoed out of the small room into the main chamber. "We've waited long enough. I'll go back to our bunkhouse to retrieve my gear. You two send your men as quickly as possible. Any other formalities should be addressed now." He waited, looking from one leader to the other. Neither spoke. He turned on his heel and strode quickly through the chamber, out the front door, and into the street.

Back at the bunkhouse, Askon double-checked his equipment: sword, knife, water, small satchel of food, generously gifted party clothes off, travel-worn shirt and trousers on, light leather armor over that, and the deep green cloak over all. He cast his eyes about the room, seeing first the things that his friends had left behind. Their weapons, armor, and supplies lay neatly stacked or folded, except for John's, which were splayed across his corner of the room.

Looking away from the reminders that his friends were gone, Askon's eyes found their way to the candles set all around the room. Several of the holders were of the same false gold as the candlestick in the meeting hall. He allowed his eyes to follow the swirling pattern of gray material that coursed through the yellow gold. Unable to resist, he reached out, grabbed one of the candle holders and pitched it across the room. It smashed into the far wall, cracking in several places along the streaks of gray. Askon left it and marched out onto the porch.

Though it had taken him little more than a few minutes to hurry through the town, enter the bunkhouse, and collect his belongings, he spent nearly an hour seated on the low porch stairs. He struggled to keep his anger in check, choosing various objects, plants, or buildings to study. He focused on the smallest details his eye could detect: a strangely spiraling blade of grass, an old barrel with rusting iron bands around its middle, a house whose doors were all wrapped in thick cloth. All of his subjects made for good practice, and his anger was not enough to bring on the fragment's negative effects though also not enough reduced to bring on the positive. Instead he sat, sulking, for another twenty minutes before his reinforcements arrived.

As if he had known Askon's mind, felt his frustration, Marten appeared, streaking across the sky. He swirled above Askon's head and landed on the bunkhouse rooftop. He surveyed the goings-on for a few moments then hopped to another corner of the roof in a noisy flutter. Another look, another hop, and he was perched on the shoulder guard, peering up the street.

They came alone. Neither Mark, nor the thane had followed them, and Askon knew why. The two men bearing the tree and quarrel of the Darts were gangly, poorly fed, poorly geared, and older than Askon would have liked. He hoped that their experience would be useful. Eldred's men seemed more alive and healthy, but not by much. Their leader, apparently one of the thane's personal guard, was no older than Thomas, and the other two were younger still. None carried himself like a soldier. And none would be half as good in a fight as Askon's friends. He sighed through gritted teeth.

The eldest man sent by the thane approached Askon and bowed formally, one eye nervously watching Marten. "Askon of Tolarenz, we have been assigned to help you in retrieving John, son of Mark, and Edward, son of Codard. My name is Anthony. And these are—"

"Oh stop with the formalities," Askon said gruffly. His tone surprised him as much as it did Anthony, who stepped back, eyes to the ground. The thane's other two selections looked at one another dumbly. Mark's elder Darts eyed them all from beneath sullen brows.

Askon rose from his seat on the porch steps. "I think we've waited long enough. Follow me."

And follow they did. For several miles Askon marched them without stopping. The wide trail led north from Dalstone, arrow-straight along the river. From the moment they had left the bunkhouse, Askon had forged ahead several paces in front of the others. Behind him followed Anthony and the thane's men, whispering to one another. Half again as far behind them, Mark's Darts dragged along, often allowing the distance between themselves and Askon to widen to a hundred feet or more.

Askon no longer cared if any of the men from Dalstone followed him at all. He pressed on, refusing to slacken his pace. More than once after hearing the thump and scrape of boots drawing nearer, he increased his speed intentionally, widening the gap again. All the while he grumbled to himself.

Dalstone. What did they understand of the workings of the world? Here they all were, hidden cowards, sheltered by their forest, oblivious to the machinations of Iramov and Codard, to the danger posed by the alliance with the Norill. Soon, they too would fall under attack. Perhaps obscurity would shelter them for a time, but after Iramov had finished with Apopsé in the south and (as Askon now fully believed) Codard in the east, the emboldened army of the Death fragment would find Dalstone. Then all of its politics, all of Mark's schemes, and all of Eldred's cunning traps would be so much flotsam in a hurricane.

They crossed the river after only a few hours. On the opposite bank, interspersed amongst the trees were wide swaths of grain and corn, peas and beans. The fields ceased after less than a mile, and Grafmark closed in again, enveloping the would-be rescuers on all sides with its gray-green embrace. Another mile or two and the trees towered above them, every bit as mighty as in the forest's eastern marches where Askon and his friends had entered not three days before. Marten, not content to tolerate the jarring ride on the shoulder guard, soared above them, appearing from time to time between the trees.

The first trap sprang just before nightfall. Askon had not seen it, a frayed strand of ivy wrapped purposefully around a short wooden stake. For hours they had marched without stopping, and Askon, at the end of his own endurance, continued to drive them onward. He would not allow himself to be the first to stop. Then as the path grew narrower, the slope of the foothill steeper, they rounded a corner between two folds of the hill.

Anthony jogged ahead, catching Askon and overtaking him. He held out a hand and rested the other on his knee. Askon halted, his own breathing ragged, his muscles aching. He struggled to control the rate at which he inhaled and exhaled and stood straight, imperious, as though Anthony had just interrupted a king's stroll through the garden.

"Askon," Anthony panted. "We need to rest. If we don't, none of us will have the energy to fight the Norill or rescue—"

Crash!

The sound boomed through the canopy. Askon spun toward it. There, on the path just behind them, an immense, rotting pine lay, bleached white like the thighbone of an enormous beast. Motes of dust and flitting bugs came down in a shower of sparkling grit. Anthony rushed forward, but Askon caught him by the shirt collar.

"Stop!" Askon commanded. "There could be other triggers placed anywhere."

Anthony twisted away, glaring back. "No. You may care little for them, but they are my friends as much as John and Edward are yours."

In spite of Anthony's omission of Thomas, Askon grudgingly released him. Always it was Edward and John who Dalstone's residents remembered. But it was for Thomas who Askon feared the most. The others, at least for a time, could handle themselves. Carefully, Askon crept back to the fallen tree.

On the opposite side of the shattered trunk lay one of the thane's men. A large gash sliced him from cheek to chin, and blood ran over his face. He was unconscious, but appeared to be breathing. Anthony leapt over the broken mass of the trap and pressed a cloth onto his friend's face. The other young man had gone pale. He shuddered, transfixed, only a few feet away from the trap's furthest reaching branches. Mark's men, who had fallen farther and farther behind, now walked briskly up the path. Their jaded faces changed little as they came around the corner and took in the scene.

Wading through the rubble of the broken tree, Askon saw that there was more to the trap than a simple falling log. All along the edges, the limbs had been broken or hand-sharpened to points. Dangling between the spear-like limbs were several broken arrows and shards of metal, probably from the weapons carried by slain Darts of Grafmark. The shimmering debris was laced between the branches with vines similar to those that held the trigger. With traps as vicious and effective as these, Askon realized, they would be forced to halt for the night. In the dark, they might all have been killed by such a device.

They risked no fire in the deep black of western Grafmark. Dinner consisted of remnants from the previous night's feast in the meeting hall. Eating heartily of the bits that would spoil, all were able to reach their fill. According to Anthony, reaching the Norill encampment by the end of the next day was not out of the question. In fact, if the trail held, and no other traps impeded their pace, Anthony was confident that they could be in a position to surveil the Norill by noon or shortly thereafter.

To this assessment, Askon grunted an assent, refusing to speak with any of his companions. They finished eating, and he organized the watches. One of Mark's men would take the first watch with

Anthony. One for Mark and one for Eldred. They would have had it no other way. The injured young man was already resting, his wound bound, his color returning. Mark's second man fell asleep without hesitation, being the eldest of those present, and soon he was snoring loudly. Askon lay back on his bedroll with his hands folded behind his head. He did not fall asleep. Instead, his mind raced with worry for his friends, as he stared through the thick, dark canopy to the stars beyond.

"Askon?"

"Yes, Líana."

"How do you trust them?"

"Trust whom?"

"All of your friends. They're all killers and so are you. I know you fight for a good reason, but you all have to do it, right?"

"Yes, that's true. I trust them because we all fight for the same cause. I trust them because they've protected me, saved me when I needed it most. And they trust me for the same reasons."

"But what if you were wrong?"

CHAPTER EIGHTEEN

Death in the Dark

A scrape and shuffle crackled in the trees. It was not Marten. Silent as the night itself, the falcon would never have made such a clumsy sound. Askon sat bolt upright, straining to hear even the slightest noise. Again it came, this time closer and more pronounced. Askon's eyes adjusted while he gazed up at the stars; the little camp was clear and colorless all around him. Sliding slowly to one knee, then rising to his feet, he padded away from the center of the camp toward the sound. It did not come again. He circled the others once fully, then gasped as a cold grip clasped his shoulder.

This time it was Marten. Askon bent close to the bird, listening as its already rapid heartbeat thudded along. Marten's head darted from one side to the other, not in the absent mechanical way that it did while he was hunting, but with purpose, as though he meant to indicate some hidden threat. Askon continued to scan the gray shapes and shadowed trees.

Then he heard it: a thick gurgle followed by a rustle of branches. Askon's eyes shot to his left, peering into the darkness from where the sound had come. Footsteps moved through the brush. Like a snake whispering through summer grass, Askon drew his sword and passed along the perimeter of the camp toward the source of the sound. It came again, eerily similar, a bubbling gurgle followed by scraping leaves. Askon wondered if Anthony or Mark's man had heard, then asked himself where exactly they had gone. Already he had circled the camp and was well on his way to a second pass.

When he came upon it, the body was curled unnaturally over the twisted remains of a fallen tree. In the dark, even with Askon's heightened vision, it was difficult to see exactly how the young man had been killed, but no pulse, no breath betrayed the signs of life. Anthony was dead. Without thinking, Askon breathed in, meaning to shout an alarm to the others. But as he did so, a shadow appeared before the sleeping form of the young man injured by the falling tree earlier in the day. The shadow bent low to the ground, its knuckles almost dragging beside it.

Askon's eyes blazed, and he roared to life. The fragment took over. Askon drove his legs into the ground, but they moved as if he were being buried in sand. The jolt knocked Marten loose from his perch, and the falcon flapped wildly into the air. Unable to move any faster, Askon watched as the crouching form slashed the young man's throat. Again the gurgling sound, only now many times more horrible and revolting than before in the agonizing slowness of the fragment's power. The body twitched and kicked. The leaves and limbs clattered.

Now Askon was upon his enemy. It looked up from its kill with a leer. But no Norill face was revealed in the darkness. The face was that of Mark's man, the one Askon had assigned to the first watch. Then, even in the fragment's unnatural sluggishness, he knew. He understood it all.

Mark had sent these two men to strike first in the battle for Dalstone. By eliminating the thane's men, the priest could gain a headstart in the fight against his rival. If somehow his assassins could kill Askon, all the better. Clearly, Askon did not support Mark, and many of Dalstone's citizenry would side with the half-elf they so revered. The explanation would be simple. Norill had come and killed the rescuers, Mark's men escaping by only a hairsbreadth.

Askon's rage surged, cresting like the foam of breakers on a rocky shoreline. Askon thrashed against the power of the fragment, but to no avail. He watched as the grizzled man rose from his crouch, the knife he held still smeared with blood. With no way to stop his forward progress, Askon's momentum carried him straight toward the knife. And then, in an unexpected and gruesome spray, the man's head came loose from his shoulders. Askon winced and fell clumsily into the decapitated corpse. Without the hand to hold it steady, the knife turned harmlessly against Askon's armor. Struggling with the dead body, he rolled onto his back, sword held before his face to deflect whatever weapon had killed Mark's assassin. In the confusion, Askon felt his blade knocked aside, and a black splotch appeared over his head. It came down hard, though oddly supple, and a burst of light erupted into his eyes. Then all was black.

"Askon?"

It was Edward's voice. Was he dreaming? What had he been doing out here in the forest? Did Mark's men really kill their fellow citizens? Then, another voice.

"Askon. Are you awake?"

"O' course he's not awake ya fool kid. Any idiot can see he's still out like a rock-slapped fish."

Thomas and John. The voices were as clear and adversarial as ever. Something heavy lay around his head, a chain? No, it wasn't cold. It wasn't a weight at all. Perhaps another sense. They all felt scrambled. He blinked, then gagged. It was a smell, a foul overpowering smell. He raised a hand and lights popped and sparkled.

"No no. Just stay there. Don't try to get up. They hit you pretty hard."

Edward again. Always calm and collected in times of trouble. Askon sat down. The ground was cold and clammy against his backside. He opened his eyes.

A cage of flimsy sticks surrounded him, twine cords twisted tightly around the overlapping bars. To add strength, it seemed, the builders had interleaved the bars so that each individual stick passed back and forth between the others. Beyond the wooden grille was another cage of similar make. John sat inside it, arms folded, eyes glaring. Just outside of John's cage stood Thomas and Edward, gazing concernedly through the bars at Askon. But there was also another figure, on Thomas's right, a girl, a woman. She lowered her eyes shyly and snaked her hand around Thomas's, the fingers interlacing tightly. Behind them the Norill encampment teemed with hunkering gray bodies.

Instantly, Askon rose to his feet and flew across the small space. He had meant to ram the side of the cell, breaking the thin sticks and freeing himself. Instead, he made only a step or two, then swayed, falling into a heap as his head throbbed. With his entire weight, he slumped against the opposite side of his cage. The bars shook, but did not give way. Marten, who had been perched atop the highest crossbar, took flight and landed on the corner of John's cage.

John laughed. "He told ya not to get up. But did ya listen? Do ya ever listen?"

Askon rolled heavily to one side. With his back to John, he closed his eyes, letting his head fall against the wall of his cell. For a few moments, Askon rested, trying to understand why he and John were prisoners and Thomas and Edward were not. Why were any of them alive at all? And since they were alive, why did neither Thomas nor Edward seem prepared to fight? All around, the Norill reek seeped into his every breath, the sound of their slow, dragging feet slipping along like lizards' tails over the rocks. Panic struck him and he fished into the collar of his shirt. There he felt the cold, sharp edges of the fragment. Under the layers of cloth, it throbbed along in that strange heartbeat rhythm.

He relaxed a bit and breathed slowly. That they hadn't found the fragment was a relief, but the gem was not the only precious thing he carried. At his right hip, his sword hung in the scabbard. When the attackers had come upon him, he had been holding it in defense. The long knife rested at his other hip, still clasped tightly in the sheath. He opened his eyes. Thomas and Edward looked on with worried faces. The girl held Thomas's hand, her eyes downcast.

"I'll try to make this simple," Askon groaned, his own eyes still closed. "Why are you not killing these disgusting creatures by the dozens?"

Thomas and Edward looked at each other, neither desiring to explain, hoping that the other would make the first move. But the response came from directly behind Askon, from John's cage.

"That kind o' talk'll get ya nowhere but right where ya are now," John said. "Been shouting at 'em, twistin', bitin', throwin' punches, and anything else I can think every time they come around. And look where it's got me."

"Indeed," said Edward. Askon's eyes were open now, and he watched as the prince shrugged. "There's something different about these Norill, Askon. Suffice it to say that Thomas and I were persuaded not to harm them, if not yet to help them. When they captured us, they were looking for you. But you split off from us closer to town, and they didn't want to risk a fight. Their leader will come soon enough. If you'll trust me, it will be better if you hear the story from her."

Askon looked expectantly at the girl standing next to Thomas. She looked up slightly with deep dark eyes, round and relaxed; the long lashes fluttered a little. Around her smooth, fair face, thick locks of raven-black hair framed the subtle cheekbones and shallow dimples.

The rest of the black tresses were tied loosely, high on the back of her head. But she said nothing.

At a squeeze from the snow-white hand, Thomas stepped closer to her. "This is Elise. She's not the one who Edward means. She's a captive like us."

"Not a captive," the girl whispered, her voice like the patter of wolf's paws in the forest.

Thomas nodded vigorously. "Right, of course. Yes. She does stay by her own will, but her arrival here was similar to our own." He glanced sidelong at the girl and two smiles bloomed, one on each face.

"Oh you'll never get anywhere talkin' to that fool boy," John barked from his cell. "Love-struck dumb, he is. Even dumber than he was to start with. We'll be half an hour just gettin' through the sighs and smiles and—" here his voice swooped up an octave, cooing, "—long aching looks." He finished with a breathless sigh, then a single throaty laugh that was as fake as the crooning voice.

"And that is why they won't let you out, John," said Edward flatly. "You can't behave yourself. Two days we've been here, Thomas and I set loose within the first few hours and you still locked in that cage glowering and yelling at the guards. You can't even be civil to your own friends."

"How do I know she's my friend?" John growled. "Hell, how do I even know if you're my friend anymore? This is a *Norill* camp. Something's gotten to yer sanity there, my prince. Can't ya see it? It's like Askon says: we ought to be fightin' 'em, not sittin' around drinkin' their tea and cuddlin' with their spies."

Both Thomas and Elise took a step away from John's cell. Thomas looked wounded. The girl moved closer to him, placing her open palm against his chest. Edward simply turned away from the cage and moved toward Askon. He grasped the bars of Askon's cell and bit his lip. He waited a moment, then tried again, this time softer. "My friend. You helped me escape just such a prison once, did you not?"

Askon's body pulsed up and down in a silent chuckle, "I did. But as I recall, I never asked you to wait around to see what would happen next."

"And rightly so," Edward replied. "You saw what they did to my guards. Those Norill had no intention of setting me free, even if they meant to keep me alive for a time as bait. You were right—we were right—to kill them, to fight our way out."

Askon gritted his teeth. He flipped the button on his knife's sheath out and in. "How is this any different?" He waved a hand at the surrounding colony.

"First of all, no one is dead."

It was then that Askon saw the Norill colony for what it truly was. A wide, well-trodden square lay between Askon's cell and a row of low, shabby buildings. Some looked to be built in Norill fashion, webs of sticks and limbs like the cages, but with grass and foliage woven between until the structure would not only support itself, but provide shelter from the wind and rain. The row of shacks extended in a circular pattern around a large fire pit that held the previous night's ashes. Between the buildings, as Askon had noticed earlier, Norill of varying sizes trundled from place to place with their unmistakable gait. But now, he saw something else. The forms were not all Norill. Several humans, perhaps ten at the most, worked at various tasks along the row. Some repaired the woven grass on an outer wall, others carried water, or hung clothes on drying lines. One man carried a large slab of meat into a hut, emerging moments later with a basket full of gleaming red fruit.

Askon's mouth hung open. "What are these people doing here?" he asked.

Edward's fingers twisted thoughtlessly about the juncture of two bars. "As I said before, I think it will be better for you to talk to *her.* I'm not sure I can explain it properly."

"Her? I thought you said Elise—"

"Not Elise," said Edward. "The Norill leader."

CHAPTER NINETEEN

Bones and Bargains

As though Edward's suggestion had been a beckoning call, all motion around the encampment stopped. It began with the workers farthest away from Askon and cascaded down until each Norill—and human—previously busy at their work, became still. From beyond the row of shacks, Askon heard what had stopped them: a drum. No deep, rumbling war-drum like the Norill sometimes carried into battle; this light, almost musical sound came like a bouncing ball past the bowed heads of the workers.

Ping! dut-dut-duh Pong!

"What is that?" Askon said, crossing the floor of his cage.

Elise turned quickly toward him. Then in her ethereal whisper, "She comes. Bow to show your respect."

Ping! dut-dut-duh Pong!

Askon cocked an eyebrow. "You can't be serious."

Without moving from his sprawled seat in the neighboring cell, John chuckled. "I told ya these two had lost it, my friend. 'Course, ya could try it their way and see where it gets ya. I'll stay right here, thanks."

Edward banged a fist against the bars. "Try not to say anything that will get you killed, John." He lowered his head as Elise and Thomas had already done. Looking first to John and then Edward, Askon made his decision.

Ping! dut-dut-duh Pong!

The Norill leader and her entourage shuffled through the shabby buildings and past the ash pile, the bouncing rhythm pounding out all the while. Behind her, three drums of different sizes hung from the waists of her small Norill companions. Each of the drummers wore a brightly feathered mask made from a hollowed deer skull. As they walked, the drums swayed against their protruding bellies. The weight of the instruments produced an almost comical wobble, their hunkering posture impossible to maintain. Instead, the drummers leaned back, further exaggerating their round stomachs, tottering with every step.

In front of them and at the center marched the leader. Upon first glance, she looked no different than her fellow Norill. Askon wondered if the creatures sent their women into battle. If they did, it would have been impossible to tell which enemies had been male and which female. Her body showed none of the telltale signs of human womanhood, and even if it had, her gruesome armor would have covered it completely. For all intents and purposes, this Norill leader could have been either gender.

Her stride was proud and tall, especially in comparison with her retinue and the surrounding bowed heads of the colony-dwellers. Atop her head rested the rounded crest of a skull. It should have been quite precarious, but it balanced solidly, even as she walked. From the center of the shining white piece of bone, several long feathers from local forest birds fanned out like a peacock's tail. Below, heavier bones, those of a cow or moose, were layered over her chest and shoulders. Between the drumbeats, the tips and edges rubbed together as she walked. From beneath the shoulder bones, a long leather tunic hung heavily down to her knees. Here, square plates had been linked with knotted twine. The dozens of whitened flat shards clattered and moved together like the scales of some awful bony fish. As she approached, Askon stood tall, refusing to bow his head, and when she passed Edward and Thomas, the permanent stench of the colony mingled with something unexpected. She smelled like wildflowers.

"Hello, Elf-kind." Her voice, like that of a hardened woman in her middle-age, reminded Askon more than a little of Ilsa, the widow who died fighting alongside them in Thomas's village. The voice came again. "It is good to see that you remember the blood of your kin. These humans must bow; my people must bow, for I am leader amongst them, their fates mine to decide. Not you. From far away the elf-kind are. Spirits of the mountain the elf-kind are. Few are left. Some say they came from stone-of-mountain itself when the Knight of Vladvir stole it away. They say he called the elf-kind from across the water, from across the sky. Many creatures of darkness swept away by elf-kind, but Norill survive. If elves come from stone-of-mountain, they decide fate of Norill-kind. If stone-of-mountain say elf-kind save humans from Norill defeat, wise of the Norill obey, for stone-of-mountain is greater than all."

Dumbstruck, Askon watched as she bowed her head, spreading her arms wide. The drummers, who had paused while she spoke, beat rapidly upon the hide heads of their instruments in perfect time as she lowered herself almost to the ground. When she rose, the drums stopped, and the echo twanged through the trees and off the mountainsides. Askon remained upright, but nodded slightly to acknowledge her gesture.

This welcome, so similar to the one he had received in Dalstone, sent shivers up his spine. Yet something in the Norill leader's tone and the well-organized ceremony of her coming made it different. When she bowed, it was no breathless, preening gesture like Mark's hollow chattering. True respect and reverence laced every word from this Norill. Many of Dalstone's people had also been affected in such a way, but not John's father.

Unsure of where to begin, or how to proceed, he stepped closer to the bars. "I am Askon of Tolarenz, son of Teral who was nearly pure in the kindred of the elves."

The round gray face looked up into his with something like wonder. Though tall amongst her people, the Norill leader stood only as high as Askon's chin. If he were to look on a level with her, he would see only the collection of feathers twitching with the movements of her body. A crooked smile crawled across the lips and crinkled the small, flat nose. "A good name, Elf-kind. We know of Tolarenz, but open plains and valleys suit not the Norill.

"I am called Brâghda. Daughter to the great Bur-ghân whose old-fathers from times long ago led our people to this place. We are the Grafmark Norill."

Edward eyed Askon, expecting some kind of reaction. And though he had complained from the moment Askon had awoken, even John remained quiet while Brâghda spoke. Thomas and the girl, Elise, watched and listened intently to the strong, powerful voice. From time to time one would steal a glance at the other; their hands remained joined.

Questions swirled through Askon's mind. What did the Norill plan to do with their prisoners? How had they, or their leader at least, learned the language so well? But the one that weighed most on his mind concerned the Tear. This was not the first time Askon had heard the words "stone-of-mountain" from Norill lips. Under the blackness of the Death fragment, near a cell not so different from the one which surrounded him now, the Norill prisoner had said it, no, screamed it into Askon's cowering consciousness.

"Where is stone-of-mountain? We will not stop. More will come."

With a shiver, Askon cast off the chill of the prisoner's words. More had come. They had come first to destroy Austgæta, then on to Shale, and according to Christopher's men, many more such villages on the Vladvir plain. If they were right, more of them gathered at this very moment in the trees of Ellmed near Codard's castle, waiting to move south, striking Lord Apopsé's young kingdom with the combined forces of Codard and Iramov.

Brâghda's eyes narrowed, and the pale skin of her brow knitted into thin lines; the feathers twitched in a spray of color against the gray. "You wonder many things, Elf-kind. I know not the questions, but I see their hold upon you like binding ropes. I would set you free, but your friend," she wagged the feathers in John's direction, "has nothing but hatred and rage within him. He is not like Codard's son, the prince, or young Thomas. What if you are like John, son of Mark. Mark, whose arrows and knives seek always the flesh of my people? Yes, I know that the Darts of Grafmark are under his father's command. What if you are like him?"

Askon said nothing. John had risen at the mention of his father, but remained silent as well.

With her long arms, Brâghda swept a wide circle through the air, twisting her palms upward, pausing momentarily at the height of the arc. She let them fall, then raised them again in the same swooping motion. This time, at the zenith, her drummers raised their mallets and with the fall of her hands pounded a shot that rang for miles through the forest. "An offering then," she crowed in her wizened voice. "I have knowledge. Using it could bring great fortune to the Grafmark Norill, could bring great misfortune to all human kingdoms and death to the elf-kind. If we meant you harm, we would use this advantage, but we do not. Will it be enough?"

Askon looked to Edward, hoping that he had already heard whatever secret Brâghda intended to share. The prince only shook his head and, with a shrug, turned to the Norill leader. "Brâghda of the great Bur-ghân, have you shared this knowledge with Thomas or myself?"

"No. Prince of Vladvir, I have not," she said coldly. "It is not yours to know. It is between the Norill-kind and the elf-kind."

Askon shook the bars of his cage. "They are my friends and closest allies!" he said too loudly. "I would have them know. If I agree, you must tell them." He paused. "And you must release John, son of Mark, as well. His harsh words do not come from his father's influence."

For the first time since she had emerged from the opposite side of the camp, Brâghda looked unsure of her next move. Everything from the bowing to the march to the drumbeat gestures had been carefully executed. Now she raised a thin, pale hand to her face. The long, sharp nail of the index finger tapped the small, flat nose and ran down across the slightly darker gray of her lips.

Then Askon noticed her eyes. He had expected dark, almost black, had seen such a color in many of his battles with the Norill. But Brâghda's eyes were not black; they were gold, shimmering gold like the sun over fields at harvest, gold like an eagle, like the treasures of kings. They glittered as they flicked from Askon to Edward to John and back again. She stretched, gaining an inch or two of height, almost to Askon's nose.

"Brâghda accepts the terms of Askon, elf-kind," she said. "But my guards will follow every step of the man John who renounces his father. If he moves against us, he will be shot like a rabid dog." Her hands swooped into the air again and the drums pounded in response. "These are my terms."

Askon nodded. "What then, is your secret?"

Once more, the crooked smile rippled over the colorless face. "You have piece-of-mountain, Elf-kind."

Beyond his control, a rush of air hissed into Askon's lungs. He felt the blood drain from his face, and his eyes widened. Without thinking, he retreated a step, his hand falling to his sword belt. Why had they left him his sword?

"Stone-of-mountain can never be whole again," Brâghda continued. "Wise Norill know this. Humans broke it many lifetimes ago: the Knight of Vladvir and his friend Morrowmen the Wise. But they were wrong to break it. Now the pieces are sick. We will not take it from you. The Lost may want it, but the Grafmark Norill do not."

Resisting the urge to grasp the jewel beneath his shirt, Askon pressed the Norill leader for more information. "Who are the Lost?" he asked.

"You know them already. In the forests near your outpost Vestgæta they live, and near the fort Austgæta in the east. They seek all pieces-of-mountain; they are not wise. The Lost would make stone-of-mountain whole again, but it cannot be done. If an armor plate is cracked and broken, it can be repaired, but its weakness will betray the wearer to her death. Clothing can be mended with thread and patching, but never does it hold out the wind as before, and so it allows the sickness-from-cold to enter and harm or kill."

"And you believe that the Tear—I mean, stone-of-mountain— will betray those who try to reassemble it?" Thomas asked, releasing Elise's hand.

Brâghda nodded. "The world is how it is," she said. Thomas looked confused. "We have a saying," Brâghda began patiently. "If something is true of a stone, it is true of a tree or a beast or of Norill-kind. From a ledge a Norill will fall, as will a stick or a bucket of water. We say, 'The world is how it is.'"

"And so," Edward said, "if something is broken, it is folly to repair it with the expectation that it should ever be truly whole again."

"Yes," Brâghda said with a nod. Then the golden eyes fell again upon Askon. "Does this ease your thoughts, Elf-kind? Will knowing about the Lost help you in your fight? Have I met my part of our bargain?"

Looking to John, who gave a reluctant nod of his own, Askon stepped again toward the woven grid of sticks. "You have my word Brâghda. No harm will come to your people from me or from John."

Surprisingly, the Norill leader clapped her hands, and her face was drowned in a beaming smile. It was not the curling grin Askon had noted during their conversation, but a radiant expression of joy. For a moment, Brâghda looked not only human, but girlish, even pretty in her own way. She clapped again and the drums resumed in a new, complicated pattern. The drummers hopped and danced as they played with Brâghda leading the way. The rhythm rolled on. She stopped, lifted a long straight knife from the belt of bones around her waist and slashed with glee at the twine cords which secured Askon's cage door. She motioned for one of her attendants to do the same to John's cage. "Welcome, Elf-kind," she said, "to Vitæsta, home of the Grafmark Norill."

CHAPTER TWENTY
Vitæsta

For nearly half an hour, the dancing and drumming continued until Askon felt as though his head might burst. When the music wound down, and the gathered Norill began to disperse, Askon hailed Brâghda as she passed, still giddy with excitement. Stepping from the dancing circle, she waited next to him, bright feathers swaying with every breath.

"What can I do for you, Elf-kind?"

Askon attempted a smile. "Though the dance has been… flattering, my friends and I are hungry and in need of time for counsel."

The round gray face grew stern; the feathers bobbed in time with the softening drumbeat. "Counsel and food are good together. I will provide these. But to our agreement, my guards must be present with the man, John."

"Thank you, Brâghda. My friends and I have much to discuss, as do you and I. When we have finished eating and talking amongst ourselves, I will come before you with Edward. You have answered many questions, but there are still a great deal to which I would know the answers."

With that, Brâghda signaled the drummers. A final beat rang out, then drifted into silence. The Norill colony went about its work once again. She waved the drummers away, and they returned moments later with plates in place of instruments. Directing them to one of the shacks on the northern side of the fire pit, she led Askon and the others to the woven walls of the small building. Outside, two of her guards stood by silently. Before Askon ducked under the low lintel, he noticed at least four more Norill guards, each with a full quiver, their arrows knocked to the string. High above, Askon caught a glimpse of Marten circling the camp. Askon slipped inside.

The dirt floor of the hovel had been swept clean of debris. Two small beds were placed head to head against the far wall. Elise and Thomas sat on one, which creaked against their combined weight. Edward sat at the other. Too tall to use the bed as a comfortable chair, he sat comically with his knees nearly bent to his chest. Askon found a seat on a three-legged stool which Brâghda collected from a corner while John was given a small crate on which to sit. Brâghda waved a goodbye and, without a word, left them. Seconds later, the drummers entered with plates piled mostly with nuts and roots, though one carried a roast chicken surrounded by the oblong red fruit Askon had seen earlier. Once the table had been set and Askon had given his approval, the drummers excused themselves, each bowing several times in succession.

After they had gone, he surveyed the room. "Where do I even begin?" he said.

"With that chicken before it gets cold, I say," John offered.

Edward agreed. "We should eat. It will ease some of the awkwardness."

"I doubt that," said John.

In the voice whose intelligence always surprised Askon, Thomas made a suggestion. "It would make the most sense to start with something easy. Something that we can fully answer with only those present. We can save the more difficult questions for later when all of the available information has been shared."

Biting into a piece of the red fruit, Askon nodded. It was sweet, with a smooth thin skin and pockets filled with tiny seeds.

"As good a place to start as any," said Edward, tearing at the chicken. "What can we fully answer?"

Thomas placed his hand on Elise's knee. "I think Elise should explain to us why the prisoners are spared and why they choose to stay in Vitæsta."

"Cause the lot of 'em are crazy, that's why," John mumbled through a mouthful. "Been brainwashed by Norill magic, they have."

"John!" Edward said. "Do you know who you sound like? My father's men say the same thing of the elves. Would you?"

"No."

"That's what I thought. Why don't we let Elise tell us why they stay? She is our only authority on the subject."

Through the black frame of hair, which hung neatly around her attractive face, Elise glanced briefly at each of the men surrounding her. Casting her eyes again to the floor, she began in a whisper.

"I am from a poor Dalstone family. My father works for Mark in service of the Darts, though he is no soldier. He runs missives and papers to Mark's supporters and subordinates. When I became old enough to marry, my father and yours, John, decided upon a husband for me. He is a captain of the Darts and from one of Dalstone's wealthier families. But I did not want to marry a man who interrogated prisoners, who hunted and killed for sport, who thought more of battle than of building a home. In our short courting period, he once said to me, 'No day is complete without blood on your hands.'"

Finding her voice and her courage, Elise lifted her head. "He is not an evil man. But I see nothing in him for myself. I tried to get to know him, hoping that some attraction would grow from familiarity. It did not. When I asked my father if another might be chosen, he laughed in my face. 'A pig barn! That's where you're likely to go without him. Nobody of any stature's going to want a weatherworn field hand for a wife. Is that what you want?'

"I wouldn't have been bothered by such a life, but it wasn't really a question to be answered. I agreed to marry the captain. When the day came, a celebration was planned for the meeting hall. We were to be wed at sunset. I cried over my father's decision and felt guilty and undeserving as the captain was a fine man. Then the Norill struck.

"They came with no intent to kill, only capture, though we did not know this at the time. I ran for my life while the captain and the Darts fought against the Norill. None were killed. No Darts, no Norill.

All escaped. I awoke here, and Brâghda came to me. She said that I had been captured in order to save me from a terrible fate. I didn't believe her.

"Then she brought before me more people from Dalstone, people we had thought lost forever: a man accused wrongly for theft, punishable by the severing of one's right hand; a woman who was thought to have committed adultery, punishable at the will of the husband; a former Dart of Grafmark who was beaten severely after having failed multiple combat tests; and on and on.

"Soon, I began to believe. The Grafmark Norill, feared for so long by my people, were rescuing citizens who were wrongfully accused, badly mistreated, or otherwise subject to the unfair laws and rules of Dalstone society. I welcomed this gift and Vitæsta welcomed me."

As she finished, a sparkling rim of water pooled in her eyes. Thomas placed an arm around her shoulder and hugged her close. She dabbed at the tears and leaned into his embrace.

The story, her story, was common in the human cities throughout Vladvir and the surrounding lands. Askon had heard of many such cases in which an ill-fitting betrothal ended badly, and too often they ended in suicide or even murder. Elise, it seemed, had been lucky in that she found no terrible fault in her suitor and that the Norill had so mysteriously abducted her. This, he decided, would be a question to ask Brâghda when they next met. She would be able to explain the Norill's motivations for collecting Dalstone outcasts and alleged criminals.

Picking his teeth with a small chicken bone, John shifted on his crate so that he was facing the girl. "Probably got plans to stew you all in a soup come ritual time, these Norill. Don't let 'em fool ya. Speakin' the language doesn't make 'em intelligent. No more than beasts, they are."

"I'll agree with language use reflecting upon intelligence in *your* case at least," Edward said caustically. John returned to his chicken, seemingly unfazed.

Askon watched as Thomas and Elise leaned closer. At times they seemed to be in a world altogether different from the others. Smiling, he carefully phrased his next question. "Thomas, it's been only a couple of days since you were taken. How did the two of you—I mean—when…"

"He wants to know if ya got a hay pile picked out somewhere, Thomas," laughed John. "Ya know, a real nice place to bed down here with the other animals."

Thomas became stone still, and anger swept over his young face. But before he could speak, Edward grabbed his arm firmly. Thomas, who had rolled up onto his toes, ready to stand and fight, sunk back to the bed. Edward released him, then promptly turned and slapped John across the face. "You have been away from home for too long. Show some courtesy, for the gods' sake. You were crass to begin with, but a life among soldiers has made you downright rude. That was simply uncalled for."

John rubbed his face, and with a glance at the two silent Norill guards, shook his head at Edward, his eyes saying, 'Wait till we get outta here, my prince. You'll get yer payment then.'

"I know what you meant, Askon," said Thomas. "It was all very fast, obviously. I think nearly anyone could see what I did when I met Elise, could hear what I heard, but what drew her to me, I do not know. Asking her to share seems more than impolite."

"That's fair," Askon said. "You met; you care for one another; that is enough, I think."

"Thank you," Elise said quietly.

John crunched audibly on a gnarled, bulbous root. A moment later, his face twisted at the bitter taste. "Alright, so we got the lovebirds outta the way. How're we gonna get back to Dalstone?"

Pushing the roots to one side of the large plate, Askon lifted a round nut and, holding it between his thumb and forefinger, examined the unusual shell. It was dense and deep brown. Little ridges and divots covered the surface on all three sides. The seam of each side was sharp, almost serrated. Despite its aggressive appearance, the nut cracked easily against the edge of the table. Askon removed the pale white center and popped it into his mouth. "That might seem like the next step, John," he said. "Though I'm not so sure there'll be much of Dalstone left to go back to."

They all stopped. John laughed, the defensive and false sound he used to redirect the conversation when he became uncomfortable. "What? You think these Norill rats can overtake the Darts and make a move on the town? I doubt it."

"No," said Askon calmly. "There is a rift in Dalstone. One side supports the thane, and the other supports your father."

"Everyone knows that. Some discovery," John retorted.

Thomas, who still leaned against Elise, sat up. "That division was fairly clear from the start. Why would it be any more of a problem now?"

Askon cast the cracked remains of the nutshell aside. "When we came to rescue you from this place—"

"An' what a rescue it was," John said cackling. Edward reached over and slugged him in the shoulder. Askon ignored them and continued.

"I requested aid from Dalstone so that I might have a chance at saving you from the Norill. Eldred sent three men, and Mark wanted to send none. It was clear that any change in the balance of supporters might set the conflict in motion. After Eldred pledged his three, John's father reluctantly assigned two men of his own to follow me. None looked like they would be terribly helpful. Mark's men in particular had ill-favored looks about them.

"I took their demeanors to be unhappiness in their assignment and forged ahead, wanting to get to you as quickly as possible. I had no idea whether the Norill would keep you as prisoners or kill you. At nightfall, I split the watch in order to avoid any conflict between sides. I couldn't sleep. And during the night, one of Mark's men began systematically killing the others. I was drawn into the fight, but it was too late. By the time I found him, all of Eldred's men were dead. Then the Norill came, killing both of Mark's men and capturing me.

"I think that Mark has already made the first move in Dalstone's conflict. And if I'm wrong, then Eldred *will* when he finds out what happened to his men."

John appeared to be unaffected by the news. "So he's finally made his bed? Serves him right. I hope Eldred knocks him around and ties him up in the square. Maybe then he'll figure out what it means to play yer part. Never was enough for him to just be the advisor. He wants to run the place."

"That could be a disaster for the town," said Edward.

"He doesn't care what happens to the town till it's been built back up in his own way," John replied. "Been a long time coming, this fight. I don't know why Eldred didn't do something about it sooner."

Askon sighed, shaking his head. "There could be many civilians lost if it comes to battle. But I suppose if it does, it does."

"The world is how it is…" Elise whispered. "As for your question about going back, I'm sure Brâghda will release you as soon as you know her purpose in bringing you here. She offered me freedom, as well as the others, but we all chose to stay. To what did we have to return?"

"That leaves only one thing," said Askon. He hesitated, looking first to Thomas, then to Elise. "Thomas, I think that perhaps Elise should—"

"Stay," Edward interrupted. Turning back to Askon, he said, "The Tear affects us all, even Elise and the Norill. Besides, the Norill speak of the stone-of-mountain quite freely. All that is left is to make the connection."

"Very well," said Askon. "We have to get the Time fragment out of Vladvir. Apopsé's kingdom might give us some much needed protection and time to plan. Morrowmen will be there waiting for us.

He will know what to do next, how to proceed, and how to defeat Iramov. He may even be able to help us regain Codard's loyalty."

"I would appreciate that," said Edward softly.

"In the South Kingdom, Elise might find the same safety she enjoys here," offered Thomas.

Elise only nodded, saying nothing.

Askon stood. "So it's settled then. We go to Brâghda, hear her purpose in capturing us, request release, and make our way to the South Kingdom as planned. Agreed?"

A long silence stretched between them: John, sullen and brooding in his corner; Thomas and Elise smiling softly, no doubt imagining a peaceful and unlikely future; and Edward slowly nodding, his gray eyes downcast and distant. He was the first to agree, rising from his seat and joining Askon at the door. Then it was John with no more than a shrug and a gesture toward them, and the Norill guards beyond. Thomas and Elise came last, stirred from their reverie. They stepped outside, leaving John behind to wait and sulk. Somewhere beyond Vitæsta's ashen fire pit and rustling circle of woven huts, Brâghda awaited.

CHAPTER TWENTY-ONE

The Enemy of One's Enemy

A sickly warmth settled on Vitæsta. Throughout the colony, gray Norill forms lay sweating in the shade. Here and there, pale pink or brown human bodies did the same, just as miserably. Few of either group remained fully clothed, yet even with the humans it was difficult to tell which were male and which female. All were thin, and the Norill fashion that they wore was virtually identical for the men and the women.

The long-term captives, now self-selected residents, had grown accustomed to Vitæsta's pervading smell, a smell which all Norill camps possessed. Askon later learned that it came from a combination of their bone-plate armor and the process by which they made the glue that helped to fasten the armor pieces together and harden the twine used in Norill construction. Under the swelter, the smell grew, though the lounging Vitæstans noticed it little.

It was into this heat and reek that Askon, Edward, and Thomas stepped with Elise following closely behind. John elected to remain in the shack after a long debate concerning his ability to be calm and respectful in the Norill leader's presence. He was still not convinced that the Grafmark Norill were any different from those whom Brâghda called the Lost. Over the years, John had fought and killed many such Norill, as had Askon and Edward. Even Thomas, in his relatively short time as a soldier had killed his share. So John stayed with the food (which pleased him well enough) and under guard (which pleased him not at all). Askon and the others made their way to Brâghda's residence, with hopes that they could leave Vitæsta behind and begin their journey to the South Kingdom where Morrowmen awaited.

Beyond the ring of shacks that encircled the fire pit, a narrow trail wound between clusters of buildings and into the towering Grafmark trees. They followed the path at Elise's direction, taking a left branch here, a right branch there until it seemed as though the trail had come to its end. Several hundred feet from the last group of Norill houses, the trail ran directly into the mountain. There, an opening gaped like a wicked mouth turned on its side. Wide enough only for one person to slide through, Askon and his friends passed single file into the gap. The light in the narrow crack vanished as they rounded a sharp corner. Blindly, they followed the opening past another corner, and another. Askon felt his way along, sliding his hand around the sharp edge until a warm orange light bloomed in the darkness.

He assumed that a torch burned somewhere within the cave. And so it did. With every step, the light grew brighter. Thin veins of metal glimmered over the walls, creating the illusion that the cavern itself generated an inner light. Finally, the entrance began to widen. Another dozen feet and the pathway accommodated all four travelers. In another dozen, the cavern ballooned into a huge chamber where many lights burned, and the ribboned stone sparkled. Above them, torch smoke swirled high into the crevices of the cavern ceiling where the Norill had dug channels into the open air. No light came down through these shafts, but as the smoke did not fill the cave, Askon assumed that somewhere above them it could escape.

The chamber was divided into four distinct sections. In the entryway an arc of torches lined either side of the opening. A large bearskin lay between the arcs, with a low bench on the left and right. This foyer of sorts led down a path outlined by two trails of small stones. Partitions, whose top edges reached almost to Askon's eye level, stretched along both sides of the stone-lined path, roughly simulating a hallway or corridor. On the left, inside the partition, was a large desk of human make. Too large to have been carried in through the crack, one of the human ex-prisoners must have constructed it on the inside. It looked old, with graying wood panels and ridges rising along the grain of the flat surfaces. A few parchments and skins, covered with what Askon assumed to be Norill runes, lay in neat piles on the desktop. A stool, similar to the one on which Askon had sat in the shack, had been left askew a short distance from the desk.

On the right side of the makeshift hallway was a bedroom, Brâghda's, Askon assumed. In contrast to the study across the hall, the bedroom showed no semblance of tidiness or organization. Scattered around the room, various Norill garments, a few of which did betray the occupant's gender, hung dangling from every chair, table and chest. The bed, of Norill fashion and construction, though of a much higher quality than any furniture Askon had yet seen in Vitæsta, had been left unmade, the thin blanket curled into a lump at the bed's footboard. Suddenly aware that he was looking into a woman's bedroom, Askon averted his eyes and proceeded between the partitions to the end of the path.

On either side of the hallway's end were the doors to the opposing rooms. The bedroom door was closed, while the study door had been left ajar. Askon smiled, thinking of how similar the Norill sometimes were to humans or elves. At the end of the hallway, they entered a large meeting room. Several bearskins, all of slightly differing colors, lay overlapping one another on the floor. At the back of the room, which was also the back of the cave, a large, ornate chair—probably made by the same hand which had assembled the desk—sat empty, its deep red cushions showing signs of frequent use. In the center of the room, Brâghda stood at a wide table. The surface reached just below chest height, though for Askon and his friends it more closely resembled an absurdly large end-table.

The Norill leader was reading something. A large skin, covered in the same runes as those in the study, lay flat before her. She looked up from her work with her strange, mesmerizing golden eyes, and reaching out to her sides, flicked her hands toward the hallway where Askon and his friends had entered. From deep in the shadows, four large Norill lumbered out of hiding and circled behind Askon and the others, blocking the exit.

Thanking the gods that they hadn't brought John along, Askon stole a nervous glance at the guards. Thomas turned to face them. "I'll watch," he said.

Askon approached the table. "Brâghda, thank you for your hospitality. Since my release, and John's, we have found the food and lodging to be quite comfortable."

"I doubt that, Elf-kind," Brâghda said flatly. "But your courtesy is appreciated." She rubbed the smooth gray skin of her forehead. "My guards will not harm you and will not repeat anything which passes between us here. You may speak freely."

How freely he could speak seemed a question of perspective to Askon. He wanted to rage at the Norill, attack them simply because of what they were and how they had captured him and his friends.

"Don't think of a salamander."

Breathing deeply, Askon smiled. In order to resist the adverse effects from the Time fragment, he picked an innocuous but interesting bit of jewelry dangling from the Norill leader's ear. A crisscross of small bones, most likely avian in nature, had been carefully notched and tied around a polished piece of glass. To Askon's knowledge, Norill technology did not allow for the making of such a substance. It must have been discovered or taken from a human settlement and repurposed as an earring. "Alright," he said to Brâghda when he was certain that he had taken control of his emotions. "We would like to leave Vitæsta as soon as possible and return to Dalstone. You speak of the stone-of-mountain—which we call Alora's Tear. You say its pieces are sick. You even mentioned Morrowmen."

Brâghda nodded. "Morrowmen the Wise, yes."

"Well," Askon continued, "I have orders from him to make my way to the South Kingdom. Do you know of it?"

Another nod.

"The more quickly we arrive there, the better. Will you let us go?"

She folded her long gray arms across her chest. The pieces of bone which made up her armor clacked and clattered at the disturbance. Then the curling smile Askon had seen at their first meeting wormed its way over her face. "Elf-kind are wise. Morrowmen is wiser. But you, Askon of Tolarenz, are only elf-kind in part. I see the human blood in you also. One green eye and one blue," she said. "Maybe the human blood makes you too hasty. You do not yet know why I have brought you here."

"Alright," Askon replied. "You have made your point. I will hear what you have to say, but cannot guarantee that I will agree with your decision."

Brâghda unfolded her arms and rounded the table's edge. When she stood only a foot from Askon, she stopped and looked at each of them in turn. "Elise," she said. "You know why we brought you to Vitæsta. My words are not for you."

The girl lowered her head, and her thick black hair slipped from her shoulders, encircling her downturned face. She backed away silently a few steps, then waited without so much as a single word.

Brâghda rose up before the three men as straight-backed as Askon had seen any Norill stand. Edward seemed relaxed in the face of her scrutiny, himself fully accustomed to such assessments by other leaders and nobility. Thomas, by comparison, looked terrible. Either the heat or the pressure had brought about thick rills of sweat which now ran freely down the sides of his face, almost like tears. He squirmed as her eyes passed over his face and body, but he said nothing. Askon, having made his demands, now became impatient at the extended introduction and slow progression of the meeting. He rubbed his knuckles, pressing each of them, one-at-a-time, until they popped.

"Well?" he said.

Brâghda smiled the crooked smile once again. "Morrowmen the Wise would tell you to have patience, Elf-kind. But I understand your need for haste, though you might deepen your own wisdom by heeding the warning." She shifted her weight to one hip, allowing her spine to curl into the natural posture of her people. "When you entered Grafmark, you were not alone. My warriors followed you closely from the moment you reached the canopy trees."

Askon shrugged. "I saw your scouts. We took them for the ones you call the Lost, the Norill who now fight alongside Iramov and Codard."

The bright feathers of Brâghda's headdress wagged back and forth. "No. The Lost were not with you under Grafmark's trees. But we were."

Edward looked skeptical. "So you followed us to Dalstone. What of it?"

"We took great risk; the Darts of Grafmark followed you as well," Brâghda said quickly, and to Askon it seemed as if Edward's comment had somehow offended her. She continued: "After it was clear who you were, Elf-kind, we began to wonder if you might be of some use to us and we of some use to you."

"Go on," Askon said, leaning against the low table.

"The Grafmark Norill," Brâghda said with a raspy, rattling breath, "tire of being the source of fear in the forest's heart. We tire of being hunted by the Darts but have no way to communicate this to the humans of Dalstone. For many years we have taken prisoners, offering them a refuge from the harsh laws and ignorance of their own people. Now we would work together with them. However, as long as Mark commands the Darts, there will be no peace."

"You can't be suggesting we get rid of John's father!" Thomas interjected.

Brâghda slowly turned to face the young man, bringing her voice low and locking her dazzling golden eyes on his. She said, "Thomas, you have already found your reason for coming to Vitæsta, I think. Stand not by these men and instead by her. Luck is not so favorable to all in such matters, the elf-kind and the prince can finish with me."

Just as Elise had done only a few minutes earlier, Thomas lowered his head and stepped back until he collided with the girl. He jumped at the contact, and her quiet laughter jostled the black tresses about her face. Wrapping his hand around hers, Thomas fell silent.

Askon resumed the proceedings. "So you would have peace, then? That seems like a simple request, but you and I both know that it is impossible for me to grant."

A thick eyebrow curled high on the Norill leader's forehead. "Still too hasty you are, Elf-kind. Let me explain what I propose.

"As you know, a great divide has grown between the people of Dalstone. Some stand with the leader of old, Thane Eldred. My spies say that almost exactly half the town would surely fight for him."

"How could your spies truly know?" Edward asked doubtfully. "They would have to keep far enough away as to remain unseen by the townspeople."

A series of hissing squeaks escaped the Norill leader, followed by the dull rattling of her bone harness. "Prince of Vladvir, you underestimate me. I did not say that my spies were Norill-kind."

With a nod and wave of his hand, Edward acknowledged his error. "A clever way for your rescued citizens to give something back," he said.

Brâghda grinned. "We also know that roughly the other half would support Mark if a conflict were to arise. If it did, and I think it will, the Grafmark Norill would fight alongside Thane Eldred as long as he agreed to peace in return."

"Then there is no time to waste," Askon said. "Your warriors killed two men in my camp. They were Mark's picked men. I had only just discovered that one had murdered the Thane's supporters who had agreed to help me find my friends."

"Yes," said Brâghda. "We know of this as well. It is why my warriors killed them."

Edward folded his arms and raised a hand to his chin. "It won't work," he muttered, shaking his head. "Norill assistance will tip the scales in Mark's favor. Think about how we reacted to my father's alliance with them."

"But the king is allied also with Iramov, the man who wiped out all of Tolarenz, the man who killed Caled," Askon argued. "Neither Iramov nor the Lost have done anything but harm. Perhaps the people of Dalstone will understand. Maybe they will listen."

Brâghda shuffled over to Edward and laid her bony gray hand upon his shoulder. Askon cringed slightly, imagining himself in his friend's position. As always, Edward accepted the gesture graciously. Brâghda leaned in, feigning a whisper. "Maybe princes of Vladvir can be wiser than elf-kind," she said. "You say what I have already long considered, but there is one thing left unsaid. When you entered the forest, I told you that the Lost had not followed your path." She retracted her hand and moved away from Edward.

"Yes, and?" said Askon.

"While that is true, it does not mean that the Lost were not already in our forest." She moved back to the rune-covered skin that lay on the opposite side of the table. "My warriors report that the Lost have indeed entered Grafmark. It is the belief of my best strategists that the Lost intend to attack Dalstone directly. If that happens, they are many and outnumber Dalstone's forces. We, however, could take them by surprise. They do not know we have settled here, and in no way suspect that Norill-kind would fight alongside humans.

"With our help, Dalstone would win easily, and we would be endeared to many of its residents. Then, if the battle between Dalstone's people must still be fought, Eldred would surely accept our support."

Askon's eyes widened. He turned to Edward and upon both of their faces, thin smiles had crept. With a shrug, Askon returned his gaze to Brâghda and her strange golden eyes. "A brilliant plan. You are correct that we have underestimated you. How close are the Lost to Dalstone?"

"They could strike at any time," she said. "Since you arrived, they have been gathering, one group at a time, their numbers ever increasing. Today they have almost as many fighters as Dalstone. In less than two days, there will be more Norill than humans."

Askon shook his head. "Then it is too late. Your warriors can't be ready to fight in less than two days. They must be spread all over the forest."

Brâghda scoffed. "Foolishness. I told Thomas that luck is not always favorable to those in love. The world is how it is, Elf-kind, and luck is not always favorable to those in war. We have waited long for this chance to make peace, and my fighters are ready to move as long as you support my plan to help Thane Eldred."

Deep down, something in Askon's gut told him to stop. It shouted and screamed, railed at the thought of allying with the Norill. The stench, the gruesome bone armor, Patrick dead at Norill hands, and Christopher's wild pursuit after his friend's death all rushed back in an instant. The calling from within continued, and he almost stopped to listen. But the plan was too well-laid, Brâghda's words too persuasive. He ignored the feeling and stepped around the table, thrusting out his right hand.

The open palm of the Norill leader met his, and in Edward's sincere fashion, Askon placed his left hand atop the two already joined. "We accept your plan," he said firmly, "and wish you the best of luck in finding peace."

Edward and Thomas looked on, unsure whether their friend had just saved Dalstone or doomed it.

They spent another hour discussing the details of the battle plan. Brâghda's fighters would stay back, remaining completely hidden for as long as possible. When the Lost struck, signal fires would be lit all around the valley of Dalstone, calling back any Darts of Grafmark who still patrolled the borders. After that, once the battle began in earnest, the Grafmark Norill would engage by first attacking key targets in secret. The sneak attacks wouldn't last long before the enemy became aware of the Grafmark Norill presence. Brâghda and her full army would then join the battle.

Askon and Edward were tasked with conveying this information to Dalstone's people so that the Grafmark Norill were not mistakenly identified as enemies. It was Edward's opinion that the job would be relatively easy if they arrived before the Lost decided to attack. With the city surrounded and outnumbered, news of reinforcements would go over well with all but the most biased individuals. Whether they would continue to be grateful after the battle had been won remained in question.

They emerged through the crack in the mountainside one after the other. Askon was first, followed by Edward, Thomas, and Elise. The latter two had remained completely silent for the duration of the discussion. Outside, the afternoon heat lingered, drawing beads of sweat onto their brows and any exposed skin. They marched away from the jagged opening and fell into step with one another. As they rounded the first corner in the pathway, Thomas stopped.

"So, who's going to tell John about all this?" he asked.

No one spoke. Askon continued walking as though Thomas had said nothing. Marten dropped out of the sky and fell onto Askon's shoulder only a few feet from the cave entrance. The bird's head jolted back, cocking to one side as it stared at Thomas. Edward gave the young man a helpless shrug. Whoever among them told John about the plan would be his target from now on. Whether he would come to accept the alliance was unclear, but his first reaction was certain to be bad.

They crossed the fire pit, sweat streaming from them all, and ducked past the two silent Norill guards into the shack. Askon had fallen to the rear of the group, and he waited as the three others entered. He lowered his head to enter, and Marten leapt from his shoulder, flapping idly once or twice before landing on the shack's roof. Inside, John lay snoring on one of the Norill-sized beds.

"Should we wake him?" Elise whispered.

Without hesitation, Askon strode across the small room and flopped onto the other Norill bed. John did not so much as twitch, but the snoring grew louder. A flick of Askon's wrist and the others made their way back to the door. None wanted to disturb John's sleep, and they wanted even less to give him the news from Brâghda. Edward, Thomas, and Elise slipped back out the door and began collecting anything they would need for the return trip.

Scooting the bed, which was surprisingly light, nearer to his sleeping friend, Askon reached out to grab John's shoulder. He braced himself for a shock, but none came. John did not jump up or startle at the touch. He just went on snoring. With both hands, Askon lay hold of John's shoulders and shook him bodily from side to side. A snort halted John's breathing, then a sniff. His head lolled to one side.

"John," Askon said firmly. "John, wake—"

"*Bah!*" John shouted at the top of his lungs.

Askon's head snapped back, and a quick intake of breath hissed through his nose. Nearly toppling off the bed, he reached out to steady himself. Inside his chest, his heart beat wildly. John cackled with laughter.

"Ha! Been plannin' that one for an hour at least," he said. "Figured you'd be the one to try an' wake me up, but I thought maybe it'd be Thomas. You should'a seen yer face! Oh, I may be trapped in a festerin' Norill rathole, but it doesn't mean it'll stop my fun." Askon shoved him hard, and he fell back onto the bed, still laughing.

"We've spoken to Brâghda," Askon said. He tried to make his voice sound severe and serious, but in the face of John's laughter, the task proved difficult. He pressed on. "You aren't going to like what we have to do."

"Who says we *have* to do anything?" John asked, trying to suppress the residual chuckles still rippling along his frame.

Askon rose to his feet, hoping it would make the words seem in some way more forceful. "I do."

John's eyes narrowed. "Fine by me," he said slowly. "But somethin' tells me it gets worse."

"It does. We're going to have to fight alongside the Norill."

Now it was John's turn to stand for emphasis. "Not a chance!" he shouted. He poked a solid finger into Askon's chest. "And you shouldn't either. I'd follow you a long way, but this is the line for me.

Ain't no way I'll draw swords with those filthy creatures. How can you even say that? You've seen what they've done, what they do. We've fought 'em from here to Ellmed and just about everyplace between. I've watched friends cut down and bashed in with Norill clubs. I've seen what happens after, and I've seen what happens when they burn a human fort to the ground." He thumped again on Askon's chest. "No."

Askon readied his arguments, but deep down a part of him agreed with John. They had witnessed the vile acts the Norill had committed on multiple fronts in their time together as soldiers. Good men had fallen to Norill blades. If the Grafmark Norill proved dishonest and allied instead with the Lost, Dalstone would stand no chance. But what choice did they have? For the moment, they were at the mercy of Brâghda and her people. If they scorned her offer, how would she react? It was simple, Askon decided. John had to be convinced. They had to go through with the plan. The people of Grafmark, both human and Norill, would be better for it.

"Then rot here John, son of Mark," Askon said with as much venom as he could muster. "Rot here while we fight to save Dalstone, while we make an alliance with Brâghda. Right now, Norill of the same kind that we fought against at Austgæta are surrounding the town. There are too many, and Dalstone's people are weakened by their infighting. Your father is to blame for that, and you know it. Do something to set it right. Brâghda will help them win and has pledged to help Eldred against your father. She would have peace. Would you?"

With that, he left John glowering on the edge of the bed. He knew not whether his friend would be convinced, but their time was running out. At that very moment, the last groups of the Lost had entered Grafmark. Within a day's time, the full force of their army would be gathered before the Dalstone gates. If there was any hope of saving the people there, Askon and his friends needed to be on their way as soon as possible, even if that meant leaving John behind.

Askon exited the shack, going from house to house, asking about supplies. He spoke only with the humans, assuming that the majority of the Norill would be unfamiliar with his language. The first few Vitæstans were of little help. They had nothing to offer but their hospitality, which was of the highest degree. Soon, Askon came to a man who could offer assistance. They exchanged greetings; the man listened intently to Askon's request; then he produced a large basket full of the red fruit. He indicated that the supply be shared amongst all of Askon's friends. After a quick thank you, Askon turned, ready to see what the others were able to procure on short notice. As he did, he saw John emerge from the shack, his face still frustrated and strained. With long strides, John paced along the row of ramshackle buildings to where the others had gathered. Speaking to no one, he shouldered a pack and folded his arms. Askon breathed a sigh of relief.

CHAPTER TWENTY-TWO

Spreading the Word

They passed the afternoon and evening upon the road. With little more than a word or two, Brâghda had released them. John refused to speak to her. In spite of his attitude, the Norill leader had lifted the terms of her deal with Askon. John, she said, was free to come and go from Vitæsta any time he pleased, a gesture of goodwill. Elise elected to follow Thomas, and the two of them walked hand in hand along the trail back to Dalstone.

When evening faded into night, the group stopped to rest only a short distance from where Askon had camped with Mark's traitorous men and Eldred's fallen soldiers. Their shadows still danced there. Askon turned away as they passed, but even behind closed eyelids he saw the faces, the bodies, the blood.

The night passed without incident, though Askon slept little, and they rose early the next morning, hopeful to reach Dalstone before the

Lost could begin their assault. Within no more than an hour of their destination, Askon prepared his friends.

"We'll need to choose only those who have Dalstone's best interests in mind," he began. "John, do you know which of the townspeople would accept help from the Grafmark Norill?"

John laughed, a deadened, hollow sound. "Oh yeah, there'll be a line set up just waitin' to hear the news."

"I know of some," said Elise. She walked a few steps ahead of Thomas, who had fallen behind to discuss something with Edward. The two men followed her closely, but their attentions were on each other, not Askon.

"Good," Askon replied.

Elise smiled, her dark eyes like flecks of blackened glass. "My father's position within Mark's ranks has its uses. I know at least who we should avoid talking to; however, the captain had friends who would be amenable to our cause, good men whose allegiance is to Dalstone, not to the politics that govern it."

Askon smiled in return. "Very good."

"Alright," John conceded. "I take the lady's meanin'. But if these Norill rats turn on us, it'll be your debt to pay." His gaze settled heavily on Askon, who tried to see past the anger in his friend's eyes. He knew that John would defend the people before letting personal feelings get in the way, but this was something more. John felt betrayed, Askon guessed, and such a wound would take time to heal. Time they did not have.

John shrugged. "There's quite a few who'll side with savin' the city. An' besides, my New Darts'll do what I tell 'em, even if it means runnin' straight off a cliff."

Thomas and Edward had caught up with them. "You wouldn't have it any other way would you?" Thomas asked.

"Damn right I wouldn't, an' you'd be smart to learn it too."

Thomas smiled, his confidence growing. "Why? So I could feel the wind in my face?"

"That's not all you'll feel in yer face if ya keep up like that," John growled, the fingers of his right hand curling tightly into a fist.

Edward stepped between them. "I'm not sure it's quite time for jokes, Thomas. Let's just make our way into town and talk to every possible supporter we can. They'll know by now that the Lost are readying an attack. In the rush to prepare, there will be no time for any meaningful argument."

He was right. They caught their first glimpse of the enemy just before crossing the river; a handful of Norill scouts prowled through the tree line. The adjacent fields had already been abandoned, and it seemed the Norill would leave them intact for the moment. Both Askon and John drew their swords when they recognized the enemy scouts—and would have killed the spies without hesitation—but Edward stopped them, cautioning that though the Norill seemed to be only five or six, there might be any number just beyond sight. Instead, Edward led them back into the trees, and taking Elise's advice, followed the river south.

The walking was easy along the border where field met forest. Shortly thereafter, as Elise had predicted, they came to a narrow, makeshift bridge. It was nothing like the properly constructed crossing north of Dalstone, but it served their purposes. On the main bridge, the Norill would likely have patrols, which Askon and the others would have had to fight or evade. By crossing farther south, they avoided such a conflict and approached the town where the Dalstone guards would be more likely to allow them entry. Had they come to the front gate, they would certainly have been turned away on account of the danger in opening the forward-facing wall.

They slipped inside with only a shocked expression from the guard at the southwest gate. Quickly, he lifted the bar and swung the row of wooden poles back just wide enough for them to pass through. Then he slammed the gate behind them, bringing the bar back down and securing it in place.

"We didn't think you would come back," he said, almost mumbling the words. The shock on his face persisted. "Let alone bring back your friends, and if I'm not mistaken, the lady El—"

"You hold your tongue!" Elise closed the gap between herself and the guard like a hunting wolf on its prey. He was taller than she was, but she remedied that by twisting her fingers into the tuft of hair which sprouted from the rim of his helmet. She yanked down hard, bringing his eyes to her level. "A wise man, such as yourself, would not remember he saw anyone who looked familiar, save the three men who returned with Askon of Tolarenz." Her voice, low and cold, sounded nothing like the airy whisper she had used throughout their time in Vitæsta. She spoke no direct threat to the guard, but the implication was clear. Her dark features, always before contributing to her shy, submissive personality, now seemed ominous: the pale skin like ice, the black eyes and hair like the devastation left behind in some great fire. She shoved the man away.

Thomas gazed with wonder as the shadow lifted from the girl's face. He looked helplessly from Elise to Edward to Askon. Then came the whisper. "He'll stay quiet now, I think."

She marched lightly into the lead, with Askon following closely behind. Thomas hesitated, and John slapped him hard on the shoulder. "Now look whatcha got yerself into with that one? Could'a told ya she was a fire-breather; that family's known for it, they are. Good luck comin' home to that!" He slapped Thomas again, laughing, and sauntered off in the direction the others had gone. Thomas stood quietly for a moment before hurrying to catch them.

They decided to fan out, covering as much of the town as possible. Thomas and Elise went together, while John, Edward, and Askon split up on their own. Askon went directly to Eldred's lodging.

The townspeople were in one of two states: panic or preparation. Many of the wives, children, and farmers stayed huddled in their houses or busily helped to fortify defenses. The men who fought in Eldred's service or with the Darts hurriedly prepared any implements that could defend the city from the siege. Piles of heavy spears were loosed from their bindings and multiple fires burned, heating kettles which the soldiers filled with oil or lard. These they posted near the gates and the weaker places in the outer wall, anywhere large groups of the Norill might gather. As Askon made his way toward Eldred's quarters, he watched the guards' preparations. Some seemed giddy with the excitement of imminent battle, while others looked as though the fight had already been lost.

The heavy pine door to the thane's personal lodging closed behind Askon with a dull *clack*. Unlike in King's City and other towns throughout Vladvir, when the guards asked him to lower the hood of his cloak, revealing the telltale signs of his heritage, they did not stop him. In Dalstone the pointed ears and two-colored eyes were the reason he was allowed to pass, not a reason to hold him back.

A long narrow hallway stretched before him and he couldn't help but remember Brâghda's cave in Vitæsta. He had expected high ceilings and ornate furnishings like those adorning the meeting hall across town, but Eldred's personal space had an impressive simplicity for someone so highly cast in Dalstone's social hierarchy. Even Caled had his indulgences in the Tolarenz town hall, with its large chambers, hidden study, and priceless artwork. Eldred's living space much more closely resembled Askon's own family home: simple furniture of quality construction, rustic decorations, and very little in the way of sparkling jewels, gleaming silver, or precious gold. Askon assumed that Mark, wherever he resided, would have a differing design sense.

Down the hall, Askon heard raised voices. An argument. He followed the sound. The voices drew closer, and he thought that he could discern only three. Whose those voices were, he did not know, though he assumed that at least one of them would be Eldred's.

Askon emerged from the hallway into a wide seating area and makeshift war room. A broad, knee-high table was strewn with maps and illustrations depicting the arrangement of enemy forces in relation to Dalstone's own fighters. Three men gathered around the table: one,

Eldred, sat with his hands pressed firmly against the sides of his face; the other two stood on either side, shouting back and forth at one another. The man standing nearest Askon, his back turned, was Mark.

"I told you!" Mark brayed. "Those creatures should have been eliminated long ago. For too long we simply patrolled the borders, and now look what has happened. They've multiplied, and we will be overrun. My Darts cannot fight so many Norill. There is little we can do to defeat them. Our best chance is to remain behind the walls and hope that our messengers reach King Codard."

The other man paced up and down his side of the table. "No. It takes nearly a week to travel from Dalstone to King's City. Even if there was a company somewhere nearby, it would take almost twice that for them to arrive here. By my estimates, we have nearly as many able-bodied men as the Norill have of their own numbers. If your Darts are as good as you say they are, each of them should be worth two Norill. I say we surprise them. We'll circle around the west side of the city, and when they come at the gates, we pour around their flanks. It'd be over quick. We don't have a better chance to win outright than that."

"And what if you're wrong?" Mark's voice shifted to a syrupy whine. "What if there are more Norill than we think, and our forces, without the protection of the walls, are flanked themselves? What then?"

Eldred rocked forward on his seat. "Then we would'a lost the fight anyway," he said. He looked old, and the latent power Askon had perceived when he first met Dalstone's thane had ebbed or faded. A voice somewhere inside told him to wait, to see what would happen, but time pressed and Brâghda's people would be gathering in the north as they spoke. Askon, up to this point completely unnoticed, stepped forward.

"I know of another way," he said.

Mark's head rotated slowly around, folds of skin piling along his face and neck until the two became one continuous, fleshy surface. "You came back!" Mark said with feigned surprise, realizing his assassination attempt was a failure. The others noticed nothing. "We were just discussing our course of action," he continued, barely missing a beat. "Have you met the captain?"

Askon reached out to shake the man's hand. He suspected that this captain was indeed the one who had been betrothed to Elise, but Dalstone might have several, even many, captains. "Greetings," Askon said. "I do have an alternative, if you would hear it." He directed the statement at Eldred, ignoring the others, then followed it with a qualification. "Though it should be presented first to Thane Eldred only, I think."

Mark's eyes popped in his round skull, and the captain's face grew skeptical. "Why?" they asked.

Casting his mind back to the days he had spent in the Tolarenz town hall, listening intently as Caled lectured him on the finer points of their people's history, and to similar lessons from the nearly pure-elven falconer, Halan, Askon did his best to imitate the wise, unassailable style of his teachers.

"Long ago, the Glittering Host came across the water, called forth by Caled, Knight of Vladvir," a point of which he himself had only been made aware in the last few weeks. "The people of that host were the elves. They swept away the threat of the Great Darkness—of which the Norill were only a small part—and saved Vladvir from a horrible fate." He drew himself up, meeting Mark eye to eye. Mark looked sharply away. "I think what remains of the elven blood still has a gift to give to Dalstone, but it can be offered to the city's leader alone. No other may be present."

Eldred seemed hopeful while Mark and the captain looked as skeptical as ever, if not more. "That was hundreds of years ago," Mark laughed. "You have no more power to summon such a host than I do. The *peasants* here in Dalstone might revere you for being born part elf, and I might even support such a belief in public, but to suggest that you have some mystical ability to help us is absurd.

"Eldred, don't listen to this—this *boy*. That's all he is after all. Why, he looks to be younger than my son, John, and what a fool that one turned out to be."

For a moment, Eldred said nothing. The captain seemed as though he would offer a word or suggestion, but instead sat down and focused on the maps laid out on the table. Askon wanted to demand that Eldred see him in private so he could reveal what Mark's men had done in the forest. But a voice called to him from some distant place in his memory.

"Patience is important, but sluggish thinking puts a man into an early grave."

And so, Askon did both. He waited, studying the Thane's face, and considered his own options. Surely, Eldred would side against

Mark if Askon told him about the murders, but then the fight between Dalstone's factions would begin, and the Norill would overtake them as they struggled to deal with each other.

Askon felt the Time fragment begin to work. Gradually, everything in the room became clearer: the sweat on Mark's brow and his subtle fidgeting, the weight pressing down on Eldred as he fought against the same worries as Askon, and the captain's idle swishing of papers, his movements betraying his desire to simply end the discussion and start the fighting.

Suddenly, the right course of action became obvious. First of all, Askon would wait for Eldred to make a move. Speaking up would only cause Askon and his offer to sound desperate. He remembered Brâghda's reaction when he had responded not as a prisoner, but as an authority. His current situation was the same, his offer final. One who is in power need not beg to exercise it.

The otherworldly clarity of the fragment made the three men appear strange and slow. Askon realized how poorly-prepared they actually were for such a battle. For years, Dalstone had been so obscure, so remote, that no real threat had ever presented itself. The Grafmark Norill acted more as a political device when Dalstone's leaders needed to impress fear upon the townspeople, but as Askon now knew, Vitæsta had never posed any actual danger.

Mark grew increasingly frustrated while Eldred made his decision. Turning to the old man, he opened his mouth to speak. Askon saw the slow twitch of muscle around the lips and the subtle motion in the throat. It was as if he could see the words forming in Mark's mind. They would be foolish and in that grating whine the priest used to agitate his listeners, but the words never came. Eldred rose from his seat, his face fixed, eyes stern.

"Come with me, Askon," he said gruffly. Then he looked at Mark and the captain, "You two go prepare for battle. If this gift fails to help us, we will use the captain's plan."

Askon smiled. For Eldred to accept the private discussion was an easy victory, one Askon considered a sure bet. Eldred would want an advantage over Mark when the battle had finished; Askon's help might give it to him. But it was the second piece that pleased Askon most. The captain's plan matched his own quite closely, though he would have fewer men attack the flanks of the Lost and use the remainder to reinforce Brâghda's fighters.

Mark stomped out of the room, but something wasn't right. Still under the fragment's power, Askon felt each step—too heavy—and the rhythm—too uniform. At the entrance to the hallway Mark looked back; there was a gleam in his eye. To Askon it said, 'Send your men to be slaughtered outside the gates. Mine will still be alive when the battle is won.' A cold ripple vibrated through Askon's mind. Unsettled, he felt the fragment's clarity lift.

Eldred limped along the hallway, leading Askon, following Mark and the captain. The old man's gray hair trailed over the back of his shirt like a mane of silver and coal. Progress was slow through the sparsely decorated corridor. Mark and the captain grew smaller, farther away, then passed through the thick door with a creak and a bang. Almost instantly, Eldred straightened and the limp vanished. Suddenly, Askon felt small in the thane's presence. In his feigned hunch and hobble,

Dalstone's true leader was shorter than Askon by a few inches. Not anymore. Eldred at his full height was easily taller than the half-elf, even taller than Edward. But though the man stood straighter than he had only moments before, the gnarled toughness and vigor did not return. Eldred breathed deep.

"I'll be glad when all this is done," he said. "Too long we've gotten fat on the milk of obscurity. I'll tell ya right now, it's my fault. I let that weasel, Mark, take over the day to day work of a thane. Now look where it's got me: Norill on my doorstep, a civil war comin' any minute after, not to mention my guards lettin' the prince of Vladvir be captured at my celebration." He stopped as they came to a door on their left and put out a hand, leaning heavily against the frame. "Maybe he deserves to win," he said, reaching toward the door handle, "or maybe it's that I deserve to lose."

Askon ignored the thane's self-pity and followed him into a room that again reinforced his memory of Brâghda's cave. In Vitæsta, the study had been on his left as he entered, the bedroom on the right. Eldred's quarters had been arranged in the opposite fashion. Inside the thane's study, a simple, well-crafted pine desk occupied the far wall. Its contents had been neatly arranged, its surface well-oiled. It looked to have been many years old—perhaps generations—but the finish had been so painstakingly preserved that it might have been commissioned only weeks earlier.

Eldred nodded to the door, which remained ajar behind them. Askon closed it and twisted the handle, securing the catch. Eldred scooted two chairs away from the wall, each one grumbling against the floorboards. They sat, and for a moment said nothing. The old man, it seemed, had no plan which could win both the battle against the Lost and the inevitable civil conflict that was to follow. He stared at the floor.

"Mark was right," Askon began. Eldred's head rose sharply, meeting Askon's eyes. On his face, lines of frustration stood out between the brows and along the mouth. Askon pressed on. "He was right to say that I have no mystical power. It is true. If the elves could use some kind of magic, it is not in this world or was only on that day when the Glittering Host arrived."

"Then why waste my time!" Eldred roared. Clearly there was little he could do while they waited for the Norill to strike, but still he raged in his inability to act.

"Don't think of a salamander."

The old man continued to shout, venting his anger on the only remaining target. Askon let his focus settle on the band wrapped around Eldred's brow. The beads, and cord with which they had been tied, were of simple make, much like everything in the thane's possession. Counting the individual beads, Askon resisted the urge to shout back at Eldred, though it wasn't enough to bring about the calm clarity of the fragment.

When the thane had finished his tirade, he stood. Askon reached out a hand and met Eldred's eyes.

"The offer is real," Askon said. "I do not have mystical powers, but the offer is real." Something in the repetition of those words seemed to strike the old man. He fell heavily back onto his seat.

"As you know, my friends were taken by the Norill. I found them, but only because I was captured as well," Askon said.

Eldred looked doubtful. "So you escaped? I don't understand how this helps us."

"I didn't escape; I was set free. Your Norill neighbors are not the threat you believe them to be."

"You expect me to believe that the Norill that've been capturin' my subjects, killin' my defenders, and that're now surroundin' the whole damn town aren't a threat? I'm beginning to think you might be missing somethin' in the way o' brains."

Askon ignored the comment. "The Norill surrounding Dalstone are called the Lost. They come from the north, beyond our outposts. I think the group outside the gates are mostly from the area around Vestgæta. They are certainly a threat."

"First the Norill aren't a threat. Now they are?" Eldred grunted. "You're not makin' any sense."

"There are two Norill factions," Askon continued. "The Lost, and the Grafmark Norill. My friends and I were captured by the latter. Their leader, Brâghda wants to make peace with you."

For over an hour, Askon explained the nature of the Grafmark Norill: whom they captured and why, how they intended to help in the fight against the Lost, why they would fight against their own people, what they would do to help Eldred take back Dalstone, and the peace they wanted in return. Initially, the thane had responded with forceful denial of Brâghda's request. But as Askon explained the plan—and how the final outcome would benefit Eldred's cause—the old man warmed to the idea.

Finally, he accepted. The Grafmark Norill would become allies of Dalstone without Mark's knowledge. Eldred's men would be informed not to attack Brâghda's fighters, who would be wearing brightly colored feathers on their armor. Usually the Norill reserved the feathers for ceremony, as the bone plates were more threatening when laid bare. The Lost would be wearing no feathers, making them easily identifiable, even in the confusion of battle. Askon mentioned nothing of Elise or their plans to leave for the South Kingdom when the battle was finished.

CHAPTER TWENTY-THREE

The Battle for Dalstone

A purple sunset glowered beneath heavy clouds in the west, the air tingling with the oncoming storm. Grafmark lay quiet in the windless threat. Near the chattering riverside, the people prepared for war. All day men and women had sharpened, beaten, tightened, and fortified. By the time the ragged mountain ridges clawed their way past the failing sun, the vats of oil bubbled sickly and the clatter of spears had ceased. The walls prickled like a net of briars.

Outside, the growing mass of Norill bodies swelled. With every spear the townspeople of Dalstone added, another of the Lost arrived from parts distant. A few times the enemy had cast out feints, groups of warriors who ran the length of the fortifications, howling and screaming at the sentries. Several now lay dead, sprawled over the edges of the deep channel which arced around the town. The guards, mostly Mark's Darts, would gladly have felled more of the creatures, but their captains had called a cease-fire in order to conserve the precious cache of arrows kept within. When the main body of the Norill force attacked, targets would be plentiful.

Distant thunder rumbled over the ridge to the west. Grafmark's mighty trees reached high, but even they found the forbidding peaks too remote, the air too thin, the ice too bitterly cold. Instead, the tufts of green descended from the heights to cover the entirety of the valley, rolling and swelling like the waves of an angry sea until they ended abruptly in the clearing before Dalstone. There, the Norill gathered, their leaders striding up and down the lines which had begun to form from the disorganized mass only an hour before.

As the lines solidified under the barking shouts of their commanders, the sheer number of Norill became apparent. Usually they squirmed and swarmed over each other like angry ants, scrabbling and fighting amongst themselves. Not in the purple sunset by the river. In that moment they were still and eerily quiet, an army of hideous gargoyles. They stared hungrily into the west, watching the fading sun and the forms of Dalstone's defenders silhouetted on the battlements.

Two of these forms stood almost as stoically as the brooding Norill army. One, tall and stern, dark haired and gray eyed, leaned on both hands against the poles of the wooden wall. The other was shrouded in deep green, his face shadowed beneath the cloak's hood. His eyes, alight with the coming conflict, stared every bit as greedily as those that stared back. Above them all a falcon circled endlessly as the light faltered then faded.

Askon's assignment in the battle was simple: command and rally the forces on the wall until the Norill began their assault. Then

Edward, who also manned the east-facing wall, would become the inspiration to those fighting from inside the city's defenses. Askon would make his way to the southwestern gate to meet John's New Darts and a large contingent of Eldred's chosen fighters. As soon as the Norill had advanced to the wall, this outside force would crash into the enemy's southern flank. If all went according to plan, Brâghda's army would simultaneously strike the northern flank of the invaders, crushing the opposition and ending the battle in a rout.

When the final fringe of sunset slipped into steely gray, Askon turned to his friend. "Watch your back up here and ours down there as well. Who knows what Mark will do when the battle is finished?"

"I think I can guess," said Edward, clapping Askon's hand in his characteristic double handshake. "A few of John's New Darts are positioned in case Mark tries anything, but I still think it unwise to send most of Eldred's men outside the walls."

"You tried to convince them," Askon said. "There is simply no way to justify putting bowmen on the ground and footmen on the wall."

Edward twitched an eyebrow to the south. "What about John's archers? They aren't on the wall."

"John and his archers are considered outsiders, inferior aim or whatever excuse Mark gave. At least if they start firing on us from above, it will have to be overt. Had they been part of the ground force, we'd have their knives at our backs."

"A fair point," Edward said. "Good luck, my friend."

"And you."

With that, as if the Norill had been waiting for the two to finish their parting words, the gargoyles sprang to life. Only a dim glow shone from behind the mountains where the sun had gone to rest. In the east, the looming clouds rolled away from the pointed ridge, revealing a sickly yellow moon. The gray-green of the forest seemed to thicken, and row after row of Norill poured from behind the line of trees. As they crossed the clearing, Askon paced up and down the wall shouting encouragements to the defenders, recalling again the voices of his teachers and the legend of the Glittering Host.

The men on the wall, and the women below who served in the supporting duties, swelled with awe as one of the elven blood spoke of the valor and bravery shown in the long ago battle against the Great Darkness. How the simple detail of his heritage brought about such inspiration, Askon did not understand, but he played hard to its strength, because though their plan was sound, their reinforcements still secret, only a fool feels confidence when predicting the tides of battle.

Askon jogged down the creaking steps, mindful of those who made their way up. Halfway to the bottom, the sound of his thumping feet vanished as the first rank of Norill ran screaming and snarling across the clearing. Above them, Askon caught sight of Marten, still circling Edward's position on the wall. In the clearing, Norill after Norill poured out of the trees toward the gate.

"Loose!" Edward shouted, and the dry wisp of bowstrings sang into the tingling air. The thin shafts arched above the surrounding trees and came whistling down into the churning mass of Norill.

Amidst the croaking screams and battle cries, the death wails went unnoticed as the arrows found their marks. And still the Norill poured forth from the trees.

Turning from the wall, Askon weaved quickly through the town. The speed with which the Norill had filled the clearing surprised him. He increased his own pace. Soon, the Lost would pile up against the defenses and eventually overcome them. Askon lowered his head and rushed past sobbing children and sheltering mothers toward the southwestern gate.

Meanwhile the arrows continued to fly, Edward striding up and down the wall, shouting and directing fire. A few arrows hissed back, some thudding dully against the poles of the wall or clattering off into the deep trenches that surrounded the city. The fallen barbs soon mingled with the fallen bodies of the Lost. Somewhere far from danger, Mark watched and laughed. Thus far the enemy had been thwarted, harmlessly gathering up and down the eastern side of the city. Elsewhere, Eldred watched too and laughed.

While the large Norill commanders brought up battering rams, the bows on the wall continued their song, volley after volley. Askon came through the southwestern gate, wasting no time, and shouted along the line of Eldred's men.

"We move silently and strike hard!" he called. "Watch for the feathers; that is how you will know friend from foe." He tightened his own harness which had been reinforced with a mail shirt and arming cap. Neither was visible beneath the hood and cloak, but he felt the weight and bulk. Both pieces of armor made him feel thick and sluggish, like a swollen, hammer-struck thumb. A few times more along the line he called the instructions, then made his way to the head of the column.

Thunder sounded in the mountains and rolled away into the dim night. Then, a dull *thud* and *crunch*. The battering rams had begun their work. Rounding a corner, he came to the front of the company. John and Thomas waited, the former lying on his back, staring into the darkening sky, the latter nervously checking every knot, loop, and fastener on his harness. Askon approached them, his breathing already accelerated under the weight of his new armor.

"Ready?" Askon asked Thomas.

The young man managed a weak smile. "What else can I be?"

"A liability," John said as he lifted himself from the ground with an effort. "That's what. A liability."

Askon shot him a glare.

"Alright," John conceded. "I'm probably the more likely to turn traitor, us fightin' with Norill allies and whatnot. The boy'll be fine. He's as ready as he's ever goin' to be."

"You give quite the inspirational speech," said Thomas. John merely grumbled and cinched a loose wrist strap tighter until it suited him. Then with a shrug, he strode to the buzzing line of soldiers.

"We got Norill so thick at the gates, our boys can't even see the doormat," he barked. "They're knockin' with their beaters, but we ain't goin' to let 'em in." He paused. "Well, are we?"

Nothing.

"Are we gonna let those slack-skinned knuckle-draggers into our city?"

"*No!*"

John grinned. "Are we gonna send 'em back to the hole they crawled out of?"

"*Yeah!*"

The shouts and cheers rippled down the column all the way to the southwest gate. By the time the sound died away, John had started them forward. Slowly, the human half of Dalstone's ground forces gathered, marching briskly along the southern edge of the city. They rounded the corner and John took off at a dead run. In a few seconds, they slammed into the bewildered crowd of Norill that stood cackling and chattering as they waited for the gate to be breached.

Askon, John, and Thomas engaged the enemy first, cutting their way deep into the Norill ranks. By the time the creatures realized what had happened, many of their fellows lay dead, and the bulk of the combined forces of New Darts and Eldred's men slashed and swarmed all around them. Amidst the slaughter, a few of the large commanders gurgled their instructions in the language of the Lost, but the Norill were confused and frightened. They crawled and stumbled over one another to escape the attack.

Just as planned, Brâghda's forces emerged on the northern side of the city, arrayed in tufts of brilliantly colored feathers. The Norill leader herself plunged into battle as had Askon and his friends, leading the way to the battering rams at the Dalstone gate. As they did, Edward reminded the bowmen on the wall to hold their fire. Seeing that the feathered Norill hacked and sliced down the attackers, most of the bowmen obeyed.

After mere moments, the press of Grafmark Norill and Dalstone humans met one another at the gate. The enemy broke and fled, running crazily and masterless into the clearing. Askon looked up. Edward stood on the wall with one hand held high.

"Hold!" Askon shouted to the soldiers around him. Brâghda snarled something in her own language at the feathered reinforcements. John bolted down the line, repeating the command as he went. Edward dropped his hand.

Another volley of arrows arced into the moonlit sky. This time, the marksmen found many targets as the Norill armor did little to protect the creatures' backs. Those who escaped sprinted for the cover of the tree line. By the time the defenders had again readied their bows, the majority of the enemy had passed out of range.

"Charge 'em!" John roared, and Askon echoed him. Brâghda shouted her fighters forward. Askon breathed deep and exhaled slowly. The fight had been easy. It wasn't yet over, but the plan had worked. He relaxed and ran hard for the enemy line across the clearing.

Somewhere between the Dalstone wall and the twisting fingers of Grafmark's trees, the fragment took over. Between the success of the plan and his focus on the fast-approaching enemy line, Askon somehow triggered the steady calm brought on by the jewel. He felt himself pulling away from the other soldiers. They seemed slow and clumsy, trudging through the field. He looked back. They did not trudge; they ran, but so slowly that they seemed to be mired in a swamp or marsh. He checked his speed, waiting for them to catch up. When their pace slackened even more, he grew impatient and plunged into the enemy line.

Askon's bloodstained steel hacked into the first Norill torso, and the battlefield came to a complete stop. The sprinting humans and Grafmark Norill stood in various states of stride while the opposing line of the Lost had once again resumed the frozen crouch of the gargoyle. There was no resistance as blade met flesh—no reaction at all—but Askon did not wait to see why. He raised the sword and brought it down directly through the bone armor plating of his next victim.

Again and again he sliced and cut and thrust his way through the surrounding creatures. Every blow was fatal or would soon prove so, but the Lost did not fall. Askon recalled the guards in Thomas's village, how they too had been struck mortally yet remained standing. He remembered Edward's reaction after Askon had rashly continued striking until the guards fell. And he remembered how human Brâghda had seemed during their time in Vitæsta. He brought the sword down again and again and again. But, unlike in the small village north of King's City, this time he did not return to strike the same enemy more than would be necessary for a kill.

As John later recalled, the men from Dalstone watched as the half-elf sprinted with inhuman speed far ahead of the group, then blurred and vanished amongst the line of enemy Norill. Brâghda's forces reached them next, and by the time John's men had engaged, Askon's early kills began to fall, one by one. Within seconds, John and the other soldiers realized that they were fighting enemies who were already dead—felled by Askon's blade faster than their eyes could perceive. Then, more of the Lost came to fill the gaps, and the battle resumed. None knew where Askon had gone.

✝ ✝ ✝

He emerged fully on the forest side of enemy lines. In his wake, a trail of slaughtered Norill remained standing eerily, a graveyard's worth of corpses that did not yet know they were dead. A hundred yards behind him, the first bodies slumped against each other.

Outside the trees, moonlight glistened on the strange field of standing dead. In that light Askon found it easy to see. He assumed that those who did not share the elven blood would not see quite so well, but that it would be more than enough to fight by. Inside the trees, darkness loomed up like a wall. Thunder crackled and lightning flashed, illuminating the forest in a brilliant instant. Askon's heart stopped.

As quickly as the lightning had come, the power of the fragment was gone. The battle came to life around him, though his movements had been so accelerated that the enemy was still unaware of his presence. But it was not the Norill behind him which had halted his concentration. In the trees, dozens of shadowy forms were gathered. Had they been additional Norill forces, Askon might have gone on without interruption, but in the lightning's split-second flare, Askon had seen who the reinforcements were.

Again, light blanketed the canopied forest floor. Fifty feet inside the tree line, a full company hid in the underbrush. Each man, and they were all men, bore either the crimson bull of Lord Iramov or the blue stag of Codard. Askon ducked behind a tree, crouching low. His breathing, heavy and loud, hissed and shuddered at the exertion of his initial attack. Rain began to fall. With his heart racing, he peered out from behind the tree.

The lightning flashed a third time, and the fragment took hold of him once again. He smiled, thinking just how easily he could single-handedly obliterate the ambush. Without hesitation, he rounded the tree, flying toward the shadowy shapes in the bushes. Suddenly, it was as if day had broken on the forest.

On one side, a line of soldiers wearing the crimson bull huddled with bows drawn, each aiming a wicked smile at the approaching Dalstone warriors. Opposite them, a row of men bearing the blue stag knelt waiting—clearly the reinforcements who would proceed on foot. At the center a man stood proudly, staring with eyes, head, and shoulders straight forward. His gaze was haughty and disdainful, or so Askon thought at first. Looking closer as the frozen spark of lighting lingered, Askon saw no subtle details of movement as he had when under the fragment's influence during his discussion with Mark and Eldred. This man was still as stone and staring fixedly ahead at a large tree, almost as if he could see through it and the battle and the wall and the mountain all the way to the end of the world. The man was Christopher. And in the shadows behind him, with the same end-of-the-world gaze, stood Patrick and Victor.

Again the power of the fragment flushed away like flotsam in a stream, and everything went black. Throwing himself to the ground, Askon rolled to one side. Sticks and limbs cracked and popped beneath his armor. The calm was gone, replaced by confusion and fear. With his back to another large tree he sat, mind racing.

How are they here? They should be dead.

In truth, Askon knew only that Patrick and Christopher had been killed. Victor's survival had been unclear. Had he fallen in the battle against the Lost when Askon's company had come too late from the caverns below Austgæta? Or perhaps he had retreated, only to be killed when they arrived at the besieged outpost. If Victor had survived, why was John in conference with the king when Askon had arrived at the castle? Over the din of rain, he heard his father's voice and felt a cold pang of dread.

"When confronted by a seemingly complex problem, son, consider that the simplest solution is usually the correct one."

Askon tried to clear his mind, to see the simplest solution. His emotions swelled: anger at Victor's support of the Codard and Iramov alliance, confusion and fear at the inexplicable return of Christopher and Patrick, worry and doubt over the outcome of Dalstone's carefully planned battle. Then an answer came to him.

The simplest solution is that they were never dead. Somehow I misread Patrick's life signs; somehow Christopher lived and escaped after we had gone; somehow Victor simply wasn't present at the time of my arrival.

The cacophony of battle added itself to the pattering rain and rolling thunder. From the bushes, the *snick* of loosed arrows signaled the ambush. Iramov's bowmen let fly a single volley, and the reinforcements emerged from the underbrush. The fragment, working in reverse now, made them startlingly quick and difficult to track. Fortunately, the faster movements of his enemies were now mirrored by his allies. Everything was happening too fast. As they swarmed past, none noticed the form huddled under the deep green cloak. Another voice—Morrowmen's voice—rose up from memory.

"Some qualities come and go as the pieces change hands. Iramov's father, for instance, would not have been able to perform the acts that you saw. That fragment, the Death fragment, as you rightly hit it, seems to feed off anger or possibly madness."

With the battle swirling around him, the tide turning as Dalstone's forces were driven back into the clearing, a sickening thought awoke in Askon's mind. What if they had been right about Victor and Patrick and Christopher? What if they really had died? What if somehow the Death fragment could bring back those who were dead? And then there was the unsettling gaze that each of them wore. They had stared forward at nothing, their eyes open but unseeing, like blind men who could only feel the world around them.

He needed another look, needed to understand what had happened. He peeked again from behind the tree, but all three were gone. Askon scanned the raging battle for those familiar, yet strangely empty, faces. He found nothing and would find nothing. They had vanished into the accelerated flashes of swords, cracking of shields, and pressing of bodies who lived and died and dealt death in the thunder and rain of Grafmark. Dalstone's forces fell back, and the fight shifted into the moonlit clearing.

CHAPTER TWENTY-FOUR

The Elf and the Arrow

A stone. Green, then brighter green, pulsing. Trickling rain and the cries of battle moving farther and farther into the distance. A silver chain of unparalleled make. Every link perfectly fused. And the setting. The setting was sturdy. Curling loops of silver all bound and beaded like ivy leaves, the round bulbs of new growth budding along the ends. Far away, a battle raged; men were dying. And then the stone again. Numberless facets refracting equally numberless reflections of moonlight. From a distance it would seem a triangle, the point facing down. But from above, the Time fragment had depth, its top a many-sided shape, nearly round to the casual eye. Originally it was the tip of the tear which fell from Alora's eye, the girl from the children's story who had been real, the girl who had cried when her lover cast himself into the sea. And here it was, a piece of the stone that had formed around her solitary droplet of grief.

✤ ✤ ✤

Askon looked up and found the world had returned to normal. The fragment's pulsing resumed its steady heartbeat rhythm. The motion of tree branches slowed. The distant figures in battle became men and Norill instead of indecipherable blurs of steel and flesh. He pushed himself away from the tree and squeezed his sword hilt. If Dalstone were to be defeated here against the forces of Iramov and Codard, Askon would kill as many as he could before he was taken.

And though he knew the same men, or men like them, had helped send his people to the place beyond the powdered circle, he realized that no amount of anger could bring them back now. Nothing could save them. But precise, mindful tactics and the flawless execution of his training could avenge them, could take a life for a life. Perhaps he would even help to save Dalstone. Whatever happened, Askon would not sit by, incapacitated by a simple pendant. He held that thought in his mind, gripped it like the hilt of his sword, knowing that it would try to escape.

Cold vengeance strode into the rain-soaked clearing under the cloak of deep green. He circled the main body of enemy soldiers. If he had burst into their ranks from behind, he might've taken many in one fell swoop, but then they would be aware of him, would surround him, would end his chance for revenge. So he bided his time, swiftly passing along the edge of the battle until he came nearly to the place where Dalstone's men had earlier sprung their trap. He followed the trench to the gate. Edward no longer stood on the wall, and the other men stationed there were few, their arrows flying intermittently from the battlements into the rear ranks of the enemy. Askon turned to the battle.

The warring forces had split into two halves. On one side, Brâghda and her Grafmark Norill in their brilliant and blood-smeared feathers fought viciously against the remaining Lost whose strength and stamina now flagged. Of all the groups present that night, none suffered more casualties than the Lost. Opposite them, on Askon's right, the men of Dalstone— also becoming quickly exhausted—fought against the smaller force of the blue stag and the crimson bull. There was no sign of the three who should have been dead.

Tactically, both choices were equal. If he helped Brâghda and the Grafmark Norill, the kills would be easier and happen more quickly, possibly allowing them to wipe out the Lost invaders and move on to the human forces. If he helped John and Thomas, he would be defending against a fresh force until Dalstone's Norill allies could finish their fight against the Lost. In his heart, Askon wanted desperately to slash and stab his way through as many of Iramov's men as was possible before he too was slain.

Edward decided for him.

From the trees on the south side of the clearing, a shout boomed over the clash of swords and cries of the dying. The roar grew louder, and soon Askon knew from whom it came. A mass of swords and spears slammed into the exposed backs of the human enemy forces. In seconds, before Askon could even engage either enemy, nearly a third of the blue stags and crimson bulls lay dead or dying in the trampled thistle of the clearing. Edward had rallied the Darts of Grafmark, pulled them from the wall, and led the attack himself.

With head held high, he drove the company bearing his own emblem into the midst of the still-raging Norill battle. Askon sprinted in the same direction, connecting first with a retreating soldier. The time had come for Askon to have his vengeance. Methodically, he batted away the man's short-handled axe and buried his sword an inch deep, just above the collarbone. Yanking the weapon free, he moved on to another and another, a thrust here, a slice there, pommel to face, swift cut to the knees, parry, slash, and on and on.

Thomas followed in Askon's wake, protecting his friend's back and finishing off those whom Askon had left alive. In this manner Askon felled enemy after enemy. Soon, a vanishingly small number of Lost and human soldiers were running for their lives into the forbidding forest. A cheer arose among the defenders of Dalstone. They had won.

Then Mark emerged from the gates.

He marched at the front of the remaining Darts of Grafmark, with stern face and flowing robe. He seemed prepared to give a sermon. The men behind him held their bows at the ready in the first rank. In the second, Askon saw the glitter of concealed sword blades and spearheads. The Darts Edward had convinced to leave their posts on the wall numbered only half of Mark's total. Like those under John's command, and the Norill under Brâghda's, Edward's Darts cheered and slapped one another on the back, glad for the victory. But Mark and his contingent marched on.

They gradually drifted north to where the majority of Brâghda's forces had gathered. When they had come within fifty feet of the

Grafmark Norill, Mark slipped to the rear of the group. Arrows slid to the string and bows drew back. Silence fell on the clearing.

"Darts of Grafmark," Mark shouted in his best commander's voice. The effect instead was an exaggerated form of the whine he put on when an argument did not go his way. "Those who followed the prince!"

The group huddled around Edward—those nearest Brâghda's army—shuffled and fidgeted nervously. Motioning to John, Askon whispered something as Mark awaited a response. Eldred's men and John's New Darts tightened their gear and readied their weapons as John slipped through the group whispering commands.

"Join us!" Mark called. "For years we've suffered these—these, vermin. They kidnap our people. They kill our defenders, raid our crops, and strike fear into the hearts of our women and children." Again the troops surrounding Edward jostled and murmured quietly. But none broke away nor made any move toward Dalstone's priest.

While Mark railed against the Grafmark Norill, Brâghda used the time to her advantage. Though they did not appear to be hostile, her warriors had reorganized in preparation for another fight. Unlike Mark, Brâghda stood at the front of her column.

"What?" came Mark's whining voice again. "Would you trade years of conflict for one day's worth of alliance? Come and fight for your people! Don't side with the enemy just because they helped kill their own kind. It's a trap! They'll corner us!" His voice pitched higher, more frantic with every claim, but still no man came forward.

"People of Dalstone," a raw, harsh voice said. To Askon's surprise, as well as that of many others present, it was Brâghda. "The Norill of Grafmark mean you no harm."

Grumbles and dissent throughout all parties. But from within the human forces another surprise came forth. The tall gray profile of Dalstone's thane strode through the murmuring troops, emerging only yards from where Brâghda stood. The men lowered their heads. He raised a hand, signaling that those loyal to his leadership should be still and listen. They did.

Brâghda continued, to all outward appearance unaffected by both the negative response and Eldred's unexpected appearance on the field of battle. "We have fought and died today in order to save this city," she growled in that weather-beaten, aged voice. "Allow us peace; it is what we wish for both our kinds." In the manner of her people, she bowed low, the same way as through a mesh of wooden bars and twine Askon had watched the other Grafmark Norill bow before her in Vitæsta.

"Kill it!" Mark shouted.

Of all who stood in the first rank of Mark's Darts, only one had the conviction to release the bowstring after the Norill leader had made her plea for peace, but it was enough. In the strange quiet, like a single plucked harp string, the bow's music rang out and died away. Askon lunged toward the unsuspecting Norill leader, meaning to shout, to scream, to somehow avert the consequence of her being struck dead before the walls of Dalstone.

And then he was running, his legs pumping like waterwheels in a flooded spring stream. The lines of Norill and New Darts and Eldred's men flicked by one by one, and he found himself at Brâghda's side. She stared straight ahead at Mark who cowered behind the bulk of his forces. She did not turn to acknowledge Askon nor did she even seem hurt by the arrow.

Following her gaze, Askon turned to face Mark's soldiers. Left with no other choice, Askon would fight them himself. He had given his word. Without Brâghda and her fighters, the men of Dalstone would have been easily defeated by the Lost alone, not to mention the reinforcements provided by Codard and Iramov.

Fifty feet away, Mark's men stood ready for a fight. The first rank had lowered their bows, though the arrows remained knocked. All except one. Near the center of the line, a man not so different in age and stature from Askon aimed his bow at Brâghda's heart. His eyes burned with anger and vengeance. Askon wondered at the man's twisted pain and raw emotion. He had lost someone to the Norill. But Askon knew the sort of people Brâghda chose to capture, the kind who didn't want to come back.

Suddenly the man's story became clear, as if he had told it himself over a mug at the local tavern. A wife that he could command and who would obey. Children who he would ignore on good days or abuse on bad days when anger or drink took hold of him. A family he neglected who one day were simply gone, taken by one of Brâghda's raiding parties.

Askon followed the lines of fury in the man's face to the bow-string, but the arrow was already gone, was already on its way to its target. For a moment, Askon wondered if the man felt the price for his revenge equal to the cost. Then he saw it.

Only a few steps away, the thin, brightly-fletched arrow hung motionless in midair. Askon studied the strange, floating missile. In the cold moonlight, the sharpened arrowhead glinted, small droplets of water clinging to its tip. Along the near side, a streak of black smudged the shaft, marring the otherwise flawless craftsmanship. A small smile rippled over Askon's lips; the man was left-handed, as Askon was. The smudge left behind by the rake of bow against arrow was evidence enough. At the base, two feathers: one from a blue-jay, the other a cardinal, had been fitted into the arrow body. *Poplar*, Askon thought, though he had seen few such trees near Dalstone. Then Askon came to his senses, reached out, and snatched the arrow from where it hovered three feet above the ground.

The power of the Time fragment dissipated with Askon cradling the arrow in his hands like a strange shell plucked from a lonely shore.

In later years, John would retell the story with an exuberance only he could muster. It became legend in Dalstone and myth in parts distant. On the best nights—nights when he had the privilege to partake in three mugs or better, and those around him had had at least two—it was almost magical.

"Blood and guts, there were, I'll tell ya, like ya never seen in yer life. One side we've got Brâghda, head down low nearly kissin' the dirt; other side we've got my father, spineless as he was, cowerin' in the back. And to think, he wanted nothin' more than to take the thane's place and lead Dalstone himself, and a Norill has the stones to stand in the front—a female no less, though I couldn't have told ya that only by lookin'. Downright disgraceful, it was for him, but it got worse."

Here John would take a mighty pull from whatever glass was handy, let out a long, contented sigh, and bask in the wonder of his listeners before continuing.

"So the enemy's run for the hills and Brâghda's layin' low. Mark orders his men to start shootin'. Ha! They don't though, see. All but one, that is. The one, he fires, and I figure we've had it. Most of us so tired from the fight we can hardly see, Norill swarmin' all around, half our guys tryin' to decide if they're with us or against us.

"It would'a been civil war for sure. Hell, after that, the real enemy could'a come back and cut us all down. But there wasn't no civil war as ya well know. And the enemy didn't come back and kill us all."

Another long pull from the drink of choice, this time punctuated with a heavy *thud* followed by several seconds of silence.

"It was like nothin' I ever seen in my life. Thomas and me and Askon (yeah that Askon) were shoulder to shoulder at least a hundred and fifty feet from Brâghda. Then he was gone, Askon I mean. Flat gone. Like a ghost, or a bolt of lightning, or the first round in my beer glass. Like he was never there at all. And 'fore I can figure out what's what, he's a hundred fifty feet (like I said) away from us, right next to Brâghda. Just like that."

A snap of the fingers for effect.

"But that ain't all. He's holdin' the arrow up like some kinda prize at a harvest festival, not two heartbeats since Mark had given the order to shoot. You should'a heard the roar. Louder than anythin' I heard up to that point or ever since. Ya ever heard a Norill cheer? I bet not. Well, I'll tell ya, them combined with our guys was like the world was about to crumble in on itself, like we'd knock the forest flat all 'round."

And so they had; so they did. Behind the line of his Darts, Mark shifted his nervous glance from Askon—arrow cupped in his hands— to Eldred, then to Edward and the others. The cheer boomed through the clearing, and if there had been thunder, none of the men present heard it, so great were the cries, so powerful the outpouring of emotion. Nearly all of the men in Mark's first rank cast down their bows, but not the man who had followed the order. He stood with mouth agape and rage brimming behind frightened eyes. Slowly, more and more weapons appeared at the front of Mark's forces. Then the unarmed men came forward several feet, separating themselves from the others.

As if it had been planned all along, they knelt in tandem on the trampled grass of the clearing, the roar around them so loud that no one on Askon's side heard what they murmured. And no one heard the next command.

Face first into the grass, a third of the kneeling men fell dead or squirming, arrows sprouting from their backs like bouquets in springtime. The others looked to one another, and to their fallen friends in shock and horror. Some tried to turn, but none survived.

Mark's dwindling forces charged their kneeling comrades, bearing down on them viciously. Askon alone saw three beheadings before he could even react. Behind the slaughter, Mark smiled his thin smile and drew a gleaming sword into the moonlight. He took a step then halted. He shuddered, and the smile went placid, the eyes empty. In the dimness, trickles of black drained down his neck, pooling a little before soaking thick into the folds of his robe; an arrow protruded from just below his jawline. He fell into the wet grass with those he had sent to their deaths only seconds before.

Askon swung around, the deafening cheer now angry and hostile around him. Only one bowman stood under the glimmer of the moon. He held not the recurve bow common to Dalstone's inhabitants but the straighter, gently sloping kind used by the king's army. Behind him the warriors came to life and started forward, eager to kill the traitors and cowards who had now murdered all those who would have surrendered to Eldred. Before the soldiers overtook the bowman who had killed Mark, Askon thought he saw a smile. John rarely talked any time thereafter about his father, and Askon never had the courage to ask if the smile had been real.

CHAPTER TWENTY-FIVE

New Leadership

When dawn broke the next morning, both battles were long over. The Grafmark Norill offered to burn the bodies of the Lost in Norill fashion while the humans did the same for their dead. For the Dalstone men who had fallen at the hands of the Lost or their reinforcements, the digging of proper graves had already begun. They, along with the men who had offered surrender would be given a burial ceremony and monument which would rest on the edge of the clearing where Edward and Eldred had emerged from the trees, turning the battle in Dalstone's favor.

Askon had managed to escape to the wall where he and Edward had watched the enemy forces gathering at the opposite side of the clearing. Now, all throughout the Norill and human armies, the soldiers spoke in excited tones of the power of the elves, of the hero who had saved them all. If they had revered him before the battle, now they worshipped him. Had he been able to hear the conversations, he might have been surprised, even angered at their words.

"I tole ya them elves was magic, I did."

"Figure he's dangerous? Helpin' us now as he is, but what about tomorrow? Suppose he means to bring his people in to rule over us all."

"Elf-kind is strong. Stronger than we thought. Maybe he helps us to take back home from the Lost."

But Askon didn't hear what they said. He sat with his back to the sharpened poles of the wall, exhausted from the exertion and emotional drain of battle. Twelve. That was how many crimson bulls fell beneath his sword. Many more were being prepared for the fire as he let his head rest against the wall's knobby surface. Twelve. He tried not to think of how many had died in the powdered circle outside the Tolarenz town hall, but the memories came anyway.

He saw his mother and his father, kneeling as the unarmed Darts of Grafmark had knelt in the clearing. He saw Halan the falconer and the girls he had grown up with: Shaylee, Natalie, Irina. Then he saw Caled, calm and cold as steel, dueling with Iramov in the main chamber of the town hall. And he saw the crossbow bolts strike as Caled brought down the blade that would have killed Iramov.

Twelve. Just two more than Askon could count on his own fingers. Another image floated up into his consciousness: his sister's bright eyes and playful smile and the blinding flash of the Death fragment. Tears spilled down his cheeks, and he clenched his jaw, forcing the painful vision back into the darkness. Twelve would not be enough.

When he awoke, he heard voices, like distant echoes originating somewhere far away, from beneath a soft blanket or thick carpet. No longer was he seated against the rough inner edge of the wall. It was dark, and the throb of bruised muscle and the burn of tired limbs pulsed through his body. He stretched, yawning widely. A quilt lay over his arms and legs. He cast it aside and swung his feet over the edge of the bed, scratching a shoulder absently as he blinked and looked around.

He was inside the bunkhouse, the curtains drawn tight, narrow lines of light glowing warmly around the window frames. Vaguely he recalled Thomas and Edward helping him down from the wall where he had fallen asleep. If they too had chosen to rest after the battle, Askon's need must have been greater, for the small room now stood empty, the beds neatly made. Outside the bunkhouse, Dalstone thrummed with the toil of its citizens. Here and there Askon heard men calling to one another while they worked. With one last stretch, he slipped on his boots and made his way to the door.

His numb, unresponsive fingers turned the door handle with a piercing squeak. Askon winced, and the creak of unoiled hinges played call and response to the handle's sharp note. But their tooth-grinding shrieks became a whimper, then a whisper as air and light and sound poured into the open doorway. All along the street, busy townsfolk paced purposefully, either preparing to celebrate the great victory or to repair the damage done by the enemy. A few men, who had collected spears cast outside the walls, now lugged precarious bundles back to their storage containers where the weapons would stay until they were needed again. In the direction of the main gate, Askon could hear the dull *thwack* of hammers, most likely the sound of repairs to the damage done by the Norill battering rams. Heavy lids clanked tight around the cauldrons of oil and lard, the fires beneath having long since cooled.

To Askon's surprise, Thomas sat on the sunlit porch facing the milling figures on the street. Not so surprisingly, Elise sat next to him, curled closely with her arms wrapped around his waist and her head resting comfortably in the hollow between shoulder and jawline. Ringlets of her raven black hair spilled over the fabric of his cloak and down his back. They breathed together.

Awkwardly, with a hesitant step over the threshold and then a retreat, Askon tried to pass without interrupting them. He stepped lightly onto the porch and turned to make his way not down the steps where they sat, but to the far side of the building where he could walk directly off into the grass. He took two or three paces before Thomas turned and called to him.

"Askon!" Thomas said excitedly. "Good. You're awake." He rose from his seat on the steps; Elise followed without releasing his hand. "I have to ask you something. I'm not sure I've decided what to do."

Askon looked slowly to either side, scratching below his eye with a thumbnail. The drowsiness of sleep lingered on him. "Where are John and Edward?" he asked numbly.

"They went to prepare for your departure," whispered Elise, her pale mouth moving so imperceptibly that it seemed her voice came not from her lips, but somewhere far away. "Please listen to Thomas. He has—we have—an important decision to make."

On each side of the porch, a short bench had been built into the outer wall of the bunkhouse. Askon sat on the nearest one while the others leaned against the railing across from him. He listened to Thomas's dilemma.

"It's obvious, I think, that I want to stay with Elise," Thomas began, in the familiar, faltering voice Askon had first heard him use when he tumbled from his horse into the dust of the Vladvir plain. "F-Fate or d-destiny somehow brought us together in Vitæsta, and it would be unwise to ignore it."

Askon smiled. "So it would."

"But I've followed you so far and would like more than almost anything to meet your friend Morrowmen. The history he must know! I could learn so much from him and test my theories against his." His words accelerated with every detail. He began to move his free hand— the one not locked tightly into Elise's—animatedly as he continued. "And then there's the Tear and the fragments. Iramov could be on his way to the South Kingdom as we speak. What should we do, Askon?"

"I think it's clear. You stay with Elise," Askon said, rising from the bench. "Do you remember what Brâghda said to you in Vitæsta? Fate is not always so kind in these matters." He gestured to indicate both of them. "Take me for example. I've never met someone who is such an obvious match as Elise is to you. And now, with Tolarenz gone, even those who might've someday been a match are no more." Staring blankly off into the distance far beyond them, he struggled against the rising tide of memory.

"We agree completely," Elise said, pulling away from Thomas slightly. "It isn't so simple for me. I was already betrothed before Brâghda took me away from Dalstone—"

"But the captain was killed during the battle," Thomas interrupted. They both looked suddenly heavy and sad. "He was in the rank that tried to surrender."

"Legally," Elise continued even more quietly than before, "I can now marry whomever I choose, though not without repercussion. My father for instance, would likely want to find me another match, and certainly the captain's family would frown upon such a quick marriage after his unfortunate death."

"In other words," Askon said, nodding, "you think Dalstone unsafe now. What about Vitæsta?"

Elise shook her head. "Brâghda and her people were kind to me, and they would take me back if I so desired, but I wish to be with my own people. The Norill ways and customs are uncomfortable sometimes. And though they are welcoming, Vitæsta is not a human city; there, I am an outsider."

"Then you come with us," said Askon flatly. "But Thomas, remember what our journey has been like so far. We've been trailed since we left King's City, nearly to our deaths. If the miles between Dalstone and the South Kingdom are anything like those we traveled before, it will be very dangerous. Are you willing to risk that?"

"I am." But it was not Thomas who answered. Nor was it the soft whisper Elise had used thus far in their discussion. It was the cold hard voice, the commanding threat which had emerged when they arrived at the Dalstone gate. "I make my own decisions, my own choices now.

Yes, I would follow Thomas wherever he may go, but not because *he* demands it. I go because *I* demand it."

A small laugh escaped around the smile on Askon's face. "Well that settles it. You will come with us to the South Kingdom. Ready your belongings, then. Bring only what you can carry on a long day's march. Thomas can help you." He pressed the smile into a hard, thin line and left them leaning against the porch rail.

By the time he found Edward and John, the preparations were almost complete. Askon slipped and skidded his way down a rocky path that slithered from the southwestern gate to the river. Marten, who had found him somewhere between the bunkhouse and the water's edge, hopped along from branch to branch in the trees. The path opened through pungent stalks of thistle and fern onto a round sandbar. Dark streaks of black sand coursed through the pale ripples covering the beach. Here and there a shock of green sprouted from the sand where the bravest plants had forged a foothold. He knew that with the new year, the water would rise, submerging the little beach, drowning or washing away any plant which dared grow. Yet he smiled at the sight.

Further down, a crew of men loaded a boat with supplies and gear. The vessel had been tied tightly to a dock which itself was tied to a higher point on the bank, far above the sandbar. Of simple construction, as were most items of craft in Dalstone, the boat bobbed anxiously in the streaming current. It was little more than an oversized canoe with three sets of oars bound to the sides. Forced to guess, Askon would have approximated that it would carry no more than eight people. On the dock, John and Edward stood waiting as another man finished stacking supplies under the benches.

"And there he is," John called. "Been keepin' bets on when you'd rise from the dead. Thomas figured you'd be up at dawn, but the mighty prince here and myself, we knew better'n that."

Edward waved a thank you to the man helping them with the boat. "We figured that you would need your rest. So, when you were still asleep this morning, John and I took it upon ourselves to ready our passage out of Dalstone. With the combined forces of my father's army and Lord Iramov's showing up at the battle, we shouldn't take any chances in getting to the South Kingdom as quickly as possible—especially if any of them saw what you did with the arrow."

"Gods damn it! Was that ever somethin' else," John shouted. "Never seen its like before. How'd ya do it? Like magic it was. I thought you said the elves didn't have it in 'em anymore."

Edward slapped him on the shoulder. "John, you know as well as I do that it was the fragment taking some kind of hold on him. There is nothing magical about Askon any more than there is about me or you."

"Why do ya always gotta ruin my fun?" John scoffed. "I figure he could at least tell us what it was like. Here one second, *Bam!* Not here the next."

Askon looked at both of them. He shook his head. The boat thumped quietly against the dock as the river rushed by. "That's how it was, John. I saw the man aiming his bow and thought how terrible it would be if Brâghda were to be shot down after helping rescue the city. And then I was there, looking across the clearing at the arrow. It just, hung there, floating. So I grabbed it."

"Ha!" John barked. "I win again." He looked expectantly at Edward. "There ain't gonna be much gold left in yer pockets if ya keep bettin' me like ya have. I told ya he'd make it sound like a day spent diggin' fencepost holes. Worst storyteller I ever heard, this one."

Reluctantly, Edward produced several coins. "Fine," he said. "Three for him sleeping till noon and two more for his lackluster story. Don't spend it all in the tavern."

"I'll spend it wherever my heart calls me to spend it," said John with a huff. "If the heart says to spend it all on the lady of the golden ale, then so it'll be. What is it those Norill say? The beer is where it is?"

"The world is how it is," Askon said, rolling his eyes. "And there's no greater example than you."

Edward grabbed them both by the shoulder and squeezed hard. "We had quite the victory, but I think it's time that we made our way south."

Askon nodded, wrapping his arm around Edward's, grabbing his shoulder in the same way. John, however, slipped out of Edward's grip and stood with his shoulders squared to them, his arms folded at his chest.

"I guess now's as good a time as any," he mumbled. "Mark's dead," he continued matter-of-factly. "With him gone, there's no one to lead what's left of the Darts. An' as ya know, I got Darts o' my own come down from Codard's army. They don't figure on goin' back, an can't all of us go marchin' down into Apopsé's kingdom without raisin' some hairs. Sure, the Grafmark Norill won't be a problem anymore, but as I said a while back, there's worse things in Grafmark than a couple o' Norill stumblin' around through the brush."

Askon dropped his hand from Edward's shoulder. "You're staying in Dalstone with your men. I understand."

But John didn't seem to hear him. "So, as you can probably guess, I've decided that I'd be more good to my Darts here, helpin' rebuild and maybe even protectin' this place if Codard sends men into the forest again. I guess, what I'm sayin' is that I'm stayin' in Dalstone with my men."

Askon and Edward laughed together. "Yeah," Askon said. "I understand."

John hesitated a moment. "That's it?" he asked. "You're not even gonna ask me to go along? Some friends you two turn out to be."

Edward looked sidelong at Askon. "Oh *please* sir, is there *any* way you could find it in your brave heart to accompany us instead?"

"Fine. I see how it is. Never appreciated my talents anyway, did ya?"

Smiling again, Askon turned away. "Your talents are beyond measurable value."

"Damn right they are!"

Askon waved to them as he stepped off of the dock into the soft sand. "Come on. If the boat's packed, we'll need to meet with Eldred before we go. John, it makes perfect sense that you would stay and keep Dalstone's remaining forces together. They need you."

The three vanished into the high stalks at the river's edge. Against the dock, the boat thumped quietly, laden and ready as soon as they had spoken with the thane.

✛ ✛ ✛

Behind them, the doors of the meeting hall boomed shut, blocking out the blinding afternoon sun. Though Askon had slept for nearly an entire day and night, he still felt tired and sluggish, his muscles still aching from the battle. Inside the hall, sunbeams spilled onto the long tables like crystal pillars stretching floor to ceiling. A musky smell drifted from the kitchens, warming the air inside the chamber uncomfortably, but Eldred had insisted that they meet here, not in his private quarters as they had done before the battle.

In the intervening hours, Dalstone's leader had commanded his men to rearrange the meeting hall chamber to more closely resemble a throne room. Had the times been different, Askon might have argued against such a display of power. Instead he felt comforted that the thane had chosen to take active control of the city once more.

They approached Eldred, who sat with an ornate chalice in his hand on the newly placed throne. It was little more than a larger version of the high-backed chairs at the thane's table, but it served its intended purpose.

"Askon of Tolarenz, the people of Dalstone thank you," he said, and all the hale strength that had for so long lain dormant shone through like the beams of light through the meeting hall windows. "We thank you and your friends, and even one of our own."

Before the thane's seat, five people bowed their heads in response to his gratitude: John, Thomas, Elise, Edward, and Askon. The latter two stepped forward, and Askon addressed the thane.

"As you know, we have important business in Apopsé's kingdom. I know by the provisions and the vessel down by the dock that you would allow us to continue on that errand."

"Yes," said Eldred warmly. "You have restored me to my proper place, saved my city, and eliminated its greatest threat. I have no right or power to command you to stay."

"And for that respect, we thank you," said Edward.

"I have to argue that you remain another night. We could easily prepare a feast, greater even than the one before. It is possible that I could be convinced to invite your friends, Brâghda and the Grafmark Norill."

"Maybe," Askon replied, "that is exactly what you should do. Invite them into the city; strengthen the bond you have forged. The allied forces of the Darts and the Grafmark Norill will be difficult for any army to defeat."

"Indeed," said Eldred, his silver-gray hair bobbing in assent. He lifted the chalice to his lips and drank. "But perhaps we should walk before we run, lest we fall instead of merely stumbling."

"What do you mean?" Edward asked.

The thane set the chalice on the arm of his throne. Empty now, he wobbled it back and forth idly between his fingers. "I mean that the feast shall take place on the field where the battle was won. The Norill shall be invited, but not inside the gates."

They all agreed that such a celebration would be worthy and respectful. If Brâghda posed any danger, and Askon believed that she certainly did not, that danger would remain outside Dalstone's walls. As the thane had said, "Walk before you run." After an offer of food and drink, they said their goodbyes and left the Dalstone meeting hall. For Askon, it was the last time he would set foot there for quite some time. And when he did, Eldred would be long since dead and his replacement a very deserving friend.

Not long thereafter, in the warm afternoon sun, they found themselves again on the soft sand near the boat. It thumped impatiently against the dock. As it did so, the five said one more goodbye.

"Now, ya take what Askon says, Thomas, and ya listen close. Listen closer than ya ever have before in the whole of yer life."

"I will," said Thomas solemnly.

"I ain't done yet," John spluttered. "Ya take his words straight to heart, like I said." He smiled broadly. "And then ya throw 'em straight to the wind and do the damned opposite!"

Askon shook his head. "Don't listen to him, Thomas."

"You see," said John. "That right there is what I'm talkin' about. That one, more than anything, ya do the opposite. Ya hear me?"

"I do," said Thomas.

John clapped his arms around the young man, slapping his back once for affection and a second time to knock the wind out of him. Thomas stepped away coughing.

"Good luck, John," said Edward. He had that look in his eyes which echoed his royal heritage. At first Askon thought John might say something flippant, as was his way, but not even John of Dalstone could disrespect Edward when he wore the face of a king. Instead, they shook hands—both hands, one over the other—firmly before Edward stepped into the boat.

"Thank you, my friend," Askon said when his turn, the last turn, finally came. "Without you, we would have been taken on the cold stones of the Greyarc. By now, we would most certainly be dead. You've done a great thing, supporting Brâghda. Dalstone may or may not appreciate just how much you sacrificed, but I know, and I will remember even if they forget." He reached out and clasped John's hand firmly. Then he pulled him in, slapping him on the back as John had done to Thomas. "And you may never know how much good you did in keeping the Time fragment out of Iramov's hands. May the gods smile upon you."

The two men pulled away from one another, Askon expecting a witty line or crack about what might happen next, but none came. Each of them tipped a small wave at the other. The next time they stood this close to one another would be under the suffocating press of the Death fragment's darkness.

Edward had already disentangled the boat. It glided gracefully away from the dock and down the rushing current of the river. John stood with his hand in the air, a small lonely figure, silhouetted against the afternoon sun as they rounded the first bend and drifted on the stream toward the South Kingdom, where they hoped to find answers. Battle awaited them.

Acknowledgements

When *Fragments* was published, I promised myself that the second book wouldn't go into production until the sales of Volume I would pay for the associated costs. As has been my idea from the start, I shared this with readers, followers, family, and friends. The response was overwhelming. To my surprise, the paperback carried a great deal of the financial weight, with wonderful interactions at local sales events, fairs, and markets.

So to all of you I say, thank you. Without your help, Askon would still be standing at the edge of the Valley of Tolarenz deciding on his next move. Edward would still (to you, at least) be a side character, seen only for a fleeting moment in the prologue. And John. Who knows where John would be? The readers make this all possible: every share, every mention, every Amazon review, every time you lend your copy to someone else.

To my students (whether in English or Marching Band) a special version of this thank you. Through all the times I've brought up the books and publishing process in class, your attention, support, and respect has been constant. For those of you who read Volume I in under a week, then waited patiently for Volume II, thank you doubly. How lucky I am to have such a great built-in audience.

Finally—and most importantly—my family. Kelli, my wife, who diligently watches our children while I clatter away at the keyboard. To Mom and Scott for all your wheelin' and dealin' (as John might say). To my brother Alex and his wife Melissa for keeping a stack of books on hand at the Farmer's Market. And to Linda Wakefield for helping with as many copies as a hair salon can. Thanks to you all.

To Zoë Markham, my editor: the text is stronger, cleaner, and just plain better every time you get your hands on it. And to my cover artist, Isis Sousa, there's little to say but *wow*. The *Fragments* cover is gorgeous, and though I'll always have a soft spot for that first glimpse of Askon, Iramov and the storm over Grafmark are everything I could have asked for in a second effort (dare I say, as my wife did, *badass*).

And one more time to Kelli, thanks for reading it again.

And again.

Continue the Journey

For now, the threat in Dalstone subsides. Askon seeks Morrowmen in the South Kingdom, though his friends—new and old—do not always agree with his decisions. Some will be lost, others will be found. And all the while, the Death fragment continues its march.

Pre-order Alora's Tear: Book 3 now.

www.barhamink.com/vol-3

About the Author

Nathan spends most of his working days with the students of Genesee Junior-Senior High School in Genesee, Idaho. Whether it's essay structure, a classic literary work, or the occasional impromptu dance routine, he strives to keep students interested in the fun and the fundamentals of the English language.

When he's not teaching, he wears a number of hats, though the one that says "Dad" is the most careworn and cherished (it says "Husband" on the back). It hangs on a hook in a house where music is a constant and all the computers say "Apple" somewhere on their *aluminium* facades. From time to time it is said that he ventures into the mysterious realm called *outside*, though the occasion is rare and almost exclusively upon request by son or daughter.

Sign up for Nathan's newsletter:
www.barhamink.com/subscribe

Connect with Nathan:
Twitter: twitter.com/natebarham
Blog: natebarham.com

www.ingramcontent.com/pod-product-compliance
Lightning Source LLC
Chambersburg PA
CBHW031131120726
47905CB00006B/1648